CW01017652

Other titles in the *Anouka* Series:

The Old Oak Tree

The Silver Chalice
The Hollow Boathouse
The Mountain & The Mirror
No Ordinary Bookshop
The Book of Immortality

THE ANOUKA CHRONICLES

The Book of Immortality

Philippa W. Joyner

Published by New Generation Publishing in 2019

First Edition

ISBN 978-1-78955-834-0

www.newgeneration-publishing.com

Oddities

Bright white snow dazzled a beanpole blonde girl, Rosabella, as she so *abominated* to be called.

Her trodden-down boots, deliberately at the heel, crunched home. And, although desperately trying to be dignified, Rosabella Joy managed to fail spectacularly.

Rosabella's large foot-skids grated down the lane; ungainly strides destroying the newly laid blanket of icy pureness. Her uneven self-chopped hair flopped into her eyes. Luckily, it wasn't a shade of green now, or maroon, just yellow-ey. And wonky. But at least her eyelashes, frozen into clumps, shielded her pupils from the ever-increasing snowy flakes falling faster from the darkening skies above.

But Rosabella's knees weren't shaking with cold. No. Just with a shivery excitement. Her overly-sized footprints were not alone this holiday. Two sets, one set much larger than the other, left deep marks in the sheet of snow that had fallen, ridiculously in volume.

Overnight.

On the whole village.

As Rosabella trudged along, her house, *4 Bank Cottages, Pilgrims Place,* slowly came into view.

"Thank GOD!" Rosabella huffed.

"Language, Rosabella!" she heard Mr Fireplace grumble from afar. His words smoking out the chimney of *4 Bank Cottages.*

"HATE that name! And *you* shouldn't keep moving further and *further* up the hill, then, should you? My house was definitely closer than that."

"I think you'll find, *Belle,* that you took the long-cut - "

"The long-cut?" Rosabella heaved her feet through the snow. "I've only been away a term. I *can* remember how to walk home. What are you *talking* about Mr Fireplace?"

"I'm talking about you taking the *long*-cut. If *Gladiolus-Viola Academy* was to teach you anything at all, I thought listening skills would be right up there."

"I did *hear* you, Mr Fireplace - "

"Did you?"

"I'm talking about me walking another way. A longer way. I most certainly did *not.* You've moved further up the hill. I can measure it if you like? My house is exactly three hundred and three metres from my old school. Look," and Rosabella started to walk backwards. Each step being one metre in length until she hit a tree. "OUCH!"

"Delusions of grandeur – the youth of today. I think we can *all* do without such stupidity, Belle," and Mr Fireplace blew himself back down his chimney. "It's much warmer inside. Hurry up. It's been rather lonesome and quite boring and, *dare* I say, painstakingly normal, I s'pose, without you being here, Belle. Not that I want to admit it."

"I guess that's a compliment," and Rosabella squinted behind to the second set of large feet. *"Don't* just stand there. Carry this!" Rosabella heaved a massive bag through the snow. "You're *supposed* to be my boyfr - "

"Huh-hmm," the feet replied. The rest of the body attached to the feet seemed to be bent and frozen.

"Don't look so worried," Rosabella twisted her head back and watched the figure drag its own bag through the blizzard. "Remind me, why did we come this way again?"

"The train. You insisted we took the *Gladiolus-Viola Express-ette*," the figure replied, its frozen mouth not moving but the words echoing through the air. "And that stops *r-i-g-h-t* down there. That Mr Fireplace was correct. It certainly feels like we've taken the *long*-long-cut."

"Oh yeah. Molly wouldn't let us ride in her, would she?"

"No, well, not *exactly.* She threw you out remember? Because you cursed her driving on two wheels," the voice hissed back.

"Don't sound so annoyed. It's good exercise walking from the train station - "

"What, freezing to death in a torrent from the Arctic? I can think of nicer ways to keep fit. Come to think of it, I can think of nicer ways to DIE!"

"Oh, stop moaning. At least you've got somewhere to stay this Christmas."

"I guess. Will I need to hide, Belle?"

"Hide?"

"Yes. As in, have you said I'm coming? Do your parents ~ *actually* know?"

"Um…"

"BELLE!"

"I *know* you looked at me in horror just then, when I looked like I was about to mention the *B* – boyfriend – word."

"Stop changing the subject. Do they know I'm here or not?"

"You'll love Mum's Stewed Star Anise. With pink custard. Well, some shade of reddy something. She doesn't even need to mix it, some unattached stick seems to do it for her. I *think* it's clean - "

"I'm not even going to bother to ask again. You haven't told them, have you?"

"Ummm..."

"And, no, I *didn't* recoil in horror with the *B* word. It's cold. My mouth seemed to just freeze. Look, like this," and Ned contorted his face so much it looked like it was morphed into a dead person. "My lips wouldn't move. Coincidence that I looked horrified *just* when you mentioned the *B* word - "

"Isn't it just, Ned. But, I wouldn't worry, I'm not picking my Mum's hat... not *yet...not ever...* ***DUCK, BOYFRIEND - "*** but Ned was too quick and his dangling arm deflected Belle's snowball right back. It smacked her square in the face. Ned watched Belle as she danced about enraged; her cheek swelling up as big as the biggest fizz-bomb he'd grown in his secret gathering of *Scientifical-Antics* lessons at *Gladiolus-Viola Academy.*

"Oops - "

"Rosabella JOY! My flames will not be able to defrost your feet unless you come in right now. Your Mother keeps using up my heat for potions!" Mr Fireplace hissed.

"You'll *never* learn, Joy," Ned barked back as the snowball bounced and then whacked Belle's other cheek. It stung so much her heart shot up into her throat. Belle pursed her lips to prevent it shooting out altogether.

"SNAKE! You can sleep with the chickens."

"Oh, *hello,"* and Ned stopped in his tracks. He looked at a stranger approaching.

"Who's there?" Belle pretended to hobble. "I've got a weapon."

"Have you?" Ned put down his bag. "Where?"

"You're such a faker, Belle. Limping like that," the stranger crept further towards them. "And weapon?"

"Course. My - " Belle scrabbled around in her bag. "This," and she held up a strange object.

"A pen?" Ned shook his head. "Unless it grows teeth the size of a lion, we're doomed."

"It has a feather on the end. A sharp one," Belle shook it, hard.

"Y'alright?" the stranger sauntered closer to Ned, scuffing his shoes into the snow and making the leather peel off. "I can see you've hooked up with the loon of the village."

"WILLIAM!" Belle threw her pen at the stranger.

"Glad your weapon worked," William replied, picking up the pen with the now limp feather, wet from the snow.

"William! I thought the reason we couldn't get that lift back from *Gladiolus-Viola* in Molly was because of that Water-Potionography project you had to finish?" Rosabella

snarled. "But it's because she was driving home *all* the way on two wheels, wasn't it? Mum'll go spare."

"Where did you find this one?" the stranger winked at Ned.

"Not sure really," Ned smirked. "You want her?"

"No, thanks. Her weapons are rubbish."

"We had to *hitch,* you know, William. Some tractor-man brought us all the way here. Mr Something-Or-Other," Rosabella butted in.

"Nice name," William sniffed. "Is that why you're still holding your *Gladiolus-Viola Express-ette* ticket?"

"Oh."

"You should have been on *my* journey."

"Why? You didn't let us come. Molly practically tossed me out."

"When did I say you couldn't come?"

"After I got out, because of your car doing her fancy two-wheel thing and then me being sick on the floor - I hate motion sickness - a letter, *your* letter, fell on top of me. Told us that it would be *foolish to all travel together* as if there was to be some massive fatality."

"I never wrote any letter."

"Didn't think it sounded like something you'd do, William."

"Naribu?" Ned muttered as a transparent wind whoosed through the trees.

"Molly took a detour," William breathed in the cold. "It's bleedin' freezing out here. Anyway, Molly, she tried not to bring me home at *all.*"

"Why not?" Belle kicked the snow and Molly steamed. Her engine revved backwards and her wheels started to grind slowly into the ice. "Has she been spooked?"

"Watch," William nodded at Molly. "Go on then. Don't show me up now!" Molly's handbrake tried to unlock herself, wrenching it nearly out of her rusty old bodywork altogether. "I had to tie up that handbrake with rope, look," William peered into Molly's side window. She automatically made it steam up, and looked cross. Her headlights flashed luminescent blinding William. "MOLLY! ***THAT*** was bleedin' uncalled for. You're insane, girl."

"S'pose I'm glad you're back, William, I think," Rosabella hissed. "But *not* so glad we had to *hitch.* ONLY to the *Gladiolus-Viola Express-ette* train station. Bit like *him,* we were," Belle nodded her head towards Ned, "staggering along the road."

"That was last term, Belle. I needed to get your attention. Anyone got any food? I'm starving!"

Belle pulled out half a packet of jelly beans. "Sorry about the sock fluff. Want some?"

"No, thanks."

"My Mum's cooking shan't be much better."

"I'll take my chances."

"Can't believe you kicked me out as we were driving, William," Belle glared at her brother.

"Guess you shouldn't have ignored that letter, then. *I'll* have one, that *blue* jelly bean hasn't got that much fluff

on it," William picked off what looked like ancient candy floss. "Quite nice. Fish flavoured, I think. Scampi. Bit of an acquired taste."

"Beggars can't be choosers, William. And anyway - "

"What? Mmmmm, Jesus! The scampi, it's changed to, to, to, I can't quite decide - "

"Your *hand,* it shoved me right out into the recycling bins, William," Belle hissed shrilly. "You're not having any more jelly beans."

"One was enough, thanks. I shouldn't have eaten it. It's turned into toilet cleaner. *How* long have they been in your pocket, Belle?"

"Hmm, three or four - "

"Three or four weeks!"

"No, three or four months. Mum gave them to me before we left for *Gladiolus-Viola.*"

"I feel sick. And anyway, it wasn't me, it was *Molly.* She was determined we shouldn't come back home. Something's wrong. I can feel it."

"Hmm."

"You were *there,* Belle! Molly totally churned up the gravel along the road, just outside *Gladiolus-Viola*'s kitchens," William rose his eyebrows.

"That was the eels, making their escape. Didn't you see their jelly solidifying on the driveway?"

"Urr, no."

"Well, *I* did. And Molly, she skidded - "

"And then opened her door, and then turned up the heated seating and popped you out onto the pavement."

"Well, there was *that.*"

Ned just stood there, motionless.

"Hello," William nodded.

"I guess you must be Belle's *infamous* brother? And that's Molly?" Ned nodded towards the rattling heap of metal.

"Yep."

"We didn't hitch. She made that bit up."

"I know."

"You *know?*" Belle screwed up her face.

"Molly's got a tracker, see?" and William pulled out a black map from his trousers. Little figures stood on the corners of it looking this way and that.

"There's *Mum!*" Belle glared closer as a tall thin lady with a floppy hair net raced round and *round* in circles in her kitchen.

"Looks like she's chasing a - carrot, with legs," Ned stared.

"She is."

"Oh."

"Anyway, look," William opened the map right out. "It's the *Amdoch Atlas,* it shows me where everyone I want to spy on currently is. Look, *there* you are Ned. On my foot, OUCH! Blimey, you're so tall, you're nearly off the top!"

"It's in the ancestry," Ned replied.

"You could actually *be* a basketball hoop, couldn't you?" Belle tried to tie her bag handle together but it just popped back open.

"I suppose. Not much of an aim in life though, is it? Being a basketball hoop."

"And there's *you,* Belle. Wearing stupid boots and arguing. It even shows me your footprints. Keeps them for three days before melting into its hard drive. That's how I knew you'd taken the *Gladiolus-Viola Express-ette,*" William frowned. "You can't lie now. This *Amdoch Atlas* tells me everything."

"Your paper map has a hard drive?" Ned stepped closer.

"Yep! Cool, isn't it?"

"Spooky, if you ask me," Rosabella butted in. "Stalking people."

"Helpful though. We can tell when Mum's about to bring home weird people to meet us," William turned to Ned. "And *you?* You must be Ted? Belle talks of you. When she actually remembers to write that is."

"Ned."

"What is?"

"Me. My name, it's *Ned.* You called me Ted."

"Did I?"

"Yes, you did."

"Blimey, the *Amdoch Atlas* must be malfunctioning," and William turned it over and stuck another feather in its hole. "That should help feed the glitch until I figure out something better."

“Is *that* one of those Reed-Warbler feathers, William?” Belle looked closer.

“Yep - ”

“But - they’re extinct.”

“Ssssh, I know.”

“How did you get it then?” Ned put out his fingers to touch it.

“GET OFF! It’ll combust. I’m growing the DNA in the lab, and it can only have one family member touching him which it recognises. It knows my skin. But if *you* touch it, it’ll think you’re an enemy and become extinct for another one thousand years with no chance of rehabilitation.”

“Oh.”

William span on the spot in the snow to face his sister. “*One* letter, *one* letter *all* term, Rosa*bella,* that’s *all* you could spare me? And you expect me to be able to remember your boyfriend’s name?”

“Urr, we’re not, you know - ”

“I know,” William winked at Ned. “You’d be insane. And, I wouldn’t have replied anyway, Belle. Too busy re-inventing dead birds. They’re Avian Dinosaurs, you know, you did know, didn’t you? - ”

“What are?”

“Birds. All birds derive from Avian Dinosaurs. Did you hear about the *Finsch’s Duck?”*

“No - ” Ned looked keen.

“DON’T get any ideas, Ned,” Belle interrupted. “One science freak in our house is more than enough.”

"Well, the *Finsch's Duck* became extinct in New Zealand in the 1870's," William smirked. "Dead as a Dodo it was. More," William looked at the *Amdoch Atlas.* "Don't worry, just checking that Mum isn't cooking us *Finsch's Duck Stew* for tea."

"Why would she be? She's a vegetarian," Belle butted in.

"Only when she remembers. Anyway, the *Finsch's Duck* is another one of the birds I'm trying to revive in the lab. I was meant to add three teaspoons of Tetrophite - "

"What's that?"

"It doesn't matter. But I accidentally added *thirty-three."*

"What happened?"

"The bird started to regenerate thirty-three times faster than I could keep up with! It burst out of its cage and fled into the mountains."

"And?"

"Well, that was it. We've a six metre tall *Finsch's Duck* on the loose. But, it's also a vegetarian so it'll only ravage turnips."

"Perhaps you should study cooking instead?" Belle frowned. "But you'd probably eat all your homework."

"Nice idea. I'll keep it in mind. Had to do Conjuration classes last term - how's Vlad's pet mouse, Belle?"

"Why?"

"No reason, but I *think* it got in the way of one of my morphing experiments, and its whiskers were shrivelled until they looked like it had been fried alive."

"*You* can tell Vlad."

"No, thanks. And, maybe I *will* have another jelly bean? Please?"

Rupert Gvist

"***Finsch's Duck Stew?*** How many ladles?"

Mrs Joy bellowed down the stairs inside. "And places at the table? Am I needing to set more?"

"How did *she* know about that duck? And, how does she even know we're home?" Belle groaned once inside the garden.

"This place is huge, Belle - " Ned looked around. "Why have you got a giant statue of a toadstool over there?" Ned pointed to a huge stone thing sitting innocently in the middle of the grass.

"Oh, dunno. Never questioned it. It's always been there," William stared at the thing. "Hasn't everyone got one?"

"Ur, no," Ned replied.

"It's to keep Mum's potions in their best condition, don't you know anything about your own family, William?" Belle replied shrilly. "The shadows that this particular *Amanita Muscaria* casts allow all of the dishes being produced in its light to be cooked to perfection, to the milli-second, apparently."

"Can't say I've noticed any perfection," William replied dully. "The last thing I ate that Mum cooked turned my toes a scaly green."

"It's because *you* were standing in the shadows cast by the Amanita Muscaria. Mum *did* warn you."

"I guess I wasn't listening."

"Hmm - and, Mum hasn't turned the outside lights on. Oh! She can *hear* us too?" and Belle watched as the string of lanterns in the garden each popped on in turn. "A *black* light? Now *that's* just weird."

"The Finsch's Duck Stew; I must have shared the recipe by accident on my Spickleweed. Damn," William shook his head. "And she can see we're here because the *Amdoch Atlas* is on Spickleweed too. Double damn."

"What the waffles is a *Spickleweed?"* Belle frowned and started to climb up and *up* the outside-inside steps to the kitchen door of *4 Bank Cottages.*

"A Spickleweed, Belle, it's a calendar you get in Year Two to record everything you do. But, it shares it with your

entire family unless you deactivate it on every entry," Ned replied like a robot.

"I'd forgotten how old you *really* are," Belle glared at Ned. "Why are there so many steps? Dad said he'd take a few away," Belle heaved herself up the last one. "Even *I* don't mind a ladle of *Finsch's Duck Stew* after that hike."

"I think I've forgotten all term to deactivate my Spickleweed," William groaned.

"That's how Mum knows you've not changed your pants, then?"

"How do *you* know?"

"GROSS! I didn't! I'm just guessing!"

"How's the Professor?"

"Stop changing the subject, William. But, he's okay, I guess, the Professor," Belle squinted her eyes at Ned. "But, Mum, she won't believe it that I came top all term."

"No, she won't," William replied. "Because it must be a lie."

"It's not! I did!"

Ned just smirked back.

"Do you think Mum'll mind I've brought Ned home for Christmas?" Belle frowned as she rattled another door leading to another set of thinner, more windy steps.

"Your Mum keeps her pet chameleons on the stairs?" Ned watched as three eleven-footed chameleons lurched behind their plates of roast dinner and glared at this stranger. "They eat *roast dinner?*"

"Course. Why wouldn't they?" Belle replied. "Weirdo."

"Where are *your* parents?" William looked Ned up and down. It took him ages. He was a tall fellow. "I think I've got vertigo."

"My parents? Oh, they're here and there. Actually, I think they're dead, but I'm not entirely sure," Ned replied.

"Not entirely sure?"

"Nope."

"Bit elusive. Dad won't like that. If it's beans on toast, it has to be beans on toast, not spaghetti on a ciabatta."

"I think your brother's been sniffing the spores of that *Amanita Muscaria,* Belle."

"Probably. It *is* the season for them to display signs of spore-bearing cultivation. It happened to Dad once, and *he* ended up growing gills at the side of his face. They lasted for weeks. When he finally got rid of them he couldn't stand the sight of a mushroom ever again. Did something to him psychologically."

"I'll do something to you psychologically in a minute, Belle," William retorted.

"If it's a problem, I can always return to my bookshop," Ned narrowed his eyes.

"Isn't that a bit, well, smoke-infested, your bookshop?" William replied. "That's what *we* heard down by the river. There's nothing left but some charred remains, isn't there?"

"Oh William, all those *books,* frittered away in a fire," Belle shuddered.

"Cheesecakes, **best** place *for* them. Who needs *books?* Especially ones with nothing written in them. I heard most of them were blank."

"Rubbish."

"Exactly! Anyway, it's freezing to frozen out here, I'm going in," and William pushed open an indoor gate at the top of the windy stairs. "To keep the chameleons out. They tend to roam. Come on."

But Ned's feet didn't want to come.

"Why are you going the other way, Ned?" Belle held the gate open. "Quick, Ned. This one will escape. He's *always* looking to. **CHARLIE!** EAT YOUR BRUSSELS SPROUTS! YOU SHAN'T BE GROWING BIG AND STRONG LIKE YOUR CHAMELEON SIBLINGS IF YOU HIDE YOUR VEGGIES UNDER THE CARPET NOW, WILL YOU?" Belle waved her arms anti-clockwise six times quickly. "There now, calm down. You're not coming further inside, remember what happened last time?" and Belle coaxed the runt chameleon into a trance and fed it a sprout. "Nice, eh?"

Charlie fell onto his back, his claws wiggling.

"Quick, Ned. Charlie's quarm charm won't last forever. When he got out last time, he fell into the gravy and nearly ended up on Dad's plate."

"Something doesn't feel right, that's all."

"If you're scared Mr Fireplace will let out your secrets, then don't worry, he takes bribes. Feed him some marshmallows."

"It's FREEZING. I want to go in, come on!" William hammered at another inner door three and a half times, and it swung open to reveal another set of even smaller winding steps.

"How many doors and steps and windy bits have you *got* in this place?" Ned glared up the next twisting dark passage.

"Enough, Ned. Dad's a precautionary. Come on."

"Is that Sicilian Spitting Cocoa?" Belle sniffed it out. "It is, that's what *I* want. Sicilian Spitting Cocoa with pink marshmallows floating in it. Don't you, Ned?"

William gagged. "DON'T try it, Ned! Last time those marshmallows blew up inside my mouth and I was sick in the rose bush. *God* knows what Mum poured in the recipe but it wasn't just sugar. Bleedin' hell, they grew and grew and *grew* until my cheeks were so puffed out my mouth flew open and even that over-cooked spaghetti bolognaise from Tuesday three weeks back shot out into those orange rosebushes. Ready to bloom, they *were.* Bloom, my foot! They died instantly. And Mum blamed ME! - *Ned?"*

"Not if it's a problem, I'm not coming in," Ned started to gradually walk backwards.

"It's not!" Belle hissed.

"Well, I don't want to just, you know, turn up unannounced."

"It doesn't matter. You can be Mum's guinea pig."

"Not sure I like the sound of *that.* What if it bites?"

"No, YOU! *You* can be the guinea pig. She can trial her new recipes on you. She's learning to be a pro - "

"Had enough of trickery for a lifetime, thank you very much. I'll just be going - " and Ned started to reverse his tall feet back down the windy steps and the doors to the road.

"Mind the **TRACTOR!"** William roared out a slitted-window as a rusty heap of junk rattled out some farm gates.

"Ned. *One* cup of Sicilian Spitting Cocoa? ONE cup. It won't ***kill*** you," Belle shouted.

"Are you *sure* about that, Belle?" William jostled with the door latch until it nearly came off. "Oh," William looked in his hands. "I only tugged it a tiny bit and look, the entire door's fallen off its hinges. Oops – come on, help me re-attach it before Mum sees."

"Alright, alright!" and Ned started to mount the stairs again.

"Okay, okay, shall we tell him, William?" Belle sighed.

"Oh your head be it. Mum likes to keep that under wraps," William shook his head.

"Tell me *what?"*

"Climb in that potato bush, that one by your side," Belle pointed to a patch of garden much darker that the rest. "Go on. It'll save you some energy."

"Um, I think I'll give it a miss."

"Ned, go *on.* It's fine. You might like it!"

"Will I?"

"Yes! Just stand on it, that blacker patch of mud - " and Belle watched as Ned slowly put one foot on it,

followed by the other. "GREAT! MUM NEEDED TO TEST *THE MULTIPLE MANOEUVRE MUD MAT!"* and Ned SHOT underground.

"WAHHHHHHHHHHHHHHH!" Ned's voice trailed off until it disappeared.

"Come on, let's see if it worked!" and Belle ran through the gate and the door, and another door, into the kitchen.

"WAHHHHHHHHH! WAHHHHHHHHHHHH! WAHHHHHHHHHHH!" William and Belle listened as Ned's voice got closer and closer and *closer* until THUD, the lanky boy landed on the rug.

"JESUS CHRIST!" Ned rubbed his behind. "WHAT JUST HAPPENED?"

"MUM! MUM? *The Multiple Manoeuvre Mud Mat* works!"

"FANTASTIC, dear Belle!" and Mrs Joy also fell out the chimney and thudded onto the rug next to Ned. "Sorry, dear."

"That's okay, I think," Ned squirmed on the rug rubbing his bottom. "Ouch - "

"I've got some ointment for that, come here," and before Ned could say no, this strange woman had pulled down his trousers and smeared a green jelly substance everywhere.

"Do you *mind?"* Ned replied coyly, trying desperately to hoik his trousers back up.

"Not really, dear tall boy. I don't mind at all," and Mrs Joy dabbed on some more of the foul-smelling green

jelly-stuff before Ned had finally pulled his trousers right up past his shoulders. Mrs Joy shook her head. Six little spiders with huge eyes shot out of her hair. "This ointment's been waiting for a good posterior to practice on, haven't you?" and Ned watched as this odd thin lady smiled at the bottle in her hand. "You're made up of, now *what* was it?" the bottle shook, annoyed, in Mrs Joy's hand. "Ah yes; earwig juice, chameleon spittle, a drop of fire-smelts and, last but not least, at *least* seven crushed dollops of goat's dung – the Nigerian dwarf variety. That's the best bit - "

"I feel a bit queasy now," Ned swallowed.

"You do, think about *me,* boy. I've been up that blasted chimney a long while now – trying to get Charlie's chameleon's cousin back, I was. Meredith, she's a wild old thing. Climbed right up inside there she did. And, if you still feel not quite right in a few minutes, swallow three of these," Mrs Joy sniffed, holding out a handful of tiny brown pellets. "Hmm - "

"NO thanks, I'm alright."

"ATCH*OOOO!* Got a bit stuck I did, my rather large hair net on the brickwork, but this person here, *hello*, we didn't really introduce ourselves, did we?"

"And you've *already* seen my bottom," Ned moved backwards.

" – well, that bottom of yours must have given me that extra little shove I needed to dislodge me. Thank you, stranger."

"That's okay, I think," Ned nodded.

"Are you a parrot, dear? You *do* keep repeating *that's okay, I think.* I've a remedy for untoward obnoxious repetition - "

"I'm sure you have," Ned mumbled.

"What was that, dear?"

"Mrs Joy, your home, it's - " Ned didn't quite know how to begin. "It's - *ginormous,"* and Ned strained his neck even taller to try and see the entire cottage. But the building was such an incredibly strange cluster of oddity that he couldn't see any top. "Are you sure, are you absolutely *sure* it's alright to stay with you? I can't believe Belle hasn't asked? - "

"Oh Ned, your name by the way, it's written on your bottom cheek, so I don't need to enquire, it's fine to stay."

"FINE?" Ned peered round and pulled his trousers slack at the back. "I've got *NED* tattooed onto my bum cheek?"

"Of *course* you have, dear. *The Multiple Manoeuvre Mud Mat* makes sure of that. Every time. Without fail. Honestly, these new people."

"Remember Angus Moon, William?" Belle sniggered.

"Yeah - "

"Mum dried him so hard he nearly disappeared altogether - and anyway, Ned, you're here now so Mum can't tell you to go. You won't be able to find your way out anyway. There's too many doors and rugs and mats and fireplaces with entrances and exits and potions in this place.

William was stuck for three days in the shower once. He was a wrinkled prune. Remember?"

"Hmm – how could I forget?" William muttered. "I was starving and no one even noticed I'd disappeared. My trousers for *Gladiolus-Viola Academy* were four sizes too big, FOUR, I'd lost so much weight."

"Nothing like losing a few pounds of cake-fat, darling," Mrs Joy cleared her throat.

"Thanks, Mum."

"You're welcome, dear. Anytime - "

"You *have* to stay, Ned. Mum needs guinea pigs to test her cooking - "

"Stop talking about guinea pigs. I really don't want to be one. I've had enough in *that* weird, muddy travel system just now," Ned glared back up the chimney. "How did I get from *there - "* he pointed back outside, " - to *here?"*

"Bewitchment, dear," Mrs Joy tapped her feet. "You'll get used to it - "

"I don't think I want to. And look at my leg, it's bruised black!"

"Oh Ned, dear, *Ned,* **dear.** *That's* just the soot from Mr Fireplace's chimney," and Mrs Joy brushed Ned's behind, hard, before she shot back up the chimney again. "WAAAAAAAAAAAAAA ~ HHHHHHHH! WAAAAAAAAAAAAAAA ~ HHHHHHHH! WAAAAAAAAAAAAAHHHHHHHH! I *obviously* haven't *quite* mastered the technique yet. I guess I didn't come out

independently the last time with your little shove, Ned, and *The Multiple Manoeuvre Mud Mat* thinks I'm a cheat!"

"I wouldn't be my Mum's cooking recipe guinea pig if I were you, Ned," William gagged. "It might leave you with crusty hair - " William scratched his head. "Mine still hasn't grown back all term from her *Gemstone Delight* modifications," and William showed Ned his bald patch. "Mu-*um?"* he hollered. "She always disappears. And her cooking, it'll certainly leave your behind on fire for weeks, Ned! Mu-*um?* WHERE'VE YOU GONE?"

"I'M UP THE CHIMNEY, OF COURSE! KINDLY HELP ME ***DOWN!"***

"But at least here, with us Ned, you'll have a bed to sleep off any allurement and fascination gone wrong," Belle looked up the chimney. It was pitch black. "MUM! *MUU-UUUM! Unbolt* the next door, it's like an icebox in the kitchen now. You've blocked up Mr Fireplace," Belle hammered loudly on Mr Fireplace's chimney feet.

"OUCH, girl! I take it all back. I didn't miss you at *all!"* Mr Fireplace curled up his poor toes.

"Right," Belle cried up the chimney.

"OUCH, GIRL! MY EARS!" and Mr Fireplace folded his ear lobes over as far as he could. "Can *Gladiolus-Viola Academy* cut the holidays short – *please?"*

"Listen, Mum. I read this at the Academy, for releasing oneself from tight predicaments – *"twist your legs slightly right, then slightly left, then drink some of that liquidised soot juice – it should be encrusted onto the inner-chimney wall."*

"Yes, dear. I can see it. Oh, it's spicy - "

" - and you'll pop out in the next room. I hope – Yes?"

THUD!

"IT WORKED, DARLING, ROSABELLA! I'VE ARRIVED COMFORTABLY ON THE RAINBOW SETTEE. OH HOW LOVELY, RUTHY-RAINBOW! YOU REMEMBERED I LIKED ORANGE-BLOSSOM JUICE IN MY FLOATY MUG! THANK YOU! NOW, WHERE **WERE** WE?"

"Like an icebox?" William's teeth had started to chatter. His tongue had turned blue. "It *is* an icebox, Belle," "*LET US INTO YOUR ROOM!* Bu-*um!"*

"WILLIAM!" Mrs Joy huffed in horror. "I'm still recuperating – I do *not* want to hear your foul tongue."

"It's not *by* fault, Bum. By tongue, it's frozen solid and I can't say by 'M's or by N's, Bum!"

"Lessons in chivalry and politeness this Christmas are *desperately* needed, SON!"

"ARE BOT!"

"All of you? Stop it," Ned heard a voice. "All of you."

"What does *that* mean, exactly? *All* of you?" Ned looked around.

No one came.

"As I said, I'll be going, for *sure* this time," and Ned started to slip back down the icy kitchen steps. *"What - ?"*

"You won't make it out alive, Ned," Belle grabbed Ned's arm. "Mum seems to have turned the steps into a slide. YOU'RE SLIPPING!"

"HE CAN STAY! *HE* CAN **STAY!"** Mrs Joy cried from the settee room. "I'm not letting *any* old waifs and strays in, Rosabella, but *he* seems an *alright* type of chap. Please don't let him fall and break a leg, though; I can't afford the hospital fees – nearly again!" Ned heard the voice of the mad woman call back from the other side of the door, closer this time. "That donkey five years ago was the *last* straw. Nearly breaking its hind legs trying to career down the garden on a sledge. The road would have been fine for breaking bodily parts, *that's* not my concern, but *my* pathway? I'd be sued!"

"Her boyfriend, Ned. He was a donkey, well, he had big ears," William started to spy through the keyhole.

"Oh," Ned cried back from a sticky tree - sticking its branches inside – "this tree's got fingers!"

"Ned, don't squirm. Keep still. The tree, it's trying to help you."

"I can't **help** squirming, William! THE TWIGS ARE GOING UP MY BOTTOM!" and William watched Ned's feet hang in mid-air as the tree pulled him upwards further and further, taller than the cottage -

The inner door to the settee room creaked.

Its hinges ground golden rust to the floor.

"GALLOPING GAZELLES, RELEASE YOUR SPELLS!" Mrs Joy tugged open the door, and she fell backwards. "DARN, it's been open all along. Oh, Ned, you still seem to be hanging there. That mustn't be the correct spell. Right. Now. Let me think - "

"WITH *ALL* DUE RESPECT, MRS JOY, I FEEL SICK! MY BRAIN CAN'T WAIT AROUND FOR YOU TO THINK!" Ned looked about, from his airy space mid-air. His face looked contorted. "I, I - "

"You don't like being constrained, *do* you, Ned?" Mrs Joy shook her head. "You'll have to be a bit more aware of your surroundings, then, shan't you? Trying to escape down an icy slide - whatever next?"

"I *don't* wish to find out whatever's next! GET ME DOWN!"

"Don't be so impatient, you wombat."

"Watch your tongue, Rosabella," Mrs Joy replied. "Ned's our guest," and she waved her spoon, and Ned fell to the floor.

"OUCH! First my bum. And now my head. Are you lot *trying* to **kill** me?"

"Yes, dear, I mean, NO dear," Mrs Joy smiled at her spoon. "Thank you, Pinkie - "

"Yes, Ned, before you say, it, my Mother names her utensils," Belle sighed as she watched Ned fall with a crash three more inches.

"Thank you, Pinkie. I didn't think you'd *quite* finished dropping our guests - I mean, returning them to the floor. You hadn't done that cute little wiggle of completedness," and Mrs Joy shoved the cackling Pinkie back in the drawer. It wriggled, furiously. "PINKIE! What did I tell you about showing off in front of our guests?"

Snow immediately seeped through to Ned's bare skin, but before he knew it he was inside the settee room,

heat blaring - his feet soaking in green glitter bath bombs - not having taken any steps under intention of their own.

Ned shuffled away from the inglenook.

It roared back.

"Nice. Bet you're related to that Mr Fireplace, aren't you?" and Ned tried to place his left foot back in the kitchen, but his legs would just not move. "What?" Ned glared at the mini Mr Fireplace. *"What,* I said?"

"Nothing."

"Oh."

"Yes, Ned. **I** *speak* too."

"Don't mind Flippin' Flaming Fiona," Belle threw herself down onto a triangular red settee next to Ned's feathery-beanie one. "She's just learning to talk."

"I am not! I'm in second grade already, I'll have you know, Rosabella. Come back from *Gladiolus-Viola Academy* a know-all, have you?"

"She already was," William replied dully.

"Well," Flippin' Flaming Fiona continued, *"I've* passed *Fume-Fogging* elementary level, **and** kindergarten, and apparently I'm way ahead in *Fire-Education Years.* Look, here's my certificate!" and Flaming Fiona turned herself out before anyone could read it. "AND, drop the *Flippin'!* I *wasn't* christened with that."

"Suit yourself," and Belle patted her arm rest whispering under her breath. Immediately, apple crumble arrived in a steaming bowl.

“What the waffles, how did you do *that?”* Ned sat bolt upright.

“That’s MY phrase, don’t wear it out. And, if you want some, tap your *own* arm rest.”

Ned tapped.

And again.

“Nothing’s coming.”

“It must be the left one then. Oh, I forgot to say, you have to whisper your desires when tapping.”

“FROG SPAWN IN CABBAGE JELLY!” Flaming Fiona cackled as Ned tapped his arm rest.

“That’s DISGUSTING!” Ned gulped as a huge bowl of wiggling tadpoles wobbled about in a bowl of steaming brown jelly on his lap.

“Told you I was clever,” Flaming Fiona burst into a red heat.

“Miss Hearth, oh Cousin Aga, oh Mr *Fireplace,* I’ve *missed* you. Not **you** *quite* so much, Fiona,” Belle scorned. “You’re getting too big for your boots. MUM? Can you turn Flippin’ Flaming Fiona off at the mains, please, until she’s sorry?”

“Yes, yes, I can do that! That Fiona’s been rather a pain since you left, Rosabella. Needs taking down a flame or two,” and Mrs Joy’s shuffling feet suddenly appeared with the most embarrassing head in huge form - mainly knotted black hair tied up in an old yellow duster-like thing - and then suddenly long thin arms emerged which tried in vain to contain the bubbling in a pot of some substance, rather wretched to the taste-buds, before it totally filled the

air asphyxiating anything within five feet of its frantic cooking.

"Belle, careful dear, *careful,* your *hair,* it's *smoking!"*

"FIONA!" Belle grimaced. "You can be turned off for two days."

"OH, I'M SORRY! I'M *SO* SORRY! PLEASE LET ME STAY ON? PLEASE?" Flaming Fiona blubbered, her tears turning down her flames until POP - she'd made herself disappear.

"Devils and demons, Flaming Fiona, you *can* do spells!"

"TOLD YOU I COULD!" Flaming Fiona invisibly hissed from somewhere.

Belle smelt a choking charcoaled aroma and, seeing wisps of black smoke from her head float up and out into the kitchen, she rushed over to the sink and plunged her head inside. After what seemed an eternity, Belle's head emerged, bedraggled and covered in strands of sickly green vegetables.

"Welcome home, dear, welcome *home,"* Mrs Joy flung out her arms. "So, tell me - "

"Tell you *what?"* Belle picked a string of spring onions from her ears. "What ARE you cooking?"

"Don't worry about that little experiment, how's *Gladiolus-Viola?* Has it *changed* you? I certainly can't *see* that it's made you any the wiser *or* any more insightful, *that's* for sure," and Mrs Joy continued to pull green leaves from Belle's scalp. "Oh! That's where the ladle disappeared

to. And these beetroot? What WAS I thinking? They're months past their best, you shan't be having *these* for tea," and Mrs Joy shook the stringy bits of stinking red vermin in mid-air and smirked at the new face which sat motionless. "Hello, Ned."

"Hello, formally, Mrs Joy," and Ned held out his hand from his settee.

"Well, Rosabella? *Gladiolus-Viola?* Are you supposing that I *guess* how you've been?"

Ned pulled his arm back.

"Sorry, dear Ned. I wasn't being rude. It's just that if I don't ask Rosabella right now what she's been up to, apart from the fleeting visit to Peru she made to see me, she'll have more time to make up precocious tales on how she's been top of the class, or some such nonsense. And, for the record, we don't shake hands in this place, we kiss," and Mrs Joy grabbed Ned and dragged his cheek towards hers. "SMACK!" she pressed her lips onto his thin face. "There. *Welcome Hello's* all done and dusted Ned."

"Thanks," Ned stared, open-mouthed.

"Stop catching flies, child. We don't do that here either."

"But, Mum! I have, I **have** been top ALL term!" Belle interrupted.

"Course you have, dear. Now, pass those baby crabettes, will you? There's a love," and Mrs Joy placed one crabette into each bowl of raw potato and the crabette claws mashed them perfectly and then heated them with their sizzling shells. "STOP! *Thank* you, Celia, thank *you,* Clive

and thank YOU, Chip-with-one-eye, you've all passed your elementary mashing with a merit!" and she gave each crabette some seaweed to roll about in.

"I think I'd rather still be hanging in that tree," Ned's mouth fell open, again.

"NED?!"

"Sorry, Mrs Joy."

"So, Belle; for *weeks* on end, mind, with not much of a word apart from that fleeting visit in your Father's ridiculous choice of car?"

"What's wrong with Molly? She's - "

"Yes, William?"

"Molly, she's - "

"Thought as much."

"Oh MUM, *love* every minute - "

"ROSABELLA, that's right in my ear. But, needless to say, I've bet you've made an impression?"

"Yep, especially with that Tabitha Squires, she's *such* a snitch," Belle threw back her hair and soaked Mrs Joy from head to toe; strands of leek still emerging from her scalp. And her ears.

"Waste not, want not, catch those leeks, Rosabella! And, shut the doors. All of them. Don't let the cold out, no, sorry, the cold *in* - " and the odd lady yanked Ned's coat and he was in, for certain this time as his feathered-beanie settee had started to float itself and its passenger towards the open door. And the blizzard.

"You were right the first time, it *is* colder in here than out there," William groaned. "What's with the hole in the

wall, Mum? I can see the shed," William turned to Ned, who was now gaining height every second by blankets of snow balancing on his brain. "It's colder inside than outside, mate, so *you* decide if you fancy staying - and don't ask about that torpedo-sized hole gaping in the brickwork. What happened, Mum?"

"Oh, just the blue turnip stew, darling. Nothing new. Took on a mind of its own it did, just last week. I was hanging out the eggs to dry, and *BLAST,* I heard it from way up by the chicken coop, and, when I returned, the turnips were on the ceiling and the pot was nowhere to be seen, lest that hole. Anyway, enough said - and, *not* if we huddle up, we *shan't* be chilly," and the bustly woman ushered everyone, magically without using any hands, to actually come inside.

Really inside.

Four more rooms further into the little cottage.

And through Flippin' Flaming Fiona's twin sister.

"Come on, Ned. Fabianna shan't hurt you. She's the cold one. Her flames are just for show."

"Oh."

"Come *on,* then! What *are* you doing standing there like a dithering lemon in the draft? Come through, come *right* through. And - " Mrs Joy looked into Fabianna's flames for a suggestion, "I guess you can call me - Pip," Mrs Joy nodded towards her new guest. "No William, not *you,* **you** can stick to calling me Mumsy - "

"What? Since when did I *ever* call you *Mumsy?"*

"Oh, well, it sounds kind of cute. Can we start?"

"Er, no."

"Oh, *Mum* then, just Mum, but *with* a capital *M*, please," and the lady threw back her head and laughed at her son. "Break a smile, boy, pleeeeease?"

"You're *so* embarrassing."

"Yes, I *do* aim to please," and Mrs Joy held out her arms to take the collection of coats that she could quite easily envisage just piling up on the kitchen floor. And then threw them inside Fabianna before walking in herself. Before she then vanished.

"Jesus Christ! Any *more* tricks she can do?" Ned glared for the third time, his mouth dropping to the floor.

"I CAN still see you, boy."

"Sorry Pip."

"Right. Anyone care for a taste of my new biscuits?" Mrs Joy shouted.

"Mum called you a *dithering lemon,"* Belle cackled. "And, go on. Walk through Fabianna. She won't bite."

"I didn't think she had teeth. Just BURNING FLAMES! I'm not getting in," Ned growled.

"Well, if you can't make the decision yourself, I guess Fabianna will have to just help you along," Mrs Joy demanded. "HONKUS-WHO, FABIANNA LET HIM THROUGH!"

And Ned found himself being lifted by a pair of flaming fingers into the air and right into Fabianna's flames –

"HELLS BELLS, WHAT *NEXT?"* Ned's body went rigid.

"Oh, there's *plenty* more. Would you like to see?"

"No! No thanks, Pip. I would not."

"You *are* a bit of a wonderer, aren't you?" Mrs Joy peered close into Ned's eyes when Fabianna's flames put him down.

"Am I? I hadn't really ever thought about it."

"Hum, yes, you look like the forgetful type."

"Huh? How did you work *that* one out, I've only just walked in the door?"

"I can tell, I can tell. Anyway, don't make yourselves *too* comfortable, there's someone here to see you, us, I guess? Strange coincidence, nice man, attended *Gladiolus-Viola* with *you* last term - " Mrs Joy nodded in Ned's direction, " - has a question for you, come further in, *all* of you, and that includes you, William. I can see you spying on my coconut-egg and gooseberry delights; they shan't be cooked for at least another fifteen point three more minutes. I've got the old whistle kettle boiling away in the piano, and the coals are firing out heat more than I can control. Come and meet Rupert, *Rupert* - sorry, I've *quite* forgotten your last name, forgive me, Rupert - ? Oh, I just need to check on my eggs."

"Rupert ***Gvist,"*** and at the sound of the low, deep voice, Ned stopped.

Stopped dead in his tracks.

"William, Belle, *don't* go in there, he's bad, *terribly* bad," Ned hissed. "It's a trap."

"Better than staying in the kitchen when those coconut-egg and gooseberry delights explode," William

muttered. “I was blinded for six days when the chocolate casserole boiled over and seeped into my socks. *And* it wasn’t even chocolate, the cheek of it. Mum just told me that to make me eat it. It was reconstituted soil, if I remember correctly. Who in their right minds feeds their children *reconstituted soil?”*

“What do you mean? Mum doesn’t know any *terribly bad* people, only Mr Svendig from the village store, and he’s only *slightly* bad. He wronged Mum last Autumn placing all the bruised plums she’d bought from him at the bottom of the shopping bag so she didn’t realise until she got home, but that wasn’t *terribly* bad - ”

“Ssssh, don’t make him aware we’re here - ” Ned slunk into the flickery shadows of Fabianna, and whispered. “That man, Rupert Gvist, I’d recognise his voice anywhere. He wasn’t in my class last term, he’s a traitor, just tried to pass through Eduardo’s fireplace, tried to gain access to *our* world. He’s reeled in your Mum but *I* am his ultimate quest as he knows I’m - ”

“You’re what? Spit it out!” Belle hissed. *“What?”*

“Don’t be so impatient - ”

“WHAT?”

“Don’t *rush* me!”

“NED!”

“Immortal.”

“You’re WHAT?”

“Sssssh,” Ned glanced around to make sure he was alone. “Well, sort of, so I’m led to believe, but maybe my Father’s book lies, I’m not entirely sure.”

"You never mentioned I had to know you *forever.*"

"I didn't say *you* were immortal, Belle."

"Really? Are you *really* immortal?" William slithered back down the darkness of Fabianna's fireplace wall, inching closer and closer to that Rupert. "And that man, in *our* living room, is here to *kill* us?"

"William!" Belle whispered with cross eyes. "Don't say *that.*"

"Might as well cut to the chase. OUCH! My foot's stuck in a mouse hole. Well, Ned? *Is* he? *Are* we all minced meat before bedtime?"

"Ned? *William?* Where ***are*** you all?" Mrs Joy hollered. "Rosa***bella?*** Ex***cuse*** me, Rupert - let me go and see where they've all got to. William and Belle, they've *barely* seen each other all term, at different sites, they are, at *Gladiolus-Viola*, a lot to catch up on, I *suspect.*"

"Of course."

"And Ned, Belle's boyfriend, would you *believe* it, someone who can keep up with her less than social ways, he's come to stay for Christmas, haven't much had the chance to ask him about his *own* parents, perhaps he's an orphan? Oh dear *Lord,* perhaps Rosabella wants me to adopt him, now that *wouldn't* be just, would it, Rupert? You don't *mind* that I call you Rupert, do you, Rupert?" Mrs Joy fussed over the kettle that bubbled ferociously balancing on Fabianna's cold flames. "Another cup, Rupert? I'll boil the coconut eggs in here to keep you company - "

"Thank you, Pippa."

"Oh, Pippa, yes. Do feel free to call me that."

"Thank you."

"PIANO? Roll yourself in here will you and get those coconut eggs boiled for Rupert to see. She's a marvel, she is, Prunella Piano, aren't you, dear?" and Rupert watched as Prunella's wheels blindly rolled themselves over Pippa's toes. "There, nicely done," Pippa winced. "Another brew, Rupert?"

"Indeed, I've got *all* the time in the world, *thank* you, Pippa," Rupert replied, slyly. "Tasty."

"Why, thank you, Rupert, and, Rupert, how *very* attentive of you to know my name. Willi-*aaam,* ROSA-*BELLA,* where *are* you? Excuse me - " and Mrs Joy with her wild hair popped back into Fabianna's darkened passageway, but when she reached the kitchen, she found it bare - the stable door swinging open on its old brass hinge. *"Really,* indeed, how *rude,* but, oh, actually, were they ever here at *all?* Did I just *imagine* all of that?" she shivered, as the gaping hole sat wider than ever, and no coats were stuffed in the flames. Mrs Joy shook her head, her chiffon scarf unravelling to the floor, and returned along the insanely dark walls, feeling for spiders and eels as she went, and not even noticing the violent blast from the Prunella as fifteen point three minutes had just struck. "Sorry, Rupert, the children, they seem to have vanished, perhaps you can come and visit again tomorrow?"

But her voice was not blessed with any answer at all.

"Rupert? ***RUUU-****PE-****ERT?"***

The Book

"Ned, can *I* see? Can *I* see your Father's book?" Belle followed Ned up the garden. "Where are you *going?* Ned?" Belle tried to keep up, but Ned's steps were three to her one, and she slipped trying to speed up. "NED! *Wait - "* Belle puffed, out of breath, *" - come BACK!"*

"I need to think," Ned's forehead creased up. "Father warned me, *years* ago."

"About what?"

"Father warned me that one day, *one* day this time would come."

"What time?"

"A boy seeking his book would come - "

"Rupert, he didn't sound like a *boy?"*

"Don't interrupt - "

"Well, you said a *boy.* That Gvist person, he sounded like a *man.* Just saying."

"This *man-boy - "*

"Ned, don't be so *ridiculous - "*

"Mum might be getting fried alive in there, and all you can do is argue about some man's age," William snapped.

"If *anyone's* getting fried alive, it'll be that *man-boy;* trying Mum's biscuits - " Belle hissed.

"AS I was *saying - "* Ned went into a weird trance; his pupils growing larger and larger.

"Did you sniff those eggy-coconut thingies?" Belle slanted her eyes. *"Did* you, Ned? You're starting to look a little flushed. That's what every new guinea pig to the house tends to be like when they take their first whiff of the *Joy* cooking."

But Ned did not reply.

He looked vacant, and his eyes started to glaze over a misty, smoky pink. *"The man-boy, he will try and befriend you by any means, but his goal? It's to get his hands on my book, 'The Book of Immortality.'*

"What *are* you talking about?" Belle shook Ned by his gangly arms. "You're speaking as if it's not you."

"He's talking as if he's his own *Father,"* William sniggered. "Weirdo."

"I *heard* that," Ned snapped out of his trance. "Don't be *rude."*

"You're the one being *odd,* Ned. Can't help but laugh."

"I wrote it, years ago, when I resided in Anouka, but I got old, frail, and I couldn't hold my quill, pen thingy - "

"Oh, *here* he goes again," William sighed. "Shall we just take a seat here? Wake me when he's finished his drivel and he's able to pick up his quill, pen thingy."

"William! Shut your trap. It's his *Father* speaking, you know."

"From the dead?"

"I guess."

"When I pass on, son, if the final chapter is incomplete, and I can ensure you it is, and my ink has run dry, remember these words. ***'Son, keep this book safe, think of it as your saviour. If you follow the right path, the life you lead, it will help you prosper and serve us well. Trust no one, but someone.'*** *Will you do that, son?"*

"That's *helpful,"* William lay down in the snow.

"So, *there* you go," Ned spluttered and brushed himself down. "What happened to my coat? It's ripped at the elbow! *Both* sides - "

"Woah! Ned, you're *back* with us? Enjoy your little delving into the dark side, did you? Oh, and *that* was Belle. She shook you *so* hard, your elbow patches must have ripped off."

"I didn't, and I *still* don't understand my Father's wisdom," Ned sat, shivering ridiculously. "Why trust *no* one, but perhaps trust *someone?* It doesn't, it doesn't make *any* sense; mind, he never made any sense when he *was*

alive. Used to feed sliced beetroot to the cat - thought it would make her more wisdom-ful."

"Is that *actually* a word? *Wis*dom-ful?" Belle frowned.

"Yes, *course* it is. I didn't become a Professor for nothing, Belle."

Apples were ripening, and it was *mid-winter.* They were getting bigger and *bigger* and rosier and *rosier* as Ned kept on staring into the distance, and then, all of a sudden, like bullets being shot from a gun, a ton of *enormous* apples fell right on his head. *"OUCH! OW!* What's *happening?"* Ned kicked about like he was being attacked by a swarm of wasps, but the apples just kept falling and falling and *falling* until it felt like every bone in his body was crushed to death.

"S-O-R-R-R-R-R-Y-Y-Y!" the frazzled voice of Mrs Joy floated up the garden. "My coconut and gooseberry delights turned out not to have been delights *after* all. Their rumblings must've made reverberations underground and shook that tree to bits. More of a terrible mishap of nature which should never have begun, these cake-things - "

"Well, *there's* a surprise," William muttered, picking pips from his sock rims. "And, *that* name hardly rolls of the tongue, does it? *Coconut and gooseberry terrible mishaps of nature which should never have begun.* I don't think *they'll* be a sell out in the shop."

"And your *Mum?* What did *she* think?" Belle looked at Ned who was desperately trying to push his leather patches back into the holes in his elbows.

“My *Mum?* Belle, I *never* knew my Mum. She was poorly from the day I was born and I grew up only knowing her through Father’s photographs. She *was* very pretty, though.”

“Pretty doesn’t pay the bills,” William scorned.

“Oh, *shut* up,” Belle hissed.

“Father spent his entire life trying to identify immortality,” Ned sighed. “Then, one day, when I was just eight years old, I heard a tremendous *roar* from his study. I was sitting alone in the kitchen, as usual - ”

“Stop trying to get pity, *Ned,”* William moaned.

“Don’t be *soooo* horrible,” Belle tried to help Ned stuff the leather patches back in place, but the more she pushed, the further up inside his sleeves they went.

“It was porridge, *again,”* Ned’s shoulders slumped forward as if remembering those solemn cereal days. “That was *all* that was in the cupboards; bags and *bags* of the stuff. I sat there, spooning in the gloop, when Father’s uproar shocked me and I fell off my stool. Father had *never* allowed me to enter his study, he had always said it was *his* room to find answers to unanswered questions. But, when he roared that day, his demand that I *never* set foot in his chambers disappeared and I ran in to see what dreadful commotion had occurred. All I saw was Father, quill and ink, writing so fast his hand could *not* keep up. He was writing his book, and then he turned to me and told me that phrase. From this day, I only trust in those who inspire me. I saw a hand, a slight wing, appear, from a bleak fireplace,

and Father's eyes, they were dazzled, he cried her name, my *Mum's* name, and *then* - "

"What?"

"He disappeared."

"Oh," Belle replied. "Did you know how to cook porridge? Did you starve?"

"No. I touched Father's shoulder as he drifted into the smouldering flames. But then, I found myself in another world. Belle, I saw *you* there, in a dimension only *Anouka* can explain. You were having a bit of trouble on your ice-skates. Anyway, *that* is why I was so attentive to you."

"Is that what you call it? I call it stalking."

"I couldn't *believe* it when you finally turned up at *Gladiolus-Viola*. I was part of Anouka, and so were you."

"Cut to the chase," William rolled his eyes. "And, there's *nothing* wrong with a hearty bowl of porridge or three, or boiled eggs, two of them, or *frog's* legs, how about toads in fact, duo legs, or *trio,* or a large, and it has to be a *large,* plate of snails. You're *so* dramatic. I can see why *you* two both get on."

"So, my *scholarship,* it wasn't *anything* to do with my verbal intelligence?" Belle dropped Ned's leather elbow patches back into the snow.

"Told you," William looked smug.

"Doesn't matter about that," Ned started to shake as he looked back towards the cottage. Wisps of green and yellow smoke were starting to appear in droves from the window seals, and even more from the edges around the back door.

"Don't worry about *that,* it'll be Mum with her new batch of frog's spawn," William muttered. *"That'll* be a change for you, Ned. No more porridge, just *newts* for breakfast!"

"There *must* have a reason Anouka took your Mum so young? - " Belle sighed.

"Who was she?" William peered closer and closer until Ned started to feel claustrophobic.

"Magenta, she was called Magenta," Ned's eyes looked to the floor. "We called her Magenta. And then, she just vanished one day. I never got the chance to say goodbye."

"Magenta?" William stared at Ned.

"Yes, what's so odd about that?"

"Isn't that a paint? We've got it in our study!"

"Imbecile," Ned sat in the snow, his trousers soaking up the winter wetness of the grass.

Belle eyed Ned up and down. He resembled a little boy, perhaps that eight year old boy. *"Magenta?* Ned, how old *are* you? That name's *ancient."*

"Old? *Me?* As old as they *come,* I guess - "

"Belle's going out with a great-great-great *grandad!!!"* William cackled.

"Father's photographs of Mum - he *called* them photographs - are *nothing* like the ones I see today, all colourful and glossy," Ned pushed his bony hand deep inside his trouser pocket and felt around. When he pulled it out, he was clutching a parchment. *"This* is my Mum, beautiful, don't you think?"

William peered at Ned's photograph. "Ned, it's a sketch – old and brown and crusty," William ran his hand over the paper.

"Careful, it's *very* delicate," Ned pulled it away.

"Ned, can we, can *we* see your book?" Belle asked. "Can you show *us* your Father's *Book of Immortality*? Did he write it because he wanted to stop others being hauled over into the dark side?"

"Stop asking so many questions. It's not a pantomime. It's my *life. And,* I don't know, I don't know the answers to *any* of your questions," Ned stood up and brushed the leaves from his trousers. "When I saw Father writing the book that day, his face was in a trance, a *demony* trance *so* intense it chilled me from head to toe. It still does. It was like he'd been p-p-p poss*essed,"* Ned shivered.

"Poor you," Belle brushed mushy apples from Ned's shoulders. They'd started to ferment. He stank.

"I was, and still am, unsure whether it was actually my Father writing the words or whether he was just the body through which someone else could express themselves."

"Someone, from *Anouka?"* William whispered.

"Sssssh - " Ned crouched as low to the ground as possible. "Maybe - " and he started to walk down the garden towards the house. "I'll show you the book, if you like?" and the back door flew open. "That smells *grotesque!* I think I'll stick to porridge."

"What if that man is still there? Rupert Gvist," Belle hissed.

"Oh, *he's* gone," Ned answered casually.

"How do *you* know? We've been up the garden all this time. You can't see the back door of the house from there."

"Mum told me, she told me it's safe to go back inside now. She always lets me know. And, that *Amdoch Atlas,* William - "

"What about it?"

"It was hanging out your pocket," and Ned put his photograph away.

"I thought only the beholder could read the *Amdoch Atlas,"* William glared at Ned.

"Obviously malfunctioning again. Can we try one of your biscuits now, Mrs Joy? Mrs *Joy?"*

"Why of *course,* you'll find them *just* at the top of the dustbin, but don't worry, they taste *far* better covered in used teabags. *And,* where *did* you get to? Rupert had been waiting for you most of the afternoon, but he couldn't wait much longer, then you disappeared, simply *left* the house without a *word,* and *really,* the back door lay *wide* open; it's a miracle we didn't all freeze in our slippers. It's winter out there, so *please,* we *really* must conserve the heat - *despite* the three-foot gaping hole, yes, William, I said it before you could throw *that* back in my face, accidents happen, accidents happen when old tiles just keep coming loose. I don't know what this house is doing save falling apart at the seams, gaping tiles that I keep pushing back, but it's like this house has an agenda of its own. It's a wonder we don't all fall prey to goodness knows what - " Mrs Joy spoke as she draped two sopping wet tea towels over the Aga to dry.

"Alright, keep your hair on," William muttered.

Mrs Joy shook her head. "Your Father's back later. The biscuits, the ones I *managed* to salvage, I think they're in the *other* purple tin by the log burner if you fancy those ones more than the binned version? Take your pick - " and Mrs Joy rushed down the passageway, " - just making up the spare room, how long *are* you staying, Ned?"

"Oh, until *Gladiolus-Viola* starts the new term again, Mum," Belle replied, choking on six entangled used teabags she had dragged off her exploded biscuit and decided to eat.

"Oh," and Mrs Joy whisked up the stairs to air some new bed sheets for the apparent long-term guest. "Right. Go and see Flaming Fiona isn't trying to creep back alight, will you?"

"My teeth ache," Ned moaned.

"Take the biscuits from the dustbin, the used teabags have softened them. And, the tea, it disguises the rancid coconuts - " Belle whispered.

"Thanks."

"That's okay."

"When I told you my Mum's name, you looked shocked. Why?" Ned sucked his biscuit this time.

"Magenta. Mum talks of a Magenta that's all. She says some people in family owes their lives to her. Centuries back in our family tree. We've – been there, apparently. Seen her. Not us, exactly, but my ancestors. There surely can't be *two* Magentas."

"You *know* her? Magenta. My *Mum.*"

"As I said, apparently we do."

“You’ve **seen** her?” Ned dropped his second biscuit.
It mulched into the floor.
“Some of have, yes.”
The floor drew the biscuit inside.
Deep down to its roots.

Rotten Coconuts & Secrets

"Yep, it *was* weird. Seeing her, Magenta. So they said - " Belle looked at Ned. "Anyway, night then."

"I'll bet. And *who* said?"

"Brodie and Kat. Some odd relations of ours."

"Bet they got a shock."

"So, you *know* then?" Belle toppled on her tip toes trying to reach the *second 'other'* biscuit tin saved for her Mum's *better* biscuits. "Why does she PUT them so high?" Belle grabbed it as it fell down.

"So *you* can't eat them all, I guess. And, know what? What do I know?" Ned clutched his stomach. I think my biscuit was actually poisoned. What *does* she put in these?"

"Your constitution, Ned, it's probably not used to it yet."

"It's happened again. You *think* you know someone - and then your *own* Mum poisons people with deadly coconuts," William sniggered.

"Stop eaves-dropping. Why don't you go and tend to your Avian Dinosaurs or something?" Belle hissed.

"I think, I think, I need … to - " and Ned dropped on the floor.

"Another one bites the dust," William nodded to the demented tree with the fingers. "Come on, *Gran Abuelo,* do your stuff and take this one to bed," and the Gran Abuelo nodded its barked trunk in appreciation and immediately spewed extra arms into the kitchen.

"GRRRR, GRAAA, GRAAAAB!" the Gran Abuelo hissed under its wooded branches. Ned was then catapulted six floors up. **"Prrrimbus, prrrimbo, grrratchint bark!"** the Gran Abuelo mumbled and Ned's clothes fell off his body which in turn dressed itself in a neat, but rather small, pair of pyjamas. "I can't help not knowing his size at such short notice," the Gran Abuelo hissed back before shrivelling up for the night in a bucket of pig's wee.

"Thanks," William replied. "We can always rely on you."

"Can we?" Belle interrupted. "It whacked me in the jaw last summer just for being - "

"Obnoxious?"

"Because I happened to know that the Gran Abuelo is part of the Patagonian Cypresses family, and that it didn't matter it couldn't come inside to reside by Mr Fireplace on wet days because the Gran Abuelo was cultivated to withstand even being buried in water due to its inherent resins."

"Right. Any more biscuits, Mum? Non-poisonous ones?"

"Crrrisp and cosy," Mrs Joy hollered, "the beds are *a-a-a-all* yours when you need them, oh, I can see our guest is already snoring. I think I'll turn in for the night too. It's been a *strange* sort of day, *really* it has. That Rupert, he did look *ever* so familiar, and his disappearance, quite unfathomable, it was," Mrs Joy mooched in and then straight back out; her knitted bed hat and microwaveable beanie slipper socks rustling as she shuffled about. "I came to find *you* children, and when *you* were *nowhere* to be seen, I returned to the settee room only to find *that* empty too. Rupert had simply vanished. Evaporated into the burning embers, you could say. Anyway, *good*night, dears - " Mrs Joy rubbed her tired eyes, " - and *that* tin, Rosabella, it's full of *hog*weed, my dear. Ni-*ight!"*, and she poured her warmed chocolate soup from the rusty stove kettle, shook her head that the cocoa had, *again,* clotted the spout, added a hearty slurp of WD40 to the rustiness for tomorrow, and nodded

before returning back up the stairs; brushing chameleon cobwebs from her hair. “Don’t forget to close the wood stoves, *both* rooms - ”

“I didn’t get to tell Ned that his Mum is now a giant butterfly,” Belle whispered to William.

“Never mind, I’m sure he knows.”

The Christmas Fayre

"Where's *Ned?"* William searched in the cupboards the following day before the sun was even up. In fact, the shadows in the kitchen were surely the *moon,* lingering. The sun was *barely* visible, its rays only touching upon the frosty shed roof.

"Well, you'll be hard pressed to find him in *there,"* Belle stirred the teapot with her left hand whilst William rummaged deeper inside the cupboard.

"And what are *you* doing, Belle?" William muttered as Belle scrubbed and chipped away at the Aga with her other hand.

"It's covered in soot," Belle replied. "It must have fallen from the chimney in that howling gale last night, and now it's *completely* welded itself to the stove. See?" Belle pointed to the sticky black tar that had stuck itself, stubbornly, to the Aga, but William's eyes were at least six feet away, trying to get accustomed to the dusty black cereal shelf.

"That's *strange,"* William's voice sounded muffled from the very depths of the porridge cupboard. "I *definitely* closed off both the wood burner in the settee room *and* in here last night. I let the fireplaces smoulder to nothing, it took *ages,* so there shouldn't *be* any soot," William coughed. "How annoying."

"Can't find the honey, to pour on your porridge, fatty?"

"No, I *was* actually talking about the Aga. I'm not cleaning it again," William was now so far inside the cupboard, Belle could have easily shut the doors and tied the knobs together, but that wouldn't give her another pair of hands for chipping. "Unless someone has been using the woodstoves? Did you say there was a storm last night, Belle?"

"Absolutely *howling,* didn't you hear? And, *I'm* cleaning it. *You* only do it as a penance; like when you accidentally drowned Dad's fish by trying to see if they could walk on the rug. Remember?" Belle stopped scrubbing and wiped her nose. "The noise was drilling, that storm, it rattled my bed. *Surely* it must have woken you, William? Cloth ears."

"Well, nope, I didn't hear anything, slept like a log," William emerged from the cupboards; six bags of porridge oats in his hands, all started, and scraped a wooden chair across the tiles. It screeched, loudly.

"DON'T do that!" Belle's ears fizzed. "Just because *you're* a deafy. You nearly burst my ear drums. And, of

course I'm sure about the storm, my bed-head cracked in two!"

"It's just that, well, look outside. Nothing's moved, see?"

"So."

"Even the leaves are still swept into that pile Dad did yesterday. Mum said. If there *was* a *howling* gale, I'm sure they'd be strewn all *over* the place. I don't mean to pick. Just saying," William pulled the teapot towards him and tried to pour out a strong stewed cup. Nothing came. "Blimey, Belle, *when* did you make this? Last *term?"*

"Oh, hours ago, I'm like Mum, nice and black and ever so strong, my tea - not insipid and made for a baby like you seem to like. Who likes dishwater with a bit of froth?" Belle stared out of the window.

"At least dishwater is more palatable than creosote."

Belle continued to stare out into the dark, austere garden through the ruched curtains that were only half drawn up. "What *was* that noise then, that gale last night?" Belle muttered to herself.

"Mor-*ning!"* Ned marched into the kitchen.

"Where've *you* been?" Belle crunched on a half-eaten carrot she'd managed to chip off the Aga.

"Urr, asleep, in *bed,"* Ned replied, startled at the question. "Where *else?* But, I wouldn't mind getting my clothes back. Look at *these* tiny things!" Ned pointed to his knees where the pyjama trousers ended.

"Your hair looks dusty," Belle squinted.

"Does it?"

"You little *fibber,* I looked at your bed covers when I woke up, peeped into your room, I did. No one there."

"Yuk! Are you one of *those,* Belle? A *peeper?"*

"No."

"What can I say? I must as sleep as flat as pancake if you didn't see me."

William looked at Ned.

"What?"

"What are you hiding from us, Ned?"

"Nothing."

"Come on, you've got that same crafty look about you that I have when I'm lying. Tell us, you're in *our* house now, and your *hair,* it's caked in black dust, *Ted,* your hair it's covered - " William looked closer, " - in *soot!"*

"It's **NED."**

"Oh, is it?" William smirked.

"Ned, you're acting weirdly. GROSS! *Aga!* STOP spitting at me!" and Belle threw her cloth at Ned. "I'm done."

"You've missed a bit - "

"Shut up, Ned, and – go and eat another poisoned biscuit if you've got nothing more intelligent to say. So, where have you *been?"*

"Alright, *alright,* don't gang up on me - " Ned skulked.

"Ned? What are you *up* to?" but Belle knew the answer. "You've been into the fireplace, *haven't* you? Mr Fireplace?"

Silence.

"You've cast a silencer spell on Mr Fireplace, haven't you?"

"No."

"Ned? You've been to *Anouka?"*

"Alright, alright! Yes, yes, I *have,"* Ned whispered, slinking about in the kitchen's shadows. "Don't tell *everyone,"* he brushed his head. Clouds and *clouds* of soot blew everywhere, and eventually landed in the tea saucepan.

"Might make it better," William tried to stir in the soot. "Don't count your chickens, though, it's stuck solid. Wouldn't drink any, Ned."

"Wasn't planning on it," Ned scraped another chair across the kitchen tiles, and Belle squirmed at the screeching.

"And you WERE planning on going to Anouka?"

"I *had* to go to Anouka last night, I *had* to. That Rupert, he's got me feared for the worst. I saw him in Anouka, when I passed over for the first time with my Father, but I've *never* seen him here, in *our* world. Never. He's come for the book. I *know* he has. We've been warned. And now, that grim day, it's come," and Ned spat out his tea. "You never said *this* batch was poisoned too?"

"It's not. They all just taste like that," William scratched his head. "Your lips, NED, look at your *lips,* they're turning purple - "

"Devils and demons, *that* was the potion from Mum's *loganberries*, not tea. Mum boiled loganberries and treacle

last September, Ned, as a **treat,** to take on that Pilgrimage. It blew a hole in the car's exhaust - "

"What was it doing in the *car?"* Ned replied through swollen purple puffed-up lips.

"Dad thought it was her home-made fuel, again, just bubbling away on the hob - like you do - "

"And, it's *still* here? *Three* months later? Stewing in the pot?"

"Yep. That's short! Mum's goose egg custard toddy sat solidifying for seven *years.* Only last Easter did she chuck it down the sink. Blocked the drains and the entire kitchen was flooded, it was. That's when we found the hole in the floor, under the rug, when we tried to clear up the sopping mess and wondered why it just disappeared into the foundations."

"I'm surprised you ever get *anywhere* at all in life," Ned scowled. "MY LIPS!"

"Well, it's never boring around here, you can say that," William scooped porridge oats into a bowl.

"What the waffles, how much have you *got* there, William? Mum'll go beserk!" Belle glared.

"Doesn't matter, it *never* rises, it's four years past its best before date."

"Yep, but remember when you did that last Christmas? The oats, they had a delayed reaction and started to swell in your stomach and your backside exploded - "

"Alright, alright, I don't need reminding."

"The bathroom was out of bounds for the *entire* weekend, Ned," Belle sniggered.

"Gross. AND, can we PLEASE do something about my LIPS! I'm starting to **float!"** Ned grabbed onto a flagging Gran Abuelo branch that had fallen asleep. It jumped, with a start.

"HONCUS PRRRINKUS PRRRONKUS SWIPE!" the branch immediately woke up and its default kicked in, flicking Ned to the ceiling.

"OUCH!" Ned hit the wall on his way back down. "But at least it popped my lips. They feel much better now. Thanks, Gran Abuelo."

"S'okay," the Gran Abuelo branch replied, casually.

"I think we're getting a *little* side-tracked here," Belle hissed.

"You ***must*** be Ned?" a tall man, sporadically shaven, but chiselled beneath the greying bitty beard, suddenly appeared and collapsed in through the back door. *"Chilly* out there. If it wasn't for that odd crisp calm sun and weird lack of wind, the weather would surely be *biting.* This coat's *good* for **nothing.** Apparently made of ostrich feathers but that *Joy* woman was duped – again - "

"JESUS! Who are *you?"* Ned shot off his chair. Eyes like daggers. "Stand back - I'm warning you, I'm armed! I've got - " Ned looked about, " - tea, ***poisonous*** tea, and ***death*** by - loganberry liquid. Stand back. Did you not *hear* me the first time? I said - *S-T-A-N-D B-A-C-K!* WILLIAM, why didn't the *Amdoch Atlas* warn us? Haven't you read all the instructions? You can set it to alert when you're not looking at it, you know."

"Can you? Awesome."

"Nothing can kill me that hasn't been tried already, sonny," the man from the blizzard stepped closer.

"I'm WARNING YOU!" Ned stepped closer too.

"DAD!" Belle threw her tea-stirring spoon to the floor; the saucepan went with it. "What are you doing in a blizzard?"

A mad wind and snowflakes as large as Mrs Joy's eyes had started to fall horizontally from nowhere.

"Woah, woah, nice to see you *too.* What are you *doing* here? It can't be *Gladiolus-Viola* vacation already, you've only been gone five minutes? I haven't had the time to hide any of my prize pigeons yet. Now that *you're* here, and whoever this gaunt-looking youth you've dragged home with you is, my prize pigeons are sure to see a sudden death by accident before fourteen minutes past whatever the next hour is - "

"I'm Ned, Mr Joy. Ooops. Sorry I was rude."

"That's no problem at all! In fact, it sounded like you were in training to be a bodyguard."

"Thanks. Oh, and, it's seven o'clock."

"SEVEN O'CLOCK! Does that mean I've *missed* tea?"

"Seven in the *morning,* Dad," Belle started to tug at his beard. "Is this thing *real?"*

"Oh, seven in the *morning,* thank the heavens. I *HAVE* missed tea, and breakfast I hope too. Don't want to be vomiting yellow lumps again. Two nights ago was *appalling!* I don't even want to reminisce. It isn't for the cooking that I stick here, I can tell you that," he sighed.

"And *Gladiolus-Viola,* Belle? You're being clever, good and all that you're supposed to be being?"

"Of *course* she is," Ned replied, holding out his hand, rather gingerly, to shake the aged man's gloved fingers.

"So, Ned, heard *lots* about you from, well - " but Mr Joy was interrupted.

"Hus-**BAND*?!* *Can*** you *h-e-e-e-e-e-elp* me, please?"

Mr Joy rolled his eyes, but Ned could spy a smirk appearing beneath his wild beard.

"Can *I* help, do you think?" Ned asked. "I *am* a guest after all?" Ned shrugged his shoulders.

"No, no, I'm sure you have more *exciting* things to do than brush off old Christmas decorations, *I must say, I have,"* Mr Joy whispered, and grabbed a large gulp of his coffee from Monday night, which had grown cold sitting on the kitchen window ledge for six days, and shuffled off down the corridor spouting ideas. *"There's the Christmas Fayre this morning, kids,"* he cried back, *"always plenty to amuse you youngsters in that village hall. Coming,* Mrs Joy - oh you *are* so full of Joy, Mrs Joy, glad we renamed ourselves as such," he muttered.

Ned looked out the window. "Odd man - "

"Heard that," Belle smirked.

"Sounds promising, shall we go? That hall thing?" Ned stared inside the cup from which Mr Joy had swigged some sort of black substance and grimaced. "No wonder he feels ill."

"You haven't said what happened last night yet, Ned. Did you *really* go to Anouka, without *us?"* Belle pulled Ned's arm as he tried to leave the house.

"I don't want to get you involved, Belle. That Rupert, he could be dangerous. He'd do anything - " Ned pulled his jacket sleeves back into place, and threw the tiny pyjamas on the floor, " - and if you rip *any* more of my clothes - " and he tightened his scarf into a knot.

"Ned, we're *already* involved. You're here, aren't you? Drinking our tea - "

"I won't hold that against you - "

"And that Rupert Gvist knows it. He knows we all know. Have you hidden the book?"

"The lights are to be turned on at noon, I read it in your village *rag.* Next to the complaint about No.7's wheelie bin being knocked over by a goat - **that** was the *headline?!* Can't believe it! Next to the escapee sheep and its Giant Poodle. Mind you, the *best* one was the *Meadow's Trust* electrifying the communal grass so little paws won't foul - what is *that* all about?" and Ned walked off. "Coming?"

Mr Fireplace *roared* blue, in defiance.

"Oh, glad *you've* been de-silenced," Belle replied. "NED! WAIT!"

"If you insist, yes, I *did* visit Anouka last night, and yes, I *have* hidden the book - "

"BLOW ME!" William shot across the kitchen. His porridge had had that delayed reaction again, but this time in the microwave. Its door blew off and the entire bowl flew

over William's head and landed in the plant pot. The azaleas immediately died under the weight of the oats and the milk had already turned mauve. "WOAH! I was gonna ***eat*** that - "

"Idiot," Belle muttered.

"Belle," Ned waited by the steps. "I can't risk Gvist getting his conniving, crooked hands on it. It's Father's book, my *Father's,* the only thing I have, truly have, left of him to remind me. That book, it has secrets on how *we* can become invincible, immortal. It needs one final chapter, but I need Father's help to write it. I needed to visit Anouka and meet - " Ned's spine chilled to the bone.

"Your dead *Father?"* Belle whispered, stunned.

"He might not be dead as we know it."

"GEES! The azaleas, they've come back to life. They're winding themselves around Dad's prize pigeons - oh LORD!" William stood rigid. "SAVE OUR SOULS!"

"Father," Ned whispered, "he said he could *not* pass his book into Anouka as he passed through as the book's pages would burn in the flames of the fireplace, but *I* am entrusted to keep it safe."

"So, you *saw* your *Father* last night?" Belle's mouth dropped open. "You saw your Father, in *Anouka?* And your - Mum?"

"I *tried* to see them both, but we need to write the last part of the book before I can pass it to him. Why are these steps so *steep?"*

"Dad's trying to keep fit by making them the steepest steps in the world. Anyway, Ned, that's impossible, you

can't take the book through the fireplace flames, you said it yourself. And, if you can't do *that,* you *shan't* be able to meet with your Father again for him to write the book," Belle looked helpless. "Or, did you just say *we* were writing it - "

"My dilemma," Ned muttered. "I can't find the solution yet. But there *must* be one, I just don't think *I* should be looking for it. *I* don't know what to write. Why *would* I?"

"Well, I know what *not* to write - " William caught up. "Any of Mum's recipes; they'd kill you outright. Nothing immortal about *them* - Go THIS way," and William grabbed Gran Abuelo.

"PUMPUS, RUMPUS, SLIDUS FROOOP!" and William shot down the steps on a massive baby Gran Abuelo root. "That's the *last* spell today, please," Gran Abuelo panted. "I'm *all* out of sap."

"But, Father would *not* have entrusted me with his *Book of Immortality* if there wasn't a way of getting it to him. I just need to wait and make sure I don't miss the opportunity. I'm convinced there must be one," Ned sighed.

"Haven't you lot *gone* yet?" Mr Joy poked his head up out the steps. His ears were lit up green from a weird entanglement of string bulbs. "The Christmas lights won't wait for *you.* I'd get on down to the village hall soonest, mmm, *hmmmmmmm?"* he peered into Ned's eyes.

The Hollingbourne village hall was awash with bustle; bustle and loud, feisty festivity.

"Did we *have* to?" William rolled his eyes. "Oh, actually, look at those lemon cakes!"

Stalls selling pots of luminescent spiced chutney filled the first table; little tasters on tiny wooden knives.

"Let's *have* some," and before Miss *Maude* Macey could stop the child, William had hoofed a hefty pile of *Purple Onion Delight* into his mouth.

At first, nothing happened.

"Pah, that's supposed to be *strong* is it? Nothing but a mere hint of tangeri - "

And then it happened.

William's eyes began to tingle, then bulge, and then his nose started to prickle and sting; mildly to begin with. THEN, before he could spit out the bits, his tongue was stuck fast to an entire raw onion which had shot up to the size of a tennis ball; crispy leaves filled his head. *"Baaww ch vhicccccc..."*

"What did you say, *child?"* Miss *Maude* Macey started to grin; the longest, meanest, thinnest smile reaching from ear to ear and further round the back of her head.

The onion grew larger and larger and *larger* still in William's mouth until his head started to turn the deepest shade of purple, and then, the *hugest* root vegetable shot out through William's lips and across the hall landing in a bowl

of raspberry-cider-vinegar cordial which had been donated by Mrs Joy.

At first, the onion looked like it was getting *smaller* and smaller and smaller floating to the bottom of the bowl in a weird bobbing fashion, but William noticed it was just a trick of the light. It was really getting bigger and bigger still until the entire bowl smashed into a million shards of glass and shattered onto the floor.

Cordial splashed everywhere; up the wall and all over the gigantic peony flower arranging tables. Ms Perennial-Burk looked *horrified.*

"There, serves you **right,** *boy,"* Miss Macey clicked her tongue in a disgusting tone. "You better *pay* for all of Ms Perennial-Burk's flowers, *hadn't* you? Did you bring your *entire* wallet of cash? I surely *hope* so, *and* there'll be an I.O.U. for at least the next three years, I'm positive of that. Greed and glutton gets you nowhere, and now, *how* are you going to explain that glass bowl to your Mother? Hmmmmm?"

"It's not *my* fault, there's not a sign telling us to take a tiny little bit of that stuff. I could get you arrested, Miss *Maude* Macey. Health and Safety would shut you down!"

"As I said, greed and glutton gets you *nowhere,"* and before William could chat back, a sign appeared, out of nowhere.

"That wasn't there before, you great horse of a *cheat!"* William jumped back as the largest wooden sign he had ever seen nearly knocked him on the head.

"Little knives for little mouths,

Please do take a dot,

Strictly no under 21's,

For fear of sudden death by shallot - "

Belle had already walked off when Miss *Maude* Macey, the eldest spinster in the village, gawped at being referred to as *a great horse of a cheat* for all the old codgers to hear.

Belle stumbled across a table filled with sugared almonds spreading themselves like rainbow gems around the room; strawberry and lime and vanilla aromas lingering in mid-air.

And, on the next table, as usual, Mr Svendig stood, scrawny-eyed, assessing eagerly who should become his next victim of deceit underselling the weight of his *Madagascan Paw-Paws.* Far too many unsuspecting villagers still fell for it *every* year.

Ned looked around. "It's simply *enormous* in here."

"It's not bad; full of cheats though who look timid and well-to-do, but they're all pocketing cash on the side despite looking old and tragic," William sauntered up, scratching his bottom. The onion aroma was working its wicked way through his *entire* body. His face was still

puffed up, and his tongue was the size of a beach ball. His arms felt numb, and suddenly, he couldn't control those cheeks. "I've gotta *go - "* and William stumbled off to the toilet; his trousers billowing out behind.

"The Christmas tree's always my favourite," Belle pointed up at the tallest green fir Ned had *ever* seen. Standing wisely as always in the corner of the hall Ned couldn't believe he hadn't seen it before. Through the plethora of needled branches, Ned squinted, narrowing his eyes so much he looked like he'd actually fallen asleep upright.

"Ned - " Belle hissed, " - Ned, what are you *doing?* Ned, are you *asleep?"*

"Course not. I'm trying to work out what's happening behind that *tree,"* and Ned stepped forward to take a closer look.

"What's he up to? Why's he doing a weird slow dance down the hall?" William had returned from the toilets. His face was dripping with water. "What's Ned doing, crouching down like that? I'm going to pretend I'm not with him. He's more embarrassing than *you,* Belle."

"You're *soaked - "* Belle recoiled, "and that water you washed in, it's stagnant," William's clothes were drenched, and *reeked.*

"Had to take a shower - " William sniffed his armpits, "I was burning up with that onion still inside me," he scowled at Miss *Maude* Macey. She scowled back mouthing *glutton, greed, glutton, greed* under her breath.

"Witch," William mouthed through a false smile. And then he gasped. "Belle, look at the *fireplace,* behind the tree, it's roaring bright orange, and a man, there's a *man* crawling out of the flames, well *bits* of a man, a figure of sorts, fingers - and - feet – and - I *think* there's a body attached?" and William fainted.

A tall, dark-haired, smartly-attired young man just stepped out from the flames.

Belle rubbed her eyes.

But when she opened them, yes, he was *still* there, looking, witchedly, around.

"What the Waffles, THAT definitely isn't Father Christmas!"

Completely hidden in the depths of the village hall, the young man managed to climb free of the grate, brush down his suit, and peer about his surroundings to ensure he had not been seen.

However, he had.

"Is he a…*ghost?"* Belle whispered.

"No," Ned whispered back.

"Is it the caretaker who died in 1898?" William joined in. "Apparently, in 1898, when the beer-swilling Christmas party ended hours past midnight, the caretaker was never seen again. Only his scuffed shoes were found hanging off the very top of the Christmas tree - "

" - And his braces in the coal bunker," Belle replied. "Never seen again - Brrr, makes my spine tingle."

But Ned, he wasn't listening.

In front of a heavily decorated nativity scene, Ned dropped his satchel to the floor with an almighty clatter. He kept hold of the handle tight, but the satchel itself swung on the floor as if it had a life of its own.

"It's *him!* It's *Rupert* ***Gvist,"*** Ned shuddered.

Rupert Gvist emerged, supposedly inconspicuously, out through the flames to the old codgers busied with buying poisoned cakes and sipping boiled-to-death hot chocolate amidst the music that *bellowed* out around the hall. But, to Ned, the secret figure was *larger* than *life* itself.

"I'm OFF!" Ned shoved his hands out to escape but managed to knock William into Miss Smock. Her stall, covered from one corner to the next in handmade iced-biscuits, shook and wobbled.

"William *Joy, watch* yerself, lad, they're *precious* my gifts, be careful, although I *know* it's *not* in your nature, *never* will be - " Miss Smock tutted and tried to straighten her tablecloth.

"Sorry."

" - you've *always* been a klutz, just like that *Mother* of yours. In a world of her own. I don't know *really WHAT* to suggest."

"Sorry, Miss Smock. And, you don't need to suggest anything, thank you very much," William tried his hardest, most convincing, apology. It didn't really wash.

"Conceited boy."

"I said I'm sorry, *terribly* sorry if you prefer? I just tripped you see, shan't happen again - "

"Don't make *idiotic* promises that you'll *never* be able to keep, *Joy - "* but Miss Smock soon changed her attitude when William gave her his crisp five pound note.

"Here, I'll have the *lot.* I'll take *all* of your tree-shaped biscuits off your hands, Miss Smock. I'm sure they'll be – *delicious - "* William licked some of the white icing from the largest shortbread. His tongue froze. *"Velishush,"* he couldn't prize his lips apart.

"I *told* that Mr Smock, that wretched brother of mine, to take them *out* of the freezer more than just ten minutes before I was leaving, never trust a man, never trust a MAN - " and Miss Smock burst into tears.

"- ny fentinents, eggsactly," William tried to reply, his lips blowing up blue as he tried to keep his eyes on Gvist.

"Thank you, boy."

"Sokay - " and William drew further and further back behind a velvet curtain out of Rupert's line of vision.

Ned and Belle cowered by his side.

"William *Joy,* what are you *doing?"*

"What *now?* Why are these oldies always picking on *me* today?"

"Come out from there this *instant,* the rest of my baking is carefully stacked behind that curtain. *Stop* pushing it so," Miss Smock rallied her church 'friends' to help pull the scrupulous threesome away from destroying her biscuits. "What *has* got into you, if it's not *bad* enough with just you and that skittish sister of yours, you've now brought

another straggler along; tall and gangly," Miss Smock *glared* at Ned, who just smiled back courteously, trying to peer behind her ridiculous skirts to see where Rupert Gvist had got to.

The commotion around Miss Smock's stall had caused quite a scene. Plenty of villagers had gathered by the biscuits to see what all the fuss was about.

"Don't look up," Ned whispered. "Let's just try and lose ourselves in the crowd. *Whatever* you do, *don't* look conspicuous or draw attention to yourself."

But – it was *too* late.

William had tried to heave himself up onto his feet using Miss Smock's tablecloth, and the entire collection of her neatly laid out biscuits, the ones that William was yet to shove into his bag, crashed to the floor; crumbs, the size of inedible bullets, scattered *everywhere.*

"I'd have broken my teeth, *all* of them, if I'd eaten those, you cheat," William glared at Miss Smock. "I could shut the lot of you down, every *last* one of you spinsters alive, cheating, conniving little - "

"WILLIAM!" Belle glared.

"Oh my *goodness, all* my *hard* work, *days* of baking ruined, *ruined* in an instant! William Joy, *take* yourself and your *friend* away from my stall this *instant!* Just *go - "* Miss Smock shrieked at the shocked threesome as they scrambled to their feet, brushing moulding biscuit crumbs and lumpy icing sugar from their clothes.

Rupert Gvist glanced over and walked, casually, towards Ned.

His eyes looked sly and relentless.

The village hall door slammed shut.

Ned had gone.

Vanished.

With his satchel.

Rupert Gvist shook his head.

"That boy, he *has* to realise *soon,* but *I* am *not* the one to tell him. It would be against the rules," Rupert muttered.

Hidden Tracks

William and Belle slunk back underneath Miss Smock's table cloth.

"Get your *feet* in, Belle, clumsy," William whispered. "He's just there. Gvist's feet are just *inches* from us, keep quiet. I know he's after Ned, but that means us too.

Remember, remember what Ned said? Rupert, he'd do *anything* to get his hands on that book."

"I don't think he'd want to smell your armpits for it."

"Shut up. I wonder how he knows about it, the book? And, *what* is against the rules?"

"Eating Smock's biscuits, surely," Belle sniffed. "I can smell the mouldy crumbs from here."

"Tell me about it? Mum'll go mad if I show her these three broken teeth - "

"They're *broken?"*

"No, but I can colour three halves in black, and then Mum can bill Smock. Serves her right, the old *cheat - "*

"Ssssssh - stop *wriggling,* William. Rupert might go away if we just hang on a bit longer."

"What if Smock catches us under here?"

"I'll cast a - *spell."*

"Cast a *spell?* What *are* you talking about? If that's *all* you can come up with your life mentally sucks."

"Mum's recipes. I read her recipe book last night - "

"And? It's not a *spell* book, it's a *recipe* book."

"William, this **is** *Mum* we're talking about. She's hand-written on some of the recipes what happened to people when she fed them - *greengage stew* was one - "

"And?"

"Well, that woman, from the Reading Group, she slept for a week after just one mouthful; couldn't get her out the door and into Dad's car for two days, until she'd lost some weight. And Mr Svendig tried one of Mum's *pickled apple strudels* last Easter - "

"Oh yes, was that when he went missing for nearly a year?"

"A-*ha.* Apparently, Svendig got amnesia. *Completely* forgot where he lived. Ended up as a sheep farmer in Bucksfarthquart; that's what his cousin said. But, his cousin also had the burnt scrapings of the strudel so none of this is for definite, but food for thought."

"How is all of this going to help *us* escape from under the tablecloth?"

"I've already poured a large dollop of pickled apple strudel filling into Miss Smock's teacup," and Belle poked out her nose. "What the WAFFLES, yep, it's worked again."

"Let *me* see," and William stood up, bold as brass.

"WILLIAM! Get back down - "

"Oh hello, *dear - "* Miss Smock bent down, carefully, and smiled into William's eyes so close that William had to lean right back. He fell over, pulling a cake stand with him; lemon drizzles dribbled to the floor and seeped into Miss Smock's handbag.

"Oh, you *poor* thing, *don't* worry, *don't* cry, it's *only* a handbag. Here, have a lemon drizzle for free, and look, a crisp five pound note in my hand! How **did** *that* get there? Go buy yourself something nice, *child.* It *is* the festive season of good will after *all."*

"Yep, it's worked alright. She's no idea who I am."

"Where do you think *Ned's* gone?" Belle took two slices of raspberry cream gateau off the table right under Miss Smock's nose and licked them. Both.

"Help yourself, *please* do. In fact, I might donate them *all* to the church - for *free.* Oh, I *do* feel a sense of Christianity about me all of a sudden, I *do,"* and Miss Smock pulled the hairband from her tight greying hair and let the greasy mess fall down. It fell and fell and *fell* as if soon it would surely reach the floor. It stopped just inches from the toilet bucket.

"Best place for it," Belle smiled through gritted teeth.

Miss Smock smiled right back, yellowing pieces of enamel filling her entire face.

"I didn't realise she was *sooo* ugly. Eugh - "

"She could sweep the fireplace with that lot," William glared at Smock's thick wiry were-wolfy locks. "No idea about that *boyfriend* of yours though."

"Ned is NOT my boyfriend."

The door was still just swinging; snow blowing in every time it flew back on its overly-sized rusty hinge.

"Guess he's just gone out of Gvist's sight, I would imagine. Do you think Ned carries that book about with him all the time? In his satchel?"

"I thought he said he'd hidden it?" Belle replied.

"Oh yes, so he did, don't believe that though," William thought. "I wonder if *we* can help, you know, perhaps throw Gvist off the scent? We could pretend *we* had *The Book of Immortality* and get Gvist to follow *us,* and Ned can then try and seek his Dad again, in Anouka?"

"But Ned can't take the book through the flames, so how will he *ever* be able to write the ending with his Father?"

“It’s us, we’re *all* supposed to help write it. I hate creative writing.”

“And why does Ned’s Father want to be immortal anyway?”

“It’s all very strange, very strange indeed. *I* wouldn’t want to be a pale, wrinkly, toothless old man, one thousand years old, when everyone around me had kicked the bucket,” William pulled a tiny corner of the tablecloth up.

Gvist’s feet had gone.

Ned scrambled around in his bag.

He felt uptight, but strangely so.

His cold fingers fell upon his Father’s unfinished book, and he shivered.

“What *is* it? What are you trying to *tell* me?” he cried in a whimper as he pulled the book from his bag and stared at its cover. *“Well?”*

The book stared back at Ned, inanimate and completely lifeless. ***“Well?*** *Stupid* thing.”

“Problem?”

“Huh?”

A crisp sound crunched in the dark shadows.

Ned jumped on the spot, and shuffled further back into the hollow of a tree.

“I asked if there was a problem, *Ned?”*

“Who goes there?”

"Me."

"Who's *me?"*

"ME!"

"Stop saying *me,"* Ned turned his head, and his eyes widened as they fixated on a silhouette. "Rupert!" Ned whispered.

"Yep."

"Rupert," Ned crouched lower onto the floor, his back pushed up against the tree's inside as far as it would go. And the snow, it started to fall heavier and *heavier* around him. Large white icy flakes drifted from the greying skies above.

Ned clutched at the book tighter still.

He cowered.

The book felt hot, to burning point, and Ned had to let go. His fingers opened out and the book fell to the snow-covered ground, sinking and melting each cold flake.

"Ned. Don't cower away. I'm here to *help.* Help write the book, help get the unfinished chapter back to your Father," a low, calm voice rang through the bare twigs that brushed against Ned's confused face. "Ned?" Rupert's voice called. "Ned, come out!"

"No," Ned told himself. *"It's a trick."* And he stayed silent.

Through the dry crisp night, the voice called again. "Ned?"

Ned covered his ears.

"Ned, *please* don't fear me, there really is no need. Your Father sent me."

"Rubbish!"

"Yes, the recycling, it *does* need sorting, I noticed that when I was at that Joy woman's house. Does she not *know* the difference between *wine bottles* and *newspapers? Clearly* not."

"My Father *warned* me about you, Rupert, years ago before he passed through those flames. Right before my eyes he disappeared following what he *hoped* could be a cure for my Mum. I'm not to trust the likes of you."

"You've misunderstood, Ned. Trust me."

"Ned, what *is* it?" Belle's voice butted in. "Who are you talking to?"

The night was now a dark navy mist. Even the moon gave no solace.

"Look, your book, you've *dropped* it - " Belle bent down and picked it up. The book was damp from the snow but it had a certain gleam to it. "It's quite something, isn't it? This book - " Belle cupped her hands and blew hot breath into them. "You must be freezing sitting in that tree. Odd place to be hanging out, isn't it?"

Ned stayed silent.

"Cat got you tongue?"

Nothing.

Once thawed, Belle's fingers began to open the book's front cover.

It wouldn't budge.

Belle tried again, to open the book from the back this time.

Nothing.

"*You* won't be able to *do* it," Ned hissed.

"Oh, the cat hasn't got your tongue."

"Surely you didn't think Anouka would allow just *anybody* to look inside? That pen, that aged jewelled pen attached to its spine - "

"What about it?"

"That pen will ensure that only the person compelled to write the final chapter can get in."

"Thank *God* it's not one of those voice-activated secret diaries," Belle spat back. "William's forever changing mine, for a joke, then forgetting what he's changed it to. I had to hand in my homework in a locked diary. Mr White thought I'd not done it and it was some kind of ridiculous excuse - and anyway, I *am* a part of Anouka, a great *big* part! Naribu, Magenta, the *Professor,"* Belle whispered the last name and then glared at Ned. "What, *exactly,* are you to do with *The Book of Immortality,* Ned? Well?"

William raced up, breathless; red-cheeked from the blisteringly icy wind. "He came *this* way, Rupert. I *saw* him. Rupert *definitely* came this way!"

"I did," the calm voice spoke again.

"WHO goes there," Ned spat. "I'm *warning* you - "

"There's no poisonous tea within two miles, Ned - unless you count the Vicar's Aunt's back at the hall. Did you see the teaspoons? They stood up on their own in the cups!"

"Show yerself, *Gvist!"* and Ned grabbed his book from Belle; stuffing it back under his arm. "Coward, *aren't* you? Thought as much - "

"You're shaking, Ned," Belle stared at him.

"Well don't tell *him,* idiot," Ned snapped back.

"I'm going - " William emptied out his bag of the biscuits from Miss Smock he had managed to stuff in. He threw one at the tree. The bark cracked and a huge bit of branch fell into the snow. The biscuit stayed whole, just levitating three inches above the ice. "My tummies turning *somersaults,* and I'm NOT eating any of those death-by-self-raising-flour biscuits. That woman, we'd have all died a slow death consuming these."

"We better tell Mum about Miss Smock's biscuit stand before she hears a half-baked story from one of the old codgers back there - " Belle rolled her eyes as if it had already happened more than once before, but it was already too late.

"Oh, Miss *Smock,* you were *what?* POISONSED?" Mrs Joy's shrill voice echoed around the kitchen. "Some sort of *what?* Sorry, the line, it's *terribly* crackly. Surreptitiously poisoned by one of *my* children? No, *surely* not. You could taste *what?* My *strudel*, in your *teacup?* The one that *what?* Ohhhh, the one that almost killed your cat - oh, well, never mind - *stupid woman,"* Mrs Joy threw the receiver into the

sink and she listened as Miss Smock's screeching voice sank to the bottom. "Much better."

William crept in first through the back door.

Eyes alert.

Belle walked behind, practically in William's underpants.

Ned trailed, sceptically, in the shadows which cast a thin black silhouette right up the garden.

The moon hung low.

It was huge; white and dimpled like a mouldy over-sized ball of cheese.

"Dear, dear, *don't* stress, I'm *sure* there must be some sort of explanation, Veronica?" Mrs Joy scratched her head.

"Oh no, it's HER. We're too late," Belle hissed.

Miss Smock was taking tea with Mrs Joy.

"But, didn't you? Weren't you - " William stared into the sink. The receiver was still sitting, calmly, at the bottom of the bowl. Miss Smock's voice was still ringing out; making vile voicey bubbles in the water.

"William? Belle? Ned? Mrs Joy hollered.

"How does *she* know we're here?" Belle hissed, hanging back in the corridor.

"Oh, sorry. I must have left my *Amdoch Atlas* behind in the settee room. Bet that Flippin' Flaming Fiona whoosed

it Mum's way. Mum's probably using it. Oops," William replied. "Sorry."

"Hi Mrs Joy," Ned walked into the settee room first.

"So you're *back ARE* you, such *deceitful* delinquents," Miss Smock muttered as she sipped her Earl Grey, a menacing glint in her pale grey eyes. Her hair was back in its tight little bun, and her yellowing teeth looked more disgusting that ever. "It was *you,* wasn't it?" she pointed a thin finger at Belle. "I can *tell,* you little - " and Belle ducked as Miss Smock tried to poke her in the ribs.

"More *tea,* Veronica?" Mrs Joy held the teapot at the most impossibly-tilted angle for the tea not to have poured all over Miss Smock's head and down her neck entirely.

"*Loved* your stall, Miss Smock. We were taken *right* aback by your festivity, Miss Smock," Belle tried to cover her tracks with compliments, but she could quite plainly see that neither Miss Smock nor her Mum believed a single word she spouted.

"*That* is debateable," Miss Smock muttered again. "You ruined *everything* I had spent many weeks creating, and you come in *here* and tell me that you *loved my stall,* you little urchins, the *lot* of you," but Belle noticed the harsh, pointed-nosed lady from the Women's Institute could not look her in the eye, not at all. Belle thought it was very strange, so she just smiled.

"Never mind, there's always next year?"

"Rosabella!" Mrs Joy spat out her tea.

"SEE what delinquent children you've raised, Mrs Joy - "

"Why, thank you, Veronica," Mrs Joy sipped from her cup.

"Curiouser and *curiouser,"* Belle whispered. "What's she *doing* here? I would have thought our house and seeing us again was the *last* place on *earth* she'd choose to be. Miss Smock was about to burst with anger when we demolished her stall - "

"I was hoping she *would - "* William muttered. "Would have paid *ten times* my crisp five pound note to see her blood splattered up the walls," William smiled through this teeth.

"Why would she drop by and risk something equally chaotic happening again?"

"Dunno - "

"WHAT are you children tittering about?" Miss Smock glared into her Earl Grey.

"Your nice biscuits," Belle replied.

"WRETCHED LIARS AND URCHINS! HOW CAN YOU STAND THERE AND SPURT SUCH RUBBISH?" Belle thought Miss Smock was about to combust.

"They're not *that* bad, Veronica! Best to be honest," Belle smiled.

"VERONICA? *VERONICA?* Mrs Joy, teach these children here some manners! It's MISS SMOCK TO THE LIKES OF YOU WRETCHED MEDDLING KIDS!"

"Such a shame about the cold winter ruining my turquoise Brussels sprouts, Veronica," Mrs Joy replied.

“Are *yours* going soft and not quite so sprouty-looking too?”

“I’m sorry, Mrs Joy. I have *no* idea what you are talking about. The likes of me doesn’t grow turquoise sprouts!”

William shook his head. “No idea *why* she’s here. Don’t really give a monkey’s, to tell you the truth. All *I* know is that Smock woman, she’s a real old twisted spinster-type. Can you *imagine* the poor man who might have had to *kiss* **her** if she’d got married? *Eugh.* I feel sick!”

“Gross, those teeth would eat you alive - ” Belle hissed back.

“She’s new to the village, Mum said. Moved here in the Autumn. Do you remember she turned up at our house just before we set off for *Gladiolus-Viola*, spying out her neighbours, questioning our behaviour? She doesn’t say a lot about *herself.* **But** she’s more than presumptuous and nosey than anyone I have *ever* met when it comes to asking after *us.”*

“Ned?” Belle whisked around. “I *don’t* believe it. He’s vanished again.”

“Fly by night.”

“You *stink* of onions, William,” Belle coughed. “Hope you’re sleeping in the garden tonight.”

“*No* chance,” and William walked off.

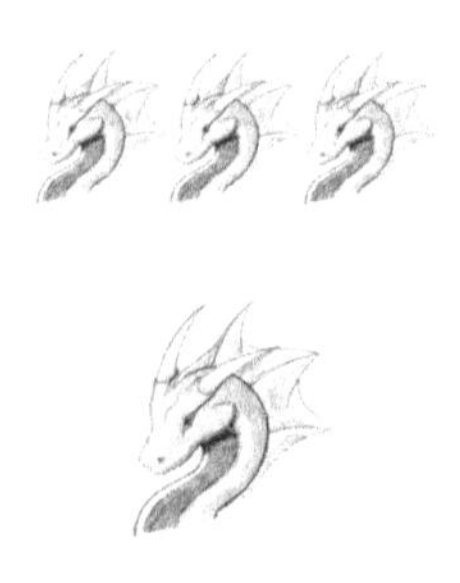

Belle heard William slam his bedroom door.

The century old windows rattled.

Tiny little puffs of blue smoke crept in.

"Suit yourself then," Belle tutted, and marched back to the settee room.

It was hot.

Flaming Fiona was blasting. Huge logs had been placed inside her. Each one roared ferociously.

"Belle, dear, how *nice* of you to re-join us," Mrs Joy stood up, forgetting her tea was just balanced between her knees. The entire mug upturned. "My *feet,* oh these *feet, bare* feet, and *slipper-less* as I totally forgot to retrieve them from their accidental trip to the dustbin, oh my *feet,* they're *dead!"*

"God, this family is *so* dramatic," Miss Smock muttered through pursed lips. "Mrs Joy, *dear,* are you *quite* alright? What a *terribly* traumatic thing to have happened to you? Mmm? *Although I shouldn't imagine for a minute it's anything out of the ordinary,"* she muttered under her tea-stained breath. "Shall I be calling the fire brigade? The ambulance? The *police?"*

"The POLICE?" Belle replied, chucking a bucket of cold, curly kale-infested water over her Mum's head so as her entire body could be relieved of heat-shock. "How on *earth* could the *police* help in a situation of burnt feet?"

"Just a thought, dear, just a thought. I'm *sure* much more dramatic things have occurred down that telephone wire of yours than a call to the police for *burnt feet."*

"She's *fine,* Veronica," Belle watched her Mum squeeze out her hair.

"It's *Miss Smock,"* Miss Smock replied.

"Of *course,* it is, Veronica. Any more tea?"

"No, please, praise the Lord, *no* more tea."

"Oh, only if you're *sure,* Veronica?"

"Yes, I am *quite* sure."

"We haven't *really* got off to the best start, have we, Miss Smock? Sorry about before," Belle rubbed her hands together as she bent down towards Flaming Fiona's burning embers. "Did you manage to sell all of your second batch of iced biscuits? I saw another bag."

"Is this some kind of a *joke,* child?" Miss Smock retorted, turning redder and redder in the face.

"A joke? *No,* Miss Smock, no *joke,"* Belle was enjoying herself. "Just interested. Hope you managed to raise a few pennies for - what was your cause again?"

"Belle, what happened? *Please* don't say you upset poor Veronica at her first Christmas Fayre since her move here?" Mrs Joy's brow wrinkled, inquisitively. "Well?"

"Mum, it was just a little misunderstanding - "

"LITTLE MISUNDERSTANDING?" Miss Smock's ears started to smoke, and she rose up higher and *higher* from her cushion which was trying to pull her back down. "LITTLE MISUNDERSTANDING? You, child, *you're* a *Little Miss Understanding,* you are!"

"Oh, *Veronica,* let her speak," Mrs Joy squeezed out her hair for the second time and this time it drenched Miss

Smock's boots; filling them with rancid water from toe to knee.

"Mrs Joy, *please!"*

"We - William, Ned and myself, Mum - well, we were rather taken aback with the turnout at the hall, and there were the *crowds* you see, a little stumble and quite strong things to taste without warning, you see, and well, we seemed to knock right into Miss Smock's biscuit stall, didn't we *Veronica?"*

Miss Smock's hair began to fizz in its bun. Three pins popped right out.

"The table legs, they must have been dodgy again," Belle lowered her head and caught Miss Smock's eye, but Miss Smock knew it was just for show. Belle might have convinced her Mum she was still angelic but Miss Smock was not so easily swayed. "Sorry," Belle whispered, slyly.

"There, Veronica, *a-a-a-all* settled," Mrs Joy rang out her hair for the third time, and this time it filled up the teapot entirely. "Anymore Earl Grey, *Veronica?"* and she tipped the pot up *so* far the lid fell off; its contents, hot water, water with bits in, Mrs Joy's strands of hair, and fourteen old teabags that looked like they had seen better days, splatted into Miss Smock's handbag. Mrs Joy pretended not to notice. "No? No to *tea?* Veronica, it doesn't look like there's enough Earl Grey to go around anyway. Where *has* all the water gone?" and Mrs Joy peered closely inside. "How *very* odd - "

"You're telling *me?"* Miss Smock added.

"Coffee then?"

"Oh, well, that sounds a better option."

"Right. North Alaskan lemon coffee with *creamy* mandrake juice? There's a *great* new recipe somewhere here, now, *let* me see, *where* did I put it?"

"Mandrake juice? Sounds positively *illegal,* Mrs Joy. I think I had better be making tracks, *and,* for the record, I suppose it *was* quite a busy turnout," Miss Smock pretended to accept Belle's apology. She had to just get out of the mad house.

"Well, *glad* we're all friends again. More Earl Grey, Veronica? Or perhaps a *Chamomile* variety this time? I can make a fresh brew? Of anything, really."

"No *thank* you, I must be getting along, crumbs to clear up and all that. It's a wonder *you* don't have that to do."

"Mum? No, *always* clean and tidy in here, *Veronica,* spick and span as you can see."

"It's *Smock, Miss Smock, Belle. And,* the *bits?* The reason you have no *bits* to clean up is because I'll be taking it all away in my *handbag."*

"Thief," Belle smirked, glancing into Miss Smock's handbag only to see everything pappy and drenched.

"Nice to see you again, *Veronica. Please* call in again; whenever you're passing?" Mrs Joy stoked Flaming Fiona.

"Yes, I suppose it's been - *interesting.* Belle. Mrs Joy. Goodbye," and Miss Veronica Smock glided out the settee room and down the corridor quite oddly. "This house is *beyond* repair."

"Yes, nice to make your acquaintance properly, *Veronica,"* Belle cried back.

"MISS SMOCK!"

"Sorry, I just love the name, *Veronica.* I couldn't help but say it. Like *Rupert,* that's a nice name too, don't you think, Veronica?"

"Rupert? Yes, I *guess* so," Miss Smock tripped over her own feet as she stumbled into the kitchen. "Not that I know anyone of that name, but if one is to be called Rupert then I'm sure it is a fine upstanding name. Anyway, I really *had* better be getting along before death catches up with us once and for all."

"So soon?" Belle followed Miss Smock to the back door, passing her her coat.

"Yes, yes, *much* to do," Miss Smock pulled on her faux-fur, inside out in haste, and disappeared out the door.

"Presumptuous old codger," Mrs Joy replied. "And making me brew *all* of that *tea,* for nothing. How very *dare* she? The nosey old coot."

"Mum!"

Oh, Belle, dear, thought you'd *gone."*

"Nope, *still* here."

"Ruder and *ruder* are these WI ladies nowadays," Mrs Joy muttered, collecting up her tea cups, smashing five, and bustling about not really achieving very much at all. "She's nice *enough-ish,* but I *really* can't seem to understand her at all. The audacity of it, her presuming that I had a house that would need *tidying.* Where *does* she get her ideas? Preposterous woman."

“Can I have a chocolate-coated celery stick, Mum?”

“Of course, dear! No need to ask.”

“Thanks,” Belle took a bite and turned green.

“And, she was most interested in us, that Veronica was. And our *guest.* But when I asked about *her* family, she just clammed *right* up. Quite a disinterest she has in divulging anything at *all* about her*self.* Anyway, where are William and Ned?”

“Oh, William? *He's* upstairs, and Ned? Well, he's somewhere about.”

Rupert's Return

"It's not that you *can't* come over, Rupert, not at *all* - oh, Rupert, *really?* My *hair?* It's glossy? *Crow black* **and** *glossy?* Oh Rupert, *really,* my dear, no need for such compliments - but a *few,* I *suppose* they don't hurt, *do* they?"

"Course not, Pippa."

"Oh. Yes. In *that* case, of *course* you can come, for a cup of tea? It's just that these children seem to be rather erratic in their ability to stay put since they came home, so I can't guarantee they'll be here. I guess they're all grown up now – *hello? Hello?* Oh, you *are* still there. Crackly line. Anyway, these children, forget there ***is*** a ***time*** for lunch ***and*** a ***time*** for tea. I would have thought *Gladiolus-Viola* would have instilled routine, but never mind, it's nice to know William and Belle are close by even if I don't always know *exactly* where."

"Right. Tomorrow? Today?"

Mrs Joy held the telephone receiver to her shoulder, majestically supported by her tipped head, as she flirtatiously spoke to Rupert Gvist *and* swept the kitchen floor, strewn with charcoal, simultaneously. "Of *course,* I'll aim for then and hope beyond *hope* that they're here," Mrs Joy shook her head, placed the telephone receiver back on its holder, and carried on sweeping the kitchen tiles muttering.

"Today or *tomorrow,* then, Mrs Joy? Hello? *HELLO?"*

Silence.

"Dithering woman," and Rupert too hung up. "I'll just have to guess then."

"I simply *can't* understand why this floor is so filthy dirty *every* morning. The fire grates are closed down, I

think, before bedtime but there's soot *everywhere.* Those children, no doubt, I don't know *how* they do it, but I can't think of any better explanation."

"I'm *starving,"* and Belle shuffled in.

"ROSA*BELLA!* **Don't** creep up like that!" and Belle watched her Mum leap into the air, the soot she'd cleared up flying back to where it had been before.

"Spinach porridge cooked yet? *Hope not,"* Belle sniffed and shook in desperation.

"Three more days for that one to be edibly divine, dear. It's a new recipe."

"Who was on the phone so *early,* it's not even seven?" Belle squinted at Mr Clock. "Is it not? Can't really read it. Why has it got *five* hands?"

Mr Clock scathingly squinted back, and then shrugged its shoulders.

Belle yawned, and, shaking the kettle to see if it held any hot water, she started to gasp. She'd inhaled some of the curly-kale fumes.

"Turned into a *fish* overnight, Rosabella? A *cod?"*

"No - *t-h-i-r-s-t-y* - **h-o-w** much **SALT** did you *put* in that *kettle* of kale?"

"Stop *gawping,* otherwise it may *well* happen. You, turning into a fish. And, the salt cellar? It was that faulty one. The entire lid fell off into the kale kettle. I'll *never* trust your Father filling it up *ever* again. And, if it's black tea you're craving, there's a pot **freshly** brewed *today."*

A *gigantic* pot hung on a hook, swaying. No steam rose from within.

"What exactly does *freshly* mean *today,* Mum?"

"Exactly what it *should* mean; fresh - today, stupid girl. What *do* you learn at this abysmal academy?"

"You'd be surprised, Mum. William's taught Molly to communicate."

Mrs Joy slurped from her own cup of drink. "Teaching *cars* to communicate, whatever next?" The liquid in the cup did not budge even when Mrs Joy tipped it up completely. "Oh, I seem to have over-cooked it again, the earth, I mean, the tea, mmm, and *Rupert,* it was *Rupert Gvist* calling, yes, I suppose it *was* quite early," Mrs Joy did not stop sweeping. "That *Veronica,* she's *not* telling *me* my house needs a darn good sweep, she can come and check *this* out, the good for nothing woman," Mrs Joy stared at her tiles as her feet started to fall a little lower.

"I think you've created a problem, Mum!"

"Problem? *Problem?* How can cleaning one's house create a problem?"

"You're shorter."

"But I thought my spinach porridge would surely make me *grow,* not *shrink.* My eye level, it was always two inches *above* the bird feeder."

"I think you've scrubbed a good two inches deeper into the floor, Mum. CHARLIE! Mum, Charlie's come in search of Miss Smock's crumbs again. He already hoovered

up the ones that kept falling out her bag and now I *think* he's addicted."

"Charlie, dear, there's a love and suck up the spilt tea too."

"UM, YUM, YUMMMM, UM!" and Belle watched as Charlie's cheeks grew larger and larger.

"MUM! He's far too young to be drinking that stuff. We *all* are!" and Belle plunged Charlie into a sleeping branch of Gran Abuelo's sap to cool down.

"PHOOOOOOOOOOO," Charlie de-puffed back to his normal size again.

"I never did understand why that bird feeder was *inside,* Mum," Belle stopped yawning and started to wake a little more, the aroma from the fresh teapot affecting her nostrils. The caffeine had started to kick in from inhaling the stuff, and her feet began to patter, uncontrollably.

"Oh, good *heavens!* My *plan!* It's *working!* **MY PLAN, it's WORKING!"**

"What *plan?"* Belle started to feel uncomfortable.

"My *'Get Clean Quick Before the Women's Institute Ladies Pop In'* plan. I boiled the pot, *that* giant pot, of tea, *three* weeks ago last Tuesday, and it's been bubbling away ever since filling the air *continuously* with a drug-induced caffeine. Surprised you hadn't noticed it, my dear?"

"There's far too much going on in this kitchen for me to notice *every* little concoction, Mum - " Belle panted, her feet dancing and skidding about.

"LITTLE CONCOCTION? *LITTLE?* Can't you see for yourself what my plan entails?" Mrs Joy clapped her hands and cried out. "CAN'T YOU *SEE?"*

"I SUPPOSE I CAN, BUT WHEN WILL IT *STOP?* I'M *EXHAUSTED,* AND THE TILES, I MIGHT POLISH THEM RIGHT THROUGH TO THE FOUNDATIONS, MOTHER!"

Mrs Joy clicked her dusters, and Belle fell to the floor, gawping.

"I did tell you to *stop* that gawping, child. You'll turn into a haddock, or at best a herring and at worst a roll mop, if you're lucky."

"I'm exhausted, I need *air* - " Belle gawped, her lips dropping to the floor.

"And - *relax."*

"WHAT THE WAFFLES! THANK GOD!"

"Oh, Rosa*bella,* these tiles! THESE *TILES!* The W.I. Ladies can shove their comments up their - "

"MUM!"

"Oh, Belle, dear, *do* wise up and get with the times. There are phrases that sometimes *need* to be aired. AND RELAX!" Mrs Joy flicked her old dusters again. *"Finally,* the plan has started to reinvent itself. I could see your soles starting to smoulder. Your feet, they're free, for now."

Belle stopped shaking the kettle. "What does he want?"

"Who, dear?"

"Gvist. He only came at the weekend. Why's he coming back again? Didn't you think it was all rather rude, his just leaving without saying goodbye?"

"Belle, dear, I have *no* idea, and stop asking such *ridiculous* questions. *You* just disappeared, so that makes the lot of you rude with *that* theory. Rupert, he's *surely* heard that Mrs Joy's kitchen is a marvel, and he wants to, you know?" she whispered.

"No."

"Steal, surreptitiously steal, some ideas for himself."

"Yep, that'll be it. He's after a new saucepan."

"Is he? Oh, well, in that case, I have ALL THESE - - - - "

"I was kidding, Mum! Put those ancient cast iron monstrosities away!"

"It's you children he wants to meet really, not me. And anyway, you can ask him yourself, he's coming around mid-morning for tea, I think, which, if I turn these dratted clock hands correctly to the correct hour, is in exactly, *three* minutes if I'm not mistaken," Mrs Joy was *still* sweeping. "This is *never* ending, I'm *sure* I've swept this bit a *hundred* times."

Mr Clock groaned.

The fireplace glowed.

Belle heard a sound, a patter of footsteps and a distant tone.

A vocal.

A voice.

She glared into the grate.

There had always been *something* else about Mr Fireplace, something alive, something more than just him answering back, an uncertainty that Belle could not quite put her finger on.

"Mum, let *me,"* and Belle pulled the sweep from her Mum's hands. *"Tea?* I'll pour you that fresh cup."

"You *are* kidding. ***I*** know what's in it."

"Oh."

"Do you think I'm *stupid,* dear. I'll not touch that tea with a barge pole, if my life depended on it. Stop *gawping - "*

"You *witch!"*

"Oh, *thank* you, Belle, but I haven't *quite* got my platinum certificate yet. My spells, they don't seem to work with exact precision, but I'm *getting* there. The *hours* I spend practicing when you're away - "

"It *wasn't* a compliment, and I didn't actually realise you were practicing to become a fully-fledged witch - "

"Not *fully*-fledged, not *yet,* but Grade B* my dear; three more levels to go before I can seriously turn your Father into a Racing Green *Ferrari."*

"Can you cast me away to a house less disorderly and full of cream cakes, please," Belle muttered.

"Don't gest and wish for things willy-nilly, my dear. And, I shan't be called a *Witch,* it's not becoming these days to be called a *Witch* - more of a - *Sorceress,"* Mrs Joy flicked her hair.

It fell right back down.

"And, Rosa*bella,* dear, I'm filthy dirty, I can't sit in here, really, on these cream sofas, what *has* got into you? You're never generally so, well, how can I put it nicely? So *helpful,* without there being some sort of an *ulterior* motive," but before Mrs Joy could flick her dusters again, she found herself being pushed into a rather overly-plumped up cushion in the settee room. Belle continued to plump, but as she looked at her Mum, she saw she was becoming higher and higher and *higher* as the cushion continued to puff up and up and *up* even when Belle stopped pumping. "Really?" she questioned, quite taken aback. *"Really,* Belle, what *has* got into you, and this cushion? What *are* you doing? *I'm* the only one with the *powers,"* and she thumped the feathers, but her words rang on deaf ears as Belle dashed back into the kitchen. "AND – RELAX!" Belle heard her Mum scream at all the cushions.

"Ned! Where've you *been?"* Belle whispered loudly as Ned stood, coated in black, coughing and shaking with cold in the kitchen. "Did you just appear from in *there?"* Belle pointed towards Mr Fireplace. Mr Fireplace stood innocent-looking. "Don't you side with *him,* Mr Fireplace. Ned, Mum and I have literally *just* left. We've been in here, cleaning the floor for hours - "

"You, cleaning the *floor?"*

"Don't ask."

"Yes, I suppose I did, come from in there," Ned coughed again, blinking and looking confused.

"Belle, *dear?"* Mrs Joy called from her height in the settee room.

"Oh Lord, get *rid* of her, Belle," Ned flicked soot out of his ears.

"Belle, *dear?* I've changed my mind, did you say you were bringing my black tea? FRESH from the cupboard? With water from the tap and *no* added extras, or shall I get it my*self?* Must say, I'm getting quite used to being waited on, especially sitting at such a great distance above all the chimneys in that lower bit of the village. I can see Veronica from here. Goodness *knows* what she's saying but her brother has fallen asleep listening to her droning voice, I do believe. *Belle?"*

"No Mum, it's coming, I'm *just* pouring it," Belle turned to face Ned who was now cleaning himself in the sink. "Didn't you know you would come out *here,* in the *kitchen,* from Anouka? I assume that's where you've been? I heard voices and put two and two together when Mum started to complain about how sooty the kitchen always was. Are you using Mr Fireplace as a door, a door to *Anouka?"*

"Well, I guessed I might come out here. That's where I normally do, but today was a little different."

"What is it? What happened in Anouka? Ned, *tell* me," Belle held her Mum's strong black tea in one hand. "Well?"

"That smells vile."

"Fairy-Jesus-and-Joseph, I've come *myself* to pour my tea," Mrs Joy appeared, covered in duck down. "Honestly, if you want something done timely in this house

you may as well do it yourself - oh Ned, hello. Are you *alright?"*

"Yes, Mrs Joy."

"Just wanted to say, we do *have* a bath, my dear, but, if this is how you do things at home, well, stick to what you're used to. Don't want to rustle with your routine - whatever *that* might be," Mrs Joy frowned and cocked her head to see how on earth the boy could actually get his entire left leg in the sink. Still wearing his shoes.

"I'm fine, Mrs Joy. Just like a walk."

"Fall down into a *coal* shed, did you?"

"Yes, yes, *that* was it. That man at No. 3, he had his door *wide* open, and I guess I just fell in," Ned shrugged his shoulders. "And, I ended up like *this."* He wiped soot off his face.

"No. 3?"

"Yep, mad man there."

"Strange, they don't have a coal shed. Just gas."

"Oh."

"Care to explain the *mess,* then," Mrs Joy was becoming particularly worried that her *'Get Clean Quick Before the Women's Institute Ladies Pop In'* plan might backfire if the tiles were covered in soot again. She had read that if they weren't *kept* clean, they would shrivel up altogether once the plan was in place, but she hadn't yet cared to think long-term.

"Sorry, Mrs Joy," Ned wiped his soiled shoes on a tea towel.

"Really? Is *that* what you do at home, is it?"

"Sorry, but I thought I could help. I thought I heard, um, heard a *bird,* up there, up inside the chimney, so I thought I would investigate, seeing as I'm a guest, and my family, well, we've *always* had fireplaces, quite a professional I am when it comes to dealing with them."

"You? You went up *there?"* Mrs Joy pointed the saucepan lid towards the flames. "Through the flames?"

"Oh, it wasn't flaming a minute ago."

"Thank you, thank you indeed, Ned. Mr Joy, he's off this week, some sort of fossiling conference, that's what he told me, so nice that you could help."

"Thank you," Ned looked smug.

"Did you find it?"

"Find *what?"*

"The bird, the bird you heard up the chimney? Did you find it? What sort was it?"

"Oh, yes, the *bird* - an *owl."*

"An *owl, gracious! Where* is it?" Mrs Joy looked alarmed.

"Outside, I set it free," Ned was beginning to run out of lies.

Belle sniggered. She *was* finding it funny to watch Ned worm.

"Belle, *she* helped me. Look, soot all over her dress, sorry Mrs Joy to create more washing. I came in from a stroll, quite nippy out there it was, at *least* six degrees colder than where *I'm* from - "

"Where's *that* then? Sorry I haven't yet had the time to enquire, my dear."

Belle sniggered again.

"Erm, well, it's an odd village, you *won't* have heard of it."

"Try me," Mrs Joy carried on thrashing the tiles with her sticky-sweep. "I'm a *whizz* at geography. Know places you'd *never* know existed, I do."

"Oh, you *shan't* know here. *Very* hard to get to. Not even the SatNav can find it. Mine blew up when I typed in the post code."

"I said, *TRY* me," and at this point Belle exploded. Luckily, Mrs Joy's tangine of blueberry meringues had had enough heating and their entire voluminous puffing up blew up Belle's dressing gown.

"More washing, oh for love of *all* the lost villages that we shan't speak of," and Mrs Joy stuck her twiggy-sweep up Belle's posterior.

"Anyway, as I was saying, Belle had her nose up the chimney, said she heard vocals, she did," Ned carried on explaining, pretending not to have noticed the calamity, "and I couldn't leave her nose, and the lost little voices, stranded, so I *heaved* myself inside and pulled out a rather soot-infested owl, flapping and hooting, I'm surprised you didn't hear. Then we set it free. It just flew away, didn't it, Belle?"

"Mmm, this blueberry meringue is a better substitute for spinach porridge than I thought," was all Belle could say, picking bits off her thighs and eating it raw.

"How *chivalrous* of you, Ned, to help Belle, and that bird," Mrs Joy ruffled Ned's head of dusty hair.

"Oh, that's *quite* alright."

"Mmm, it's even sweeter than you would *ever* imagine," Belle narrowed her eyes. "Oh, I've finished it *all,* never mind."

"Sit here, Ned. Don't worry about *that* glutton. Her teeth are sure to fall out. I might as well make us all some black tea - "

"Don't mind if I do -" and Ned poured his tea into the azaleas whilst Mrs Joy examined the chimney to see if anymore owls were in residence.

"It was my Mum, I saw my *Mum,"* Ned whispered to Belle. "She was there, but that's not all, she was talking with - "

"Sugar, Ned?" Mrs Joy interrupted the deep conversation that was making Ned and Belle frown. "What *is* it? Why the solemn faces? Bit grey - "

"Ned's got something in his eye, soot I guess."

"Oh, *dear.* What do your parents use to get it out? We can try that."

"My *parents?"*

"You know, at *yours* with your *professional* experience with fireplaces? You said so yourself. Must have happened a lot, soot in your eyes - " Mrs Joy tossed between holding the hot tea pot in one hand and teasing with the corner of a handkerchief in the other. "Let me, I can't *see* anything, are you *sure?* It must have slipped out on its own, there's no soot now," Mrs Joy turned her attention back to the brew. "Needs more cardamom pods this one," she grimaced as she tasted it. "It's even too strong for *me,* I'll

get the other pot, there's tea brewing by both fire places, I completely forgot – oh now, Mr Fireplace, *don't* get jealous, Flaming Fiona only brews cold tea," and Mrs Joy's skirts disappeared into the dark hallway.

"She was talking with who, your Mum?" Belle hissed. "Well?"

"Him, Rupert Gvist," Ned hissed back.

"Rupert Gvist? Are you *sure* it was him, I mean, he was talking to Mum on the telephone this morning, apparently he needs to see *us*. He's coming, well, *now - "* Belle gabbled as she heard her Mum's skirts sweep back along the hallway.

"Yes, absolutely *sure* it was Rupert," Ned whispered. "But Belle, listen - " but Ned was cut short. William fell in, tripping over his Mum's skirts; three spiders falling out.

"Ned, he's ***coming!*** Rupert's walking up the steps, *our* steps - " William blurted out, breathless.

"At least he's going to use the door," Ned muttered.

"Why *wouldn't* he? He'd hardly come down the fireplace now, *would* he?" Mrs Joy glared.

"No."

"And yes, I invited him for a cup of tea. What *is* wrong with you all? He's quite nice you know, quite normal actually compared to these last few days - " and with a rap of her toes on the skirting boards, the back door flew open. "Come in, Rupert, come *in!* Easier said than done, but I *somehow* managed to keep all three rascals in sight, Rupert. Honestly, *do* come *right* in," Mrs Joy held the door back, awkwardly. *"Oh,* ***will*** *you be-have,"* she muttered to the

door panels. "I know that the spell is a *'Quick In, Quick Out spell',* but, cut Rupert some slack, the poor man. I'm *only* a novice sorceress," but the door *still* tried to prize itself shut; its hinges bulging as Mrs Joy's cheeks blew up crimson trying to outwit its strength. "Your *coat,* Rupert?"

"Me?" Rupert looked about, cautiously.

"Yes, *you,* there's no one *else* behind you, is there?" Mrs Joy peered at the Gran Abuelo. "You're not up to your tricks, *are* you?"

"HMPHHHH," the tree snorted.

"Hmm, I'll be keeping an eye on you in your adolescence."

"No no, Mrs Joy. I'm alone," Rupert cleared his throat. "It's just that I can't stay too long, just a small task to be adhered to. It shan't take a minute," Rupert Gvist widened his eyes towards Ned.

Belle tensed, the blood drained from her cheeks, and she took a step backwards. *"Ned?"*

"Oh, the *kettle,* all that water has gone, it's boiled *dry.* Heavens above," Mrs Joy prattled about the kitchen in an unfathomable whirlwind.

Ned exchanged books with Rupert.

"What *is* he doing?" William whispered.

"Beats me, but Ned knows *more* than *we* do. He was about to tell me something before you flew in," Belle spied Ned with questioning eyes. She leant closer to William. "And he's been to Anouka. *More* than once."

"When?" William hissed back. *"When* did he go?"

"The last time was just now, I had to get Mum out of the kitchen before Ned bounded out that fireplace." Mr Fireplace's flames roared as if he knew Belle was talking about him.

"Your tea, Rupert, *dear?"* Mrs Joy wiped her brow, but as she spun around with her tray piled high with tea and pickled artichokes, her eyes only fell upon an empty kitchen of which she was the only person left. "Not *again,"* and she flopped into the rocking chair. "This family? What *is* it with them? Just one pickled artichoke puff then, just one for me, I suppose," and as she took a bite, the brown sugar exploded into her face like an overly blown-up balloon.

Mrs Joy brushed off the sticky stuff as if she did not care, and closed her eyes. "Just like me back then, in Anouka, I guess," Mrs Joy dreamt, just hearing the faint echo of voices to which her tired mind did not question.

Magenta & the Strange Young Boy

"Where *are* we?" William whispered as fierce blue flames shot past his eyes and a deafening roar of fire, sky high, hurt his ears. "Where *is* this place?" The kitchen disappeared to a dot, then, it was gone completely.

"Where do you *think?*" Belle cried. "It's where we *always* end up, but I've never come *this* way before."

A long charcoal tunnel twisted and turned as the three, no four, heads somersaulted further upside down.

"It's *Gvist,* he's come with us. Gvist's up ahead. I *told* you there was something strange going on, William," Belle hissed.

The tunnel fell abruptly to an end. Down and down it circled.

"Our *house,* blimey, Mr Fireplace, we actually entered Anouka through MR FIREPLACE! In*cred*ible," William checked his hair. "Is it all burnt off?"

"No."

"Phew, I've been growing it into a new fashion," and William twisted his head back from where he'd fallen. "He always had a sense of *life* about him, but I thought the Mr Fireplace just hated drying my underpants. They always come back burnt to a crisp - "

"You aren't meant to put your pants *inside* the fire, William."

"How *else* are they to get dry, then? I've *never* got enough pairs - "

"No, you *shan't* if you keep incinerating them - "

"I needed a *'Get Dry Quick Pants Plan'* - thought that would be a suitable answer." *THUMP!* William clonked to the floor. Belle landed on his backside.

"Of *all* the places - " Belle cried, " - of *all* the places to squelch into, it *had* to be your *backside,* William," and she screwed up her face at the smell. "I'm sure I've let out unsavouries - "

"Well, you've let out my *appetite.* Anyone got any food, I'm *starving?"* William rubbed his stomach as if it hadn't seen even an *apple* for three weeks.

"You're always *starving,"* Belle mumbled. "Rupert, I always thought you were - " Belle scratched her head.

"Didn't anyone *hear* me? I'm going to *die* if my stomach doesn't get filled this *instant,"* William panted and fell to his knees, groaning. "Jam tarts? Just the *one?* No? Okay, then, rhubarb crumble, with just a *smidgen* of custard? No? *Really?* I don't need a very big bowl - "

"Were *what,* Belle?" Rupert replied, slowly raising his eyebrows. "You thought I was *what?* Can't wait to hear what you thought I might be. A *three-headed dragon?* I might try being that next time," Rupert narrowed his eyes. "Do I look like the bearer of *evil?"*

"Yeah - " William found his tongue.

"William," Belle dug him in the ribs. "We aren't entirely sure he's *not* a bearer of evil yet, not *entirely - "*

Rupert wrenched the corner of his mouth apart and pretended to blow fire. "Now, if I'd read page 101 of your Mother's *recipe* book, I'd probably be able to do that, the fire-blowing dragon thing."

"I thought you were a *being that ought never to be trusted,"* Belle overheard Ned tell Rupert as she got closer.

"A BEING! A *BEING* THAT OUGHT NEVER TO BE *TRUSTED!"* Rupert grimaced, then threw back his head. "I *wouldn't* trust myself with boiling an egg, but – *secrecy - "* Rupert whispered, leaning *further* in, and Ned followed his line, their noses practically touching, " - *secrecy,* now *that's* one thing that I *can* do."

"Father, he always told me a tale, one that I'll *always* remember from a boy, but a story that always made me just so aware, perhaps *too* aware."

"Never to kiss Belle," William stammered, but before he could stand straight again, his finger had poked himself in the eye. "Ouch! Who did *that?"* William looked around.

"I think you'll find you did it to yourself, William," Rupert replied.

"Did it to *myself?* Don't be so *ridiculous - "* but before William could speak anymore, he'd poked himself in the *other* eye, *harder* this time. "RIGHT, THAT'S *IT!"* William wiped his nose free of tears that had started to stream down his face. "Why would I poke myself in the eye, *twice?"*

Rupert twitched. And smiled.

"You *did* read a bit of Mum's *recipe* book then?" Belle muttered. "Clever thing. Was it the spell about shutting annoying boys up?"

"You can never be *too* aware. You were right to cast judgement, Ned. Really you were," Rupert sounded soft. "Your Father and I were friends, *are* friends, and, believe *me,* he has sent me here, but the lengths I had to go through

just to avoid that brew she makes," Rupert shuddered. "Chills me to the spine knowing what she throws in there from time to time, that Joy woman. Anyway, as you know, your Father cannot come back into our world. He's now part of Anouka. He gave up the right to flow freely like ourselves when he became your Mum's guardian. He is that, you know, her *guardian* from an evil of which you must now quash - "

"What's *that* when it's at home? Some type of weird vegetable?" William snapped out of his mini-trance.

"Eradicate, Ned. It was to *you* that your Father entrusted *The Book of Immortality,* and to you that must fulfil the task of writing the end, before - " Rupert Gvist looked around, slowly, as if spying the presence of an evil, " - before it really *is* too late."

"Too late?" Belle cried, trying to escape the darkening forest that seemed to be closing in around her. "What do you mean *too late?"*

"Exactly what he says, ***too late,*** *cloth* ears," William started to jitter again; his tummy had started to growl.

"Looks like you're fancying another trip down *Poke me in the Eye Lane,* William, mmm?" Rupert glared, clicking his toes inside his shoes.

"No, *thanks."*

"Father, he told me I would prosper one day," Ned muttered to the floor. The trees started to rustle around him, and their leaves began to fall; slowly at first, then faster and *faster,* and their skins started to turn a rusty orange, burning in fury as they looped and whizzed around Ned's head like

wasps in a dustbin, smelling out mouldy cabbages. "I felt *I* should look into how to prosper, to win, but now I realise *you* have found *me,* Rupert. Father meant *you, you* are the one I must trust, and *all* these years seeing you in Anouka, watching over me when I passed through the fireplace from my bookshop, *you* were protecting *me - "*

"Give it a *rest.* I left home without my breakfast, I did, and all you can talk of are these incidentals? What about some cheese and pickle incidental sandwiches around here, it must *nearly* be lunchtime?" William kicked the dry earth, but before he could duck, his thumb stuck itself up his bottom. *"CHEESECAKE! THAT HURT!"*

"Well, *stop* being such a gloomy irritant."

"It was *you, you* all along, Rupert - " Ned whispered to the fiery leaves that had started to bind themselves together, *" - you,* keeping an eye on *me* to make sure I was unharmed?"

"Is there a broken record around here?" William fought with his thumb and his bottom.

Father told me this. *"Son, keep this book safe, think of it as your saviour. If you follow the right path, the life you lead will help you prosper and serve us well. Trust no one, but someone."*

"My THUMB! It's stuck, **completely** *stuck!"* William hopped about, tugging and *tugging* his entire arm from his behind. It would *not* budge.

"I had to wait for the right time to come, Ned," and Rupert plucked the hugest pear from above his head.

“How d’ya get *that?”* William hopped over, sideways.

“If you look around, and not just complain all of the time, Joy, then you’ll notice more. But, *I* can’t teach you these things, you’ll have to work it out for yourself,” Rupert took an enormous slurp from his pear. His eyes rolled.

“Idiot. You can’t bring us here and then *throw* it all back in our face.”

“Suit yourself,” and Rupert stalked into the deepening forest.

Burning leaves had started to fall upwards.

“BUT - ” Rupert cried back. “I WOULDN’T STAY THERE, WHEN THE SKY BECOMES ABLAZE, I SHAN’T WANT TO BE *YOU* - GOODNESS *KNOWS* WHAT WILL FALL BACK DOWN,” Rupert shouted before his shadow disappeared.

Completely disappeared.

“Wait up, then - I said, *wait up!* There’s a limit to how fast a boy can walk when his thumb is stuck up his bottom!”

Ned crouched in the shadow cast by a huge oak tree.

It seemed that the forest’s leaves couldn’t see him if he hid. The shadows were like a saviour. The leaves shot and fired themselves about, but as soon as they came close to his shadow, an invisible wall seemed to knock them right

back to the floor, and the little lanterns, ablaze in their hearts, just burned out.

"I had to wait until you had found William and Belle, Ned. But *that* was no easy task," Rupert rolled his eyes as they all hunched together, " - thought you were going to pop your clogs in that fire. All *three* of you of on many occasions. Defying nature by drying pants, William? Talking to the flames so close, Belle? And you, Ned – popping in and out as if you are immortal - "

"But I am?"

"Hmm, maybe."

"Pop our *clogs?* What's *that* supposed to mean? And, if you hadn't noticed, my *thumb?"* William tilted his head backwards. "It's still, you know - "

"Oh, if we *must,* then - " and Rupert chucked his pear core at William's stuck hand. It immediately fell free.

"Finally - but *now?* Those *pears,* they're miles back - "

"William, just give up, will you?" Belle curled up against Ned in the darkest part of the shadow. The ground felt slightly moist, and a warmness started to fuel her limbs.

"All of you are needed," Rupert continued.

"Needed for *what?* AND, don't *worry,* I don't mind *starving* until whatever has to be done is done - " William grumbled.

"We're not just playing *football,* William. This task, it's for real," Rupert was suddenly at William's feet.

"How d'ya get there, so fast? Are you - a *ghost?"*

"Save Anouka."

"Sorry?"

"Save *Anouka.* You asked what you're all needed for, and that's it. You're *all* needed to *save Anouka."*

"Alright, alright, you don't need to say it *three* times."

"But we're *here, in* Anouka. So, if we fail, we'll just *die* here?" Belle sat up. "I didn't sign up for this. I came home for Christmas. Is this some kind of nightmare. Dying - *here?"*

"If we don't die of *starvation* beforehand - " and William felt his fingers start to wend their way back towards his face. "But, of course, I can *always* wait until tea-time - when *is* that?" He felt his palms tighten, and his fists curl up towards his cheek. "BUT, I'll wait, yes, wait until breakfast three weeks on Tuesday, if not *more,"* William forced his arms down before he gave himself two black eyes.

"Yes, Armageddon; *that's* what we fear. Your Mum, Ned, she was not ill, she was not taken from you for no reason. It was destiny, *destiny* for her to protect Anouka. She was needed. Your Mum was born to enhance and to save Anouka. The butterfly, the butterfly effect that she could save Anouka time and *time* again was the key, and she did, but this time, *this* time is different. *This* time, a black hole has approached that *cannot* be reversed - "

"Oh Mama-Mia - " William clutched his hunger pains.

"UNLESS, the end of that book is written. You see, *The Book of Immortality* does not refer to a person, it refers to the *whole* existence of Anouka. We need to close off the

evil that's chasing this book," Rupert pulled back a small corner of his anorak and revealed an old leather corner. It was the book that Ned had exchanged with Rupert in the kitchen. "I'll keep this safe here. An evil wants this book. And you keep mine as an imposter; a pretence. Guard your backs," Rupert looked about, slyly, "but you *will* find your book, when you least expect, it will suddenly dawn on you, one morning, within arm's reach and where you've been residing for always. Tiles, homely, in a place where the passageways to Anouka ultimately lie."

"Oh, for *heaven's* sake - " and a pear, the size of a tennis ball, stuffed itself in William's mouth. *"Awww awwww awwwwww - "*

Ned looked at the book he held in his hands. It looked the same, but he knew it was not the original. It felt light and empty of soul. "I shall, I shall keep *this,"* Ned replied with a nod, although he had no idea what to do with it.

"You can't be *seen* here, you *must* leave," Rupert inched further back until the roots of the oak tree curled around his spine from the ground up, and he pushed his hands away as he shut his eyes. "Be gone, *BE GONE,*" and he urged the gawping faces back to the smoke-filled tunnel. "Wend your way back, *quickly* now. The forest always has ears and eyes. It's *not* safe for you," and just as quickly as Rupert Gvist's words left his lips, *he* was gone, swiftly and quietly into the Anoukan night sky; not a trace of the man left behind.

"Awwwwhat noooow?" William tried to force his lips wider than the pear still stuffed in his mouth could go. "Eee'z gong...."

"Sorry?" Belle tried to look innocent. "Sorry, William? Are you *ill?"*

"Aaa-ooow!" William's cheeks bloated in anger.

"Oh, are you saying what shall we do *now?* Now that Rupert's gone? Well, I don't *know,* William. *I'm* not the man with the spells, *am* I? Perhaps Mum's recipe book will help - it'll be a while though - "

"AWWWWWWW!"

"Oh, if we *must, then,"* and Belle threw her pear core at William's steaming face. The tennis ball-sized pear shrivelled to the size of a pea.

"IDIOTS! I *hate* you! The lot of you!"

"Hadn't we better get back? You heard what Rupert Gvist said, this forest has eyes and ears," Belle quivered. "Come on - "

"No, *not* yet. I need to see my Mum. And my Father. I need to find out what to do next, with this false book," Ned stared at the imposter. He had held the real *Book of Immortality* for as long as he could remember knowing that one day, *one* day, its final inscription could help his own Mum. Now he could see the bigger picture, the book's final inscription was to save Anouka. And *his* Mum was the hub. He had never known Magenta was the heart of this entire world.

"Ssssssh, what's that noise?" Belle hissed, tugging Ned's arm.

The roots of the oak tree started to wriggle and creak.

Little cracks appeared in the earth, and stinking termites fled.

"Don't tear any *more* of my clothes, Belle. I don't revel your Mum asking about my sewing skills. She keeps on and *on* about where I come from - "

The oak tree was starting to close in. Little by little its branches groaned and its bark started to crack away revealing new flesh beneath its ancient skin.

*"A*s you said yourself, *don't* go searching for answers," Belle hissed.

"I know, I *know,* I just feel - *vulnerable,"* Ned's brow started to sweat. He twiddled his fingers over and over.

"See, you *would* be good at sewing," William butted in. *"Those* nimble fingers. Aren't we *going* yet? What are you two *whispering* about?"

"You, Ned? *Vulnerable?"* Belle hissed. "That's the *last* word I'd use to describe you. In fact, I'd never use it all. Come on, it's getting dark and I *don't* fancy getting lost in this forest. The roots, they're getting irritable," Belle looked down as miniature spirals of turnip-like stumps started to twist and turn, working their way to her ankles.

Belle shifted.

"Bit like your tongue. Irritable," William uttered back.

"Oh, *shut* up. Look, Mr Fireplace's embers are fizzling out in the distance. We've drifted. And the moon, it's nearly gone. Where's the time disappeared to?"

"It's Anoukan time, Belle," the boys hissed together.

"JINX, Ned. Same time, same words - "

"Yes, well, I think that's where it ends," Ned continued to flick his fingers round and round.

"Where *what* ends?"

"Any similarities, between you and me."

"Tell me about it, there's no *way* I'd be dating *her,* and your hair, it's just *too* dorky. Yep, you're right, there's not much we share."

"Me dorky?" Ned whispered.

"Oh, just *ignore* him," Belle cut in. "He used to have a mullet hairstyle. I put it in a ponytail one year, and he thought he was a *rock* star, so he hasn't got *much* going for him. But you're right, you *do* come from an era, Ned. We could be in Anouka at any time. Any dimension. You remember that sketch of your Mum? *Ancient."*

William cast his eyes about.

He was certain at least eight pairs stared back from somewhere, somewhere hidden.

Suddenly, a movement in the trees ahead made William stop and stare, " - what was *that?"* William froze.

"Or *who* was that?" Belle grabbed Ned's elbow. "Did you see a *figure?"* A chill ran down her spine.

"No," but Ned looked alarmed. He glanced around, and, without consciously doing so, he slunk further and *further* to the ground. Dry twigs and the brittlest of leaves

broke beneath each footstep. The forest felt different. The trees looked taller, thinner, blacker, *drier.* More light filtered through the branches which had started to break and fall in bits to the floor. Red sky pitted the mud underfoot, and the once mossy sponge that had felt soft to the touch now became hard and chalky. "William, *Belle?"*

"What?" Belle was now practically on her knees; inches from Ned's nose. *"What?"*

"Anouka - "

"What about it?"

"It's *dying."*

"Dying?" Belle whimpered. "How? *Why?* Anouka doesn't *die."*

"Well, I think it is."

"I feel sick," William crawled alongside Belle.

"Did you eat some of the earth?" Ned whispered back. "Don't even joke, William. I saw a snake's head explode into more bits than strawberries have pips once. I wouldn't trust *anything* here."

"No, I'm not *that* dumb, eating earth, pah," William spat out a mound of sludge into a hole that had started to dig itself deeper, and brushed grit from his lips from a mouthful he'd inhaled, "but it *does* look at bit like cocoa flapjacks, the floor, all gooey and speckled in dust," William's eyes fizzed, and his mouth started to moisten again as if he couldn't help but hoof in another stodgy pile of gunge.

"That *rustle - "* Ned's eyes shot about.

"What rustle? *Where?"* Belle shook, her nostrils flared and her eyes darted about, jittering.

"Over there, *look,* it's a tree, an *entire* fallen dry tree. Lifeless," Ned looked back. The fireplace through which they had entered was but a small deep red flame burning lower and fainter. "*The Book of Immortality*, it's *got* to be written before the heart of Anouka fizzles out - *forever."*

A face, a *sour* face appeared in the dying flame, blurred at first before becoming icy crystal clear. *"Miss Smock!"* Ned glared in horror.

"Blimey, it *is!* It's Miss *Smock,"* William stared closer as a fierce wind blew him flat to the ground.

"Magenta?" Belle whispered through the gale as an enormous pair of translucent wings silently brushed the top of Belle's head.

"Mum?" Ned raised his arms and stretched out his fingertips trying to touch one of Magenta's wings as she swooped, pale, towards her predator. *"Noooooooooooooo!"*

But Ned's voice was lost to the deep hisses.

"I've only just found you again, MUM!" and Ned covered his eyes as a battle commenced. *"I'm* to help, *I'm* the one to intervene - " but Ned's head felt crushed with an intense pressure and, helpless, he fell to the ground clutching his wordless book.

"Ned? *Ned?"* a light voice penetrated him, and an incandescent silver oasis blurred his vision. Ned put his hands over his eyes.

"Mum?"

"Ned, are you al*right?"* It was Belle. "You fell."

"*Fell?"* Ned croaked.

"Yes, you fell in pain. You were clutching your head. And that book. Can you hear me, *can* you? Say something if you can? *Ned?"*

Ned scratched his hair.

It flopped back over his eyes.

And he sat up.

His head was banging.

His mouth felt dry. "Where *are* we? Where *is* this place? Where's my *Mum?* Where's *Magenta?"*

The forest lay still.

It felt calm.

Silent.

Empty from torment.

"She's gone," Belle whispered.

"When Belle says *gone,"* William butted in, "she doesn't mean *dead."*

"Of course I don't, *idiot."*

"Well, it was a bit confusing, it *could* have meant dead."

"Alright, stop saying that," Ned tried to sit up taller. His head was still pounding. "What happened?"

"She simply vanished," Belle looked into the distance at the dot of a flame that then popped out. "Magenta, Magenta

and Miss Smock, they were pulled into the night sky, leaving us with this - " An intense silver light lit up the forest. All the trees looked like immense charcoaled silhouettes against the silver sky. "I just hope we can get back home. These trees, they're far too thick to know which way we came. I don't want to end up heading further and deeper inside."

Although the light shone a bright sense of serenity, there was also a deep feeling of fear.

It was quiet.

Deafeningly quiet.

Anouka was not normally so.

"Mum? Where *are* you?" Ned whispered to the silver stars. "I have this book to fill, you see."

"Look!" William squinted into the forest.

"What?" Belle was picking brittle sticks off her clothes.

"Look over there - "

"So you keep *saying,* what *is* it?"

"Why don't you look for yourself?"

"Because I only know that you'll *think* you've seen a chocolate bar tree, all melty and sticky with caramel, and so we'll head over, and you'll start licking the trunk, embarrassingly, and then it'll take me *ages* to get you to understand that it's *all* a figment of your imagination, and - "

"No, Belle, look, *really* - " Ned butted in.

"Not *you* as well."

"It's, it's a little *boy,* over there in the woods. He's running really fast. See?" Ned pointed.

"No."

"I wonder who he is?" Ned took a step forwards.

Belle followed Ned's finger. "Oh," there *was* something there. Moving in the trees. "Wait, *wait!* Hello, young lad, where are you headed?" Belle started to walk, although it was more of an incoherent swagger, towards the fair-headed boy. "Hello. Why are you running? And, *excuse* my friends, they didn't even *think* to tell me you were here - "

"You, *liar,* Rosa*bella,"* William hissed.

The little boy was now running faster in the opposite direction. His foot kept tripping over his other foot as if he was trying so hard to get away, but he continued to stumble along through the brittle trees, a beige canvas satchel tightly clipped together flying out behind him as he tore along with speed. As Belle called out to him again, he finally twisted his head towards her.

"What in *heaven's* name - " Belle gasped, and the blood drained from her body. She recognised his face, she *absolutely* did.

The boy turned his head fast back around and continued to stumble on further and *further* into the dry black bracken, then as quickly as he had appeared, he vanished into a patch of glowing circular embers whispering. "Sorry, I *can't* stop, I was told *not* to stop and talk to *anyone.* I *really* mustn't. You look *awfully* nice, but I really *must not* stop," he panted, breathlessly, clutching his satchel even tighter.

"WAIT! Who *are* you?"

"What do you mean? Do you *know* him?" William caught up.

"Yes, I mean *no,* not really, but I feel I *ought* to," Belle replied.

The Fossiling Conference

"Is it *me* or is Mr Fireplace ridiculously eager to display heat tonight?" Mrs Joy dragged her rocking chair away from the soaring flames and swiped her hot rosy cheeks with a damp dish cloth. "And where *is* your Father? That fossilling conference is taking up far too much of his time. How am I supposed to keep this place running all alone?"

"Mum, are you *okay?"* Belle slurped from her glass. Water dripped like waterfalls down each side of her mouth.

"Belle, *please* be careful, and clear that up."

"What?"

"The *flood*, right there, on the floor! Look at that lake you've made. Did *any* of it actually go in your mouth? We're not *made* of money, and if you're going to be tipping pints and *pints* of water all over the place, then you can clear it up and at least - "

"At least *what?"*

"Take a bath in it. Yes, *that's* it. Shovel it into the pot, *that* one over the fire, heat it up and take a bath. Come to think of it, why *are* you so muddy? Or dusty? Look at your fingernails, and your hair? What *has* happened? Looks like you've been dragged through a forest - "

"Tell me about it."

"Sorry?"

"Nothing."

"Get going then, get shovelling that lake before it seeps away altogether," and Mrs Joy tried to tap her tongs on the floor in such a way that Belle knew another amateur spell was about to break free.

Mr Fireplace *raged.*

"Miss Smock?" Belle whispered into the purple flames which had started to dance mysteriously. *"Miss Smock,* ***what*** *do you know?"*

"Sorry? Are you talking to *me?"* Mrs Joy was still tapping her tongs, harder at each crash to the floor and wondering why nothing was happening. "I'm *sure* I'm

tapping it at the correct angle; thirty six degrees tipped slightly at the top, and *tap.* What's *wrong* with this thing?"

"What do you know? And why, why are you here?"

"Why's *who* here, Rosabella? ROSA*BELLA,* who? And, *why* aren't you paling that water into the pot?" Mrs Joy thumped her tongs on the floor for the seventeenth time and this time the purple flames shot *so* high they knocked the entire pot onto the floor and it started to gather up the puddles of water itself. "Oh! *OH!* I've *cracked* it! I'VE *CRACKED* IT! HEAVEN'S ABOVE, IT *WORKED.* NOW, THAT'S ENOUGH, POT, THAT'S *PLENTY*...POT? *POT?* I SAID THAT'S *ENOUGH,* STOP! *STOOOOOOOP!* BELLE, DO SOMETHING, *DO* SOMETHING. THE POT, IT'S NOT ONLY PALING UP THE WATER, IT'S HACKING INTO THE *FLOOR!"* and Mrs Joy tapped her tongs *so* hard that the tiles cracked in two and the pot hurried, impishly, back onto its hook. "That's *better,"* she glared as the pot bubbled away, steam filling the entire kitchen. "Must be these tongs, it says always use new ones and I've had these for twenty *years."*

"I can hear footsteps," Belle jittered on the spot. "Who's there? I said, who's *there?"*

William pulled back the curtain.

"William! Don't *shock* us like that," Mrs Joy jumped. "My heart is in my *throat."*

"That's not the best place for it," William answered back. "What *has* happened in here? Why is it so thick with steam?"

"Oh, it's just my *'Scoop up a Waterfall'* spell," Mrs Joy flicked back her hair, showing off. "Worked a *dream.*"

"Really? Looks like it went astronomically wrong."

"William, I'll have you know that this place looked like we were about to *drown* until my tactics moved the oceans into that pot, and now, now it's heating up ready for a bath - a bath that *you'll* also be taking by the looks of things. Where *have* you both been?"

"He's back - "

"Who's back?" Mrs Joy stared at her tongs which had started to sharpen themselves on the broken tiles. "Will you *stop* it?" she glared at them. "And, don't test me, I'm warning you. I have no patience for naughtiness in *my* kitchen," but the tongs still jittered and didn't sit still.

"Dad, he's *back - "* but William's voice was drowned out as his Dad crashed in through the back door.

"Mr *Joy!"* Mrs Joy fell off her stool. "What *is* up with you?" she sat, breathless, on the floor.

"ME? What's up with *me?* I think *I* should be questioning *you?* Why are you on the floor, and *why* is this place full of steam?" Mr Joy coughed.

"And, where *have you* been? You missed the inauguration of my *'Scoop up a Waterfall'* spell."

"It's *that time! That* time dear, you know? The fossil, if it's still there, as I left it years ago, **that** time," and Mr Joy disappeared out of the opposite kitchen door to where he had fallen in.

"What *time?"* William scratched his head. Dry leaves just seemed to fall out of his scalp. "What time, what *is* Dad

talking about? If he means time for breakfast, then he's right on cue, but if he means time for a bath, then I'll just be going - "

"Oh, *that* time," and Mrs Joy disappeared as curiously as the first parent out of the kitchen and across the unevenly tiled hallway surfaces. "Gracious, *that* time. I'm all a quiver," Mrs Joy muttered over and *over* again, fainter and *fainter* her voice became as she moved further and *further* away.

"What was *that* all about, odder and odder they are," Belle looked at Ned. "Why can't we just have normal parents?"

"It's not odd, Belle," Ned replied. "Not odd at all. It takes me right back. It reminds me of my youth. The secrets, the antics, the whole sketch. I think perhaps your parents are part of the plan - "

"What *plan?"*

"I have the strangest feeling - "

"You must need the toilet, then. I get the strangest feeling when I've eaten too many big sausages - " William stood, awkwardly.

"I haven't had any big sausages."

"Oh, it doesn't need to be big sausages – or sausages at all - "

"William, stop making everything about you, you and your intestines."

"Fossilling conference indeed, I'm sure that's a cover up," Ned crept towards the kitchen door and listened.

"Can you hear anything?" William whispered, although he was not entirely sure why. *"Well?* Can you hear any voices? *I* can't. It seems silent up there."

"That's what worries me," Ned squinted his eyes so much they practically closed altogether. "It seems suspiciously quiet, *too* quiet," Ned whispered back. "Your cottage, it's so old there's *never* a time when even at the furthest point of the house your Mum's footsteps can't be heard. Or that Stick of your Mum's crashing on the floor. Even when any of us are just shuffling about the floorboards creak. William, I don't think they're here. I think they've, well, they've *disappeared."*

"Disappeared? Disappeared *where?"* Belle whispered as she managed to push herself between Ned and William, "get out my way," she continued to shove herself sideways between their hips, "unless they've jumped out of the window? *I* wouldn't though. Have you seen the drop?" and Belle crawled along the floor, deeper and deeper into the passageway and further down the tiles towards the foot of the staircase. *"Mum?"*

Silence.

"Dad?"

Silence.

The loudest silence rumbled for a remarkable length of time.

"Well? What can you see?" William stayed in the kitchen. His voice was slow, and calm, but his heart was beating so fast the pot on the hook started to judder at the same pace. "Belle?"

Suddenly, Belle jumped back. She crashed to the floor.

"What *is* it? What did you see?" William tripped, clumsily, over the tiles. "Belle? What did you see? Or *who?"*

Belle's eyes widened.

Her jaw dropped.

"Have you laddered your tights?" William whispered.

"Don't be an idiot."

"What *is* it, then, Belle? *What* can you see?" William tried to force his head between his sister and the bottom of the stairwell, but there wasn't enough space and his jaw didn't fit. "Belle, *speak* to me, *what* did you see?" and, with a shove, William peered up the stairs through a crack between Belle's legs. "Belle, there's nothing, nothing but thick smoke. What did you *see?* Why are you pale? Are you dead? You *are,* aren't you? Ned, she's *dead - "*

"They - "

"Yes?"

"They - "

"Yes?"

"They vaporised," Belle spoke in a trance.

"Who vaporised?"

"Mum. Mum and Dad. They vaporised. They, they simply vanished. Gone. There one second - and thin air the next," Belle muttered. *"On the top stair one minute, and then flash, grey smoke - and nothing. Nothing but her Wandy-Stick-Thing -* " Belle whispered, and her words floated up the stairs.

"Oh no, not that *Stick.* If it gets involved with those tongs, we're minced meat. *She* can't control them; they'll play havoc with *us.* Probably tie our dressing gown cords together and hang us from the rafters; and then pretend we just went AWOL."

"Don't give them *ideas,"* Belle hissed. "Mum said they store up every idea and then spring it on her when she's up to her elbows in hawthorn and goat's milk soup."

Anyway, how do you know they're not just sitting upstairs, in the study? Or in the loo," William whispered, twisting tufts of his hair around his fingers.

"Since when does Mum *ever* sit in the study? *She* can't sit still," Belle scratched her eyebrows.

"The mist, it's probably smoke from the fire. Yes, *that's* it. When I was in the study, the grate was near to burning out, just dry crackly old wood and charcoal. Simple explanation," William started to slowly mount the stairs, pushing the mist carefully from his face. He twisted his head half way. "What are you waiting for, Belle? *Ned?* Come *on."*

"You're just scared," Belle hissed again.

"Am not, and stop acting like a snake. I'm not scared."

"Are *so.* Since when do you *ever* want us to help you discover something new? Hmm, let me think. That's right, *never* - and, what's that smell, that *musty* smell? Where have I smelt *that* before?" Belle frowned.

"In the *forest,"* Ned whispered. "That smell, it was in the forest when my Mum and Miss Smock vanished in battle. And when that little boy led us back."

Belle didn't think her eyes could in fact grow any larger. "My *Mum?* My Mum and *Dad* in Anouka? I must have banged my head."

"Fossiling conference, I thought it was to *never* end. *Fossiling conference,* could you have *thought* of anything less likely?" Mrs Joy whispered.

"Not really, no, I don't think I could," Mr Joy replied.

"It was a *rhetorical* question, dear."

"Oh. Did your *tongs* teach you that?"

"Teach me *what?"*

"Long words."

William listened from the top stair.

"Did you get the go ahead, the *sign?"* William heard his Mum ask Mr Joy. William stood perfectly still. In shock. "Well? Mr *JOY? Did* you?"

William stood, rigid.

Only a faint voice caused him to flinch.

It was a young voice – young and innocent. *"Who does that voice belong to? Who else is there? And that musty forest smell,"* William sniffed it as it started to seep out from under the cracks of the study door and to wend its misty fumes down the stairs. It had a sweet, sickly aroma and it began to make William feel strange, light-headed, dizzy, and momentarily he lost his footing as his head flopped from side to side. His brain felt airy.

"William!" Belle cried, as she sat, curled up, petrified at the foot of the stairs. "WILLIAM, you're *falling!* Hold *on!"* but William, he only heard his sister's muffled warning. He had no self-control and his body tumbled and crashed the entire length of each of the thirteen roughly-carpeted stairs.

"William? *William,* can you *hear* me? Willi-*aaam? Please* don't try that kamikaze jumping thing down the stairs, again. You'll end up breaking my vase, or worse still my *Spell* Stick. Can you *imagine* if that broke? All manner of spells would escape half-baked and utter *utter* chaos it would be," Mrs Joy rapped her knuckle on the handrail.

"Thanks, Mum. Glad that you're not worried about me breaking my legs," William rubbed his head.

"You? Breaking your *legs?* No danger of *that,* dear. You seem to just bounce. No, my Stick is *far* more precious. Can you imagine - "

"No, Mum, I can't."

"Don't be so facetious, William, dear, you fell, you fell *all* the way down the stairs. What *were* you thinking? There's a concrete wall at the bottom - not much give there

for your trousers not to rip. What were you *doing* hanging from the handrail so precariously? Honestly, you should know better, *really* you should, although - "

"Sorry - "

"Hmm, *are* you though? *Sorry?* Hmm, *I'm* not so *sure,"* Mrs Joy squinted her eyes. "There's something else - hmm, I can't quite put my finger on it, but something smells fishy - "

"Lunch, Mum?"

"CHRIST, *YES!"*

William sat up from his crumpled position in a heap on the floor. He stared at his Mum. "What are *you* doing there? *Here,* at the bottom of the stairs? You were at the top, the *very* top, in the study, sort of in the study, we think."

"Deranged, *quite* deranged, I do believe, that's all I have to say," and Mrs Joy held a cold wet cloth on William's head. "Press hard, just here, come *on.* You children, such scrapes."

William glanced at Belle, then Ned, in turn. "Unbelievable. She's lying, for sure," he whispered.

"I'm *sorry,* did you say I was *fibbing,* William? *Did* you?" Mrs Joy pulled an overly-sized, overly-baked cod from the Aga. It stank. Wisps of dried skin flaked from its bones, and one eye popped out altogether. "Oh *dear.* I *was* going to use the carcass for tomorrow's soup-dish too but now it's not even fit for *tonight.* So, *fibbing?* Did you accuse me of *fibbing,* William?"

"No, Mum. *Course* not."

"Hmm."

Belle and Ned shrugged their shoulders.

A key turned in the door.

Mr Joy walked in. “Crisp out there, it is, crisp and *cold.* I wouldn’t want to be outside for longer than the quick trip from the car up the steps to the back door, not tonight - and what *is* that smell? *Revolterous* - did the cat from next door die - again?” Mr Joy threw his green overcoat onto the back of the rocking chair and blew a kiss.

“Oh, Mr Joy, my cheek, it’s *burning.* Your kiss slapped me right across this bit, just here,” and Mrs Joy tapped her Stick three times on the floor at which the cloth in William’s hands flew out and stuck to Mrs Joy’s face. “Ahh, *that’s* better. How was the fossilling conference?” Mrs Joy enquired, not looking up from washing a baked-on sponge cake from its tin. Her Stick just sat there, now propped up against the wall. Lifeless. “Yes, *you’re* not much help, are you? Mind, I haven’t gotten on to non-stick cakes or self-washing ones *quite* yet.”

The Stick still played dead.

“So, fossils, Mr Joy?”

“Oh *that* - ”

“Yes, *that* - ”

“Yes, *that* - a success, a *great* success, that fossilling conference,” and Mr Joy threw a knowing look across the kitchen. The cloth on Mrs Joy’s face then slopperty-slipped from her cheek to where the knowing look had landed on her posterior. A light musty smelling mist fogged from Mr Joy’s overcoat, and the kitchen fire roared with a knowing

approval. “Yes, a most delectable outcome indeed, Mrs Joy, *most* delectable indeed.”

“Oh, such a relief. *Stew?* We’ll have to settle for last week’s.”

“Mmm, I can see *that.* What happened to the cod?” Mr Joy looked into the bin where the one-eyed cod stared back.

“Such a long-awaited relief. *Apple crumble?”* Mrs Joy ignored her husband and continued to chisel away at the encrusted tin muttering, “at least *some* things are easy to appease, *some* things, and that old cobwebbed fossil was one that *absolutely* needed appeasement.”

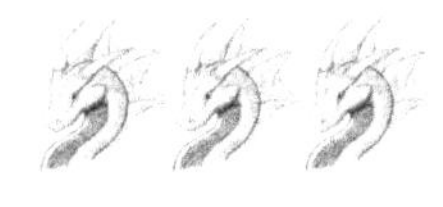

Jacintha

A harsh relentless wind rattled the top attic room window. Howling, it was. But William lay oblivious to its horrific winter's doom.

The cottage, built of ancient solid rock, stood perfectly hardened to the elements. But late night conversations lay steeped in unanswered questions as the day drew further and further to a close and miserably darker in atmosphere. Not even a jagged flying piece of molten

stone from an abyss beyond the realms of the village crashing onto the cottage roof stirred the people indoors.

Apart from Mrs Joy.

She wasn't even asleep.

"It's started," Mrs Joy sat bolt upright.

Her bed creaked.

"We need a new bed, it can't cope with your antics *any*more," Mr Joy rolled over and snored. Dust flew up and then down upon each of his large loud breaths.

"Not the *bed,* that's *always* been a wreck," Mrs Joy elbowed the lump next to her. ***"It,*** *it's* started. And, there's nothing wrong with my antics, Mr Joy. It's the bed. It creaks when there's ill-blood in the air."

"Ill-blood? What *ill-blood?"*

"As Magenta warned, *it's* begun. The beginning of the end, it's begun," Mrs Joy pulled her thick crocheted blanket further up towards her ears. "Innocence won't help anyone now. It's up to *them.* And can we get a *goose*-down duvet next time please? I don't care about the price, I'm sick of this woollen thing from decades past. Plays havoc with my spells this synthetic load of unreal stuff."

"Mrs Joy, Mrs *Joy,* have you no *faith?* No faith in our offspring?"

"I'm talking about a good night's sleep, with *goose* feathers."

"I'm talking about you rolling your eyes when you say *them.* When you tell of our offspring being the *ones* now. Have you no faith? Have you *not?"*

"Mr Joy, I'll have you know I can tell last night was no easy rest for *you* either. The kicking out of your feet and the loud continuous chanting from your lips - I heard it *all,* you're no hero, you fear the dangers Anouka could bring, I know you do, you cannot fool me, despite thinking you can with that snoring."

"Yes, dear, you know best," Mr Joy pretended he hadn't been listening, but beneath his squares of coloured crocheted knit he was equally, if not more, anxious that Armageddon was nigh.

From the top attic room, a slight movement occurred. Mutterings sounded, which turned to vast loud scrapings and a very strange tapping which got louder and louder and so quick the sequential noise turned into one continuous beat.

The drumming woke Ned first.

His eyes flicked open and he clenched his knuckles. They cracked in turn.

"Belle? *Belle,* are you awake?"

Silence.

Not a rustle.

"William? Are you there?"

The attic room was roasting.

Globules of sweat dripped down Ned's chest, and his head was on fire. The heat was too much and he pushed his voluminous duvet over the side of his bed to a crumpled heap on the floor. *"Belle?"* Ned shouted this time.

"What? I've been covering my ears hoping that Mum would stop that banging. It's been going on for ages. My eyes are popping out my head."

"I don't think it's her. She'd have got ratty with that Stick ages ago if it played up."

"Is it you?"

"Me? No."

"My *ears,"* Belle stuffed her fists into the side of her head. "This *heat.* Baby-ette Fireplace in here is only smouldering. Why this insane *heat?"* Belle stumbled from her bed and shook her brother.

"It's not *me,* I'm not making any noise at all, it's coming from the grate, look, even the wood is rumbling, shaking about - " William tried to pretend he could ignore it and get some more shut eye, " - if I wake up now, I'll need food, and I can't be bothered to go downstairs - "

"Trunchons and dragons, it *is - "* Belle snuck closer, and closer.

"What *is?* What is *what?"*

"Baby-ette Fireplace," Belle could see its kindling rustling on the spot, and its hunks of wood scrape from side to side. "What *is* it?"

"BELLE! WATCH OUT!" William lurched from his bed, but his feet got tangled in his sheets.

"WATCH OUT! Blimey! *Talons,* talons and claws, they're forcing their way in!" Ned leapt from his mattress and pushed Belle across the room just in time before a deep green dragon shot out into the cindered grate; ash and embers burning holes in the carpet.

"Mum'll be *furious,"* William hissed.

"Are you kidding?"

"No! She *will!"*

"I think the most of our worries at the moment is *THAT!"* and Belle shot her fingers towards the gnarling, fire-breathing, intoxicating beast that wriggled and spat on the floor, smoke blasting from its nostrils. The beastly dragon stretched out one entire foot laden with orange talons and simply plucked William from his bed.

"WILLIAM!" Belle screamed from her screwed up place on the floor. "Ned, William's *gone!"*

Ash and soot, rocks and burning embers had fallen everywhere, and the chokingly black smoke that the dragon had infiltrated around the room during its timeless intrusion were disorientating. Belle had no idea where to run. Only the dragon drawing its breath led her towards an exit - a hole.

"Ned, where *are* we? Ned? NED? Did you come? Are you here? *NED?"*

"I feel sick."

"Where in heavens name *are* we?" Belle scrambled about.

"I think I inhaled that eye - "

"What eye?"

"The eye from that cod when it popped out. I saw that ridiculous Stick trying to locate it; tap about for fodder, but I think *I* swallowed it."

"Apparently, so says Mum's recipe book, cod eyes are the most nutritious eyes in the fish family."

"That forest - we're back in that *forest,*" Ned gagged and pointed his arm far into the distance. "That peak, the dragon is on that peak, and look, it's, he's protecting William, protecting him from some figure," Ned squinted. "Can you see a figure looming? I can't work it out," Ned peered closer, his neck straining and his oesophagus stretching as far as it would go before his throat spewed up a little green ball.

"OH NED! That's *disgusting!* You've sicked up that eye!" Belle grasped her stomach and started to heave.

"Want it? You said it was nutritious - "

"GROSS!"

"Gracious, it's - it's - it's *Miss Smock?"* and then Ned ducked, as, quite insanely, the dragon swept down, its scaly emerald wings scraping across the top of Ned's scalp. "HUH, *aah,* dragon, you caught my *hair.* Can't you see where you're *going?* What *is* he doing, Belle?"

"I'm so *terribly* sorry - " dithered the dithery dragon, " - I'm the biggest clumsiest clot I know," and it looked around as if to actually check its own admission. "Yes, I really *am.*"

"No, *we're* sorry, *aren't* we Ned? *Ned?"* Belle poked the boy hard in the ribs.

"Sorry? What Belle?" Ned hadn't been listening to a word Belle had been saying, he was too busy rubbing his head for he was adamant that careless, ridiculous beast had actually torn out a large clump of his hair. "You hurt me, dragon!" Ned scorned, still riling with pain. "In fact, you've given me a seething headache."

"Gracious, I *am* most *awfully*, *painstakingly* apologetic. You see, I'm *far* too used to having to be threatening in my role to protect this world, and I'm so incredibly *not* used to, or prepared to, being dainty and genial. That's why I came to your room, sorry about the insidious mess, and plucked Ned from his bed," the dragon licked his moronically unclipped talons. "That imposter, Miss Smock as *you* know her, she wants to be immortal, she is after that *book* Ned holds - " the dithering dragon looked about, " - so I had to make sure she didn't find it, so I simply stole Ned away. Miss Smock, she's an evil tyrant, wants to make Anouka all-powerful where *she* rules, and only she. She wants that book, and *nothing* will stop her from getting it. If *she* fails, she wants *everyone* in Anouka to fail, everyone who has *ever* set foot in Anouka will fall foul to its abhorrent collapse, an Armageddon from which nothing and no one can possibly escape. Oh, and by the way, I'm a *she*," the dragon replied, quite courteously Belle thought for a dragon that oozed hatred.

"Explains the lack of co-ordination and endless nattering, I suppose," Ned still rubbed his sore head.

"At least we make sense and don't *constantly* think of our stomachs," Belle retorted, and she turned to the dragon. "But, *dear* dragon, *this* is Ned," and she touched Ned's bony shoulder. "*That* boy you plucked is William, my brother. It's Ned who has the book. Here look," Belle pulled Ned's thin beige anorak apart revealing the jacket of the imposter book. "And, you see, also, this book - it's not actually the real - "

"AWWWWW, MY HEAD," Ned grimaced.

"You were rubbing the other side a minute ago," Belle let go of Ned's anorak.

"Was I?"

"Yes, you *were.*"

"Must have been something **you** *said,* then," Ned glared silently. "Threw me right off track, Rosabella."

"Oh, Ned, can't you see this dragon is, well, a little, well, how can I put it? *Challenged?* You know, in the brain department."

"Am I? Is that a ***good*** thing? ***Is*** it? I haven't had a compliment in ***years!"*** the dragon replied, a smile trying to creep across her sticky cheeks.

"Yes, Belle? *Is* it? *Is* it a compliment, or were you suggesting our friend here is a little under par, intellectually-wise?" Ned replied.

"Intellectually-wise, that *does* sound mighty," the dragon puffed a thick turquoise smoke from her stuffed up nostrils. "I *would* love to be *intellectually-challenged."*

"Would you now?" Ned replied, quite enjoying himself. "Well, Belle can explain - "

"That's *enough,"* Belle snapped. "You're fine just as you are, dragon. But, William? Well, he looks a bit precarious up there, don't you think?"

"Sorry, I *do* beg your pardon and please *do* forgive me, but, did you say *you're* Ned?" the dragon peered closely and more wide-eyed than ever at the lanky boy standing tall and helpless at her feet.

"Haven't we just done all this?" Ned frowned.

"Oh, a little more statuesque, and not *quite* as formidably proportioned, and *ever* so gangly in the leg department, and much more, how shall I put it? Let's see, oh cut to the chase, Jacintha, more of a *geek* than I thought possible, but I *was* expecting someone far more robust, you know - "

"Well, of all the *rude* remarks I've heard in my years, and I can tell you I am *far* older than you could ever possibly guess, dragon. Of all the past I've truly encountered and the people I've met, you must simply be the ***rudest*** dragon I've had the misfortune to have clapped eyes on. Really, indeed."

"And - " continued the dragon, " - and, how many dragons exactly *have* you clapped eyes on? *Mmm?"*

Belle grinned - "Well?"

"Oh shut up, stop ganging up on me. Aren't we losing track of the *real* problem here? William, and, well, trying to stay – urr - *alive?"*

"Ned, really. Can't you see, the dragon - oh, *Jacintha,* did you say that was your name? Jacintha is playing you. Ned, we're on the same side, aren't we Jacintha?" Belle walked over to the beast that had now managed to stop haphazard fire steaming from her nostrils, and stared up, very high she thought, into the dragon's eyes. "I don't think I've introduced myself properly, so *hello.* I'm *Belle,* and there, enchanted in some sort of sleep state and surrounded with your daggers, is my brother, *William,* and *this* here, *this* lengthy bony boy, is in fact whom you seek, *Ned. This* is

Ned, for sure. Well, he was when I last looked anyway. How are *you* to help, and who *sent* you?"

"Hush, I hear something, quick," and Jacintha opened up her gargantuan wings, spanning the entire forest floor where they stood, then whacked them down over Belle and Ned. "Not a word now."

"I'm not bony, I certainly am *not,* just *tall,* and *that* is what accentuates my rather thin, no, *sculptured* body, certainly not bony, bony indeed," Ned spoke out from beneath the darkened cave like place they now seemed to be.

"I SAID SSSH, **NOW!"**

"Ned, really, is that *all* you can think about? Your body, really, there are *much* more pressing worries, right *here* right *now*," Belle hissed, her loudest she could afford, reply.

"Well, who *does* she think she is, *Jacintha,* criticising me? And, *Jacintha?* What type of a name is *that* for a dragon? It's pathetic."

"Don't always judge a book by its cover, Ned. And, stop being so vain, we're all trying to save Anouka so stop complaining, we don't know whoever, or *whatever,* is out there to hear us. Ooh, I've just found a jammy dodger in my knickers."

A wind whipped up outside, then calmed itself. The silence was deathly. Jacintha stayed deathly still.

"Can you hear anything?" Belle whispered.

"Well, no, not really, just some sort of crunching, like feet on dry leaves," Ned replied. "Can you?"

"I'm not entirely sure. It's a bit eerily quiet out there. *Jacintha?"* Belle called from the darkness of her hiding place. *"Jacintha?"* she called a bit louder. "Who can you see? What came along?"

"Who said that?" Jacintha shuffled.

"CAREFUL! You nearly stepped on my feet this time!" Ned snapped. "Clot."

"Oh, *dears,* oh my *dears* I *quite* forgot you were under there," Jacintha heaved her great wings from cowering over her victims and coughed, loudly. A red flame shot out across the dry forest carpet and caught a collection of branches. They immediately set on fire.

"JACINTHA!" Belle cried.

"Oh, it's nothing, don't worry yourselves about a little house fire."

"A LITTLE house fire? That entire bush is blazing alight! It's three times the height of even *you!"*

"It's fine, it'll burn itself out soon, and if not? Well, I can try my new spell - "

"New *spell?"*

"Yes, my new *spell.* Learnt it just yesterday and I've been waiting for the opportune moment to see if it *really* worked. I've been practicing the words all night, that's why I'm half asleep really. Tired of preaching the verse."

"Go on then, *now* would be a good time!" Ned stared at the flames that were now so tall the peak on which William lay was completely blocked. The sparks had even covered the moon.

Jacintha went into a trance. *"Cast it out, blow us free, fire burning, look at me…*oh, I appear to have forgotten the rest, and I knew it *so* well last night. Three o'clock it was when I finally managed to close one eye, but the other was still flickering excitedly, now, *what* came next, Jacintha? Think, **do** *think - "*

"JACINTHA!"

"OH yes, it's coming back now. Jacintha became trance like again. *"Cast it out, blow us free, fire burning, look at me. Please stop the heat, or you'll defeat, not only them, but ME!"* and immediately the fire disappeared.

"That was all a bit odd," Ned scratched his scalp.

"This whole thing is a bit odd," Belle stared at the bush which now lay in a cremated black mess on the floor.

"It was no one, nothing," Jacintha licked her talons again.

"What wasn't?" Belle sat down.

"Oh, the noise. When I scooped you up like prisoners. It was nothing. *I* am indeed the most *terrible* clot. It was in fact only my own tail swiping the ground that made me make you jump and hide. Sorry for that distinct dithering of mine, simply my stupidity, most ridiculous and clumsy of me, I might add, how *am* I to rectify it, never have managed to up to now, once a clot *always* a clot; can't keep my mind on anything in particular – ooh, is that a jammy dodger, Belle? - " but Jacintha was cut short as this time an enormous shadow *did* loom over her taking away the dragon's breath with a formidable result.

"Yes, it is jammy dodger. Do you have them here? Would you like a bite - "

"R-U-N!" Jacintha puffed. "Run from me, Smock has tracked us down - R-U-N!" Jacintha stumbled off into the darkest part of the forest huffing. "Run as far as you can go - save yourselves!" and she was gone.

The burnt orange sun lowered fast.

And Belle and Ned were alone.

Very *much* alone with her.

With Smock.

"Smock! What *is* she?" Belle gasped as she faltered looking all around completely undecided as to which way to run. "What on earth *is* she?"

"I've no idea, but I'm not hanging around to find out! I really am *not. This* way, Belle, Jacintha ran *this* way, and as I have absolutely no idea which way leads where I'm following that clumsy old dragon!"

"Oh, so you *want* to be with her now, do you?" Belle cried as her feet tried their utter fastest to keep up with the speed of the long-limbs that ran one step to her four. "You don't mind following in the footsteps of insult if it'll *save* you?"

"NOPE! And I'm sure *you* don't either, and stop your constant natter; save your breath for running! What *is* it with females and incessant chat, chat, chat, nag, nag, nag at the most inappropriate times? Don't get it myself. Really I don't! In fact I don't think I *ever* will, not in all my long life, will I ever understand them - - oh!"

Darkness fell.

"Belle? BELLE? Are you alright?" Ned cried out as he began to fall further and further somewhere. ***"B – e – l – l – e ?"***

A Strange Set of Circumstances

Mrs Joy picked up a pile of broken china that lay scattered, clumsily, everywhere on the kitchen floor. She muttered as the tiniest of her new spell brushes swept shavings of white chippings into the dustpan. “What a most *terrible* clumsy

clot I am. Really, Jacintha Joy, even your *name* is quite a mouthful. It's just a blessing Anouka doesn't allow names to be taken from *its* world to *this* world. I guess I'll have to console myself in being fortunate that my constant clumsiness hasn't gotten me into much *more* trouble. Just imagine, just *imagine* if that Smock knew? Just imagine if my sister, brrr I shudder at the name, knew *I* were Jacintha. Gracious, she would undoubtedly *never* have passed the time of day with me here, sat in my own *kitchen,* sipping my *tea* and complimenting me on my *biscuits,"* Mrs Joy chuckled, and tripped up over her annoying tail, from which she could never quite escape, and she could never quite disguise beneath her apron skirts bursting out as usual.

She stumbled backwards as she heard a distant scraping.

And voices.

Mrs Joy pushed the last few remaining jagged bits of broken china into the bin. "If I hadn't piled all those tea cups right in the chimney, what *was* I thinking, I obviously wasn't, then I wouldn't be throwing them all away. Shame, shame, I *did* like those. Now I'll have to re-spell a new set and it took three Sundays in a row to make those cups conform and brew the tea and spit out the grouts themselves. Anyway, never mind, I totally forgot that last bit from the forest was such a brutal drop into the kitchen, I'll remember one day, one day I might," and she brushed down her ripped frilly apron with her dry scaly hands, and shoved her ancient dustpan and brush into the, already bulging, kitchen

cupboard and flung herself, breathless, into the rocking chair.

"Dears," she smiled calmly as Belle and Ned tumbled, muddy and speechless, into the kitchen.

"Hi Mum."

"Shut the back door, there's a good girl."

"But, but, but we didn't come in through the back door - "

"Tea? You *do* look exhausted. What *have* you been doing? And *where* is your brother? Not left somewhere, I hope, alone? You two are as thick as thieves lately together. Don't leave him out. Lest hungry. Can you *imagine* the state his stomach would be in if it was even slightly empty?" Mrs Joy babbled on.

"We'd rather not," Belle muttered.

Mrs Joy eyed Belle closely, and then sat further back down. She found it terribly hard to leave Jacintha behind. Even her nostrils felt full of hotness from their constant firings of ridiculous flames over which she had absolutely no control. "So, where *is* he?"

"Who?" Belle tried to cover her tracks, not very well.

"Who? What do you mean, *who?* Your *brother,* William, remember him? Robust, ponderous, you know? Perhaps not, you do both seem rather elsewhere. I'll leave you to it. Brush up though - " Mrs Joy hit one of her hands harshly down onto her skirts - *"blessed tail."*

"Oh *Mum,* we haven't got another charcoaled fish for tea, *please* say we don't? I couldn't eat a stiff old tail, not tonight."

Mrs Joy pulled on her rubber gloves. "Well, your Father will be back soon, and he'll want to have some time with you children. Have we sat down to tea, I mean *all* of us, together, since you broke up for Christmas? I don't think we have, I *really* don't think we have come to think of it, a must, a *must* - "

"That means we *do* have another charcoaled fish for tea - " but when Mrs Joy turned to grimace and tell that tale of the starving African children, again, Belle and Ned had long gone.

"What *is* it with my conversations that the audience just keeps disappearing?" Mr Fireplace roared a tall blue flame. "Thank you, *thank* you, at least *someone* is listening. Are you, William? *Are* you listening?"

Silence.

A loud tap made Mrs Joy jump. *"Who's* there?"

The tap tapped louder.

"I said, who can that be at this time of night? Honestly, has *nobody* anything better to occupy themselves? It's past, *very* much past, social visiting hours, invasion, *invasion* of my time - Oh, Miss Smock, what a *pleasure,* an *absolute* pleasure," Mrs Joy lied through her clenched teeth as she forced open the stable door, which appeared to want to have no desire to let anyone in, and smiled incredibly falsely.

"Where *is* he?" was Miss Smock's first seething introduction.

"I'm *sorry,* Miss Smock. I must have missed something? To *whom* are you referring?" Mrs Joy stood in

the doorway, neither letting Miss Smock in nor Mr Fireplace's incensed flames out.

"Oh, nice, incredibly, forcibly nice innocent Mrs Joy whose undeniably farcical virtuousness has paved its way *far* enough."

"I don't quite follow."

"You're hiding something. It's obvious now. You're *no* saintly Mum. You know far more than you care to let on, with your *cups of tea* and your *pretence at baking biscuits.* It's simply *no* cover up. I'm not a fool."

"Miss Smock, Miss Smock, really, you come to my house in the darkness of night and throw around insane ridiculous accusations on my own back doorstep - " Mrs Joy whacked down her scaly tail that had decided to become involved. "Really, Mr Joy will be home soonest and what will he say seeing me beaten to demeaning shreds of indignity," Mrs Joy totally surprised herself with her pleasing false outrage.

"Oh Mrs Joy, *spare* me the sobbing innocent details, *pleeease,* there is *no* time for award winning spectacles of grief and self-pity. Just GET OUT OF MY WAY!" and she pushed past her suitor and fell in to the hottest kitchen ever. "Mrs Joy, *no* sane person can live like this, it's *far* too hot! Now, *where* is that boy of yours, that guest who has invaded your home? TELL ME!" Miss Smock's voice resonated throughout the kitchen, but before Mrs Joy's lividly-powerful tail could no longer be self-contained, it forced its way outside of her multitude of skirts and simply swiped Miss Smock to the ground.

"Sister, sister *Smock,* indeed. Oops."

"Huh?"

"I really *did* warn you," Mrs Joy straightened her skirt tails and continued to wash the dishes.

Miss Smock, Jacintha & Rupert Gvist?

Belle and Ned crouched upstairs, in their attic room, waiting, waiting for what neither knew, but they were waiting none the less.

"This carpet, it's ruined. Surprised Mum hasn't mentioned it, she's always the first to know everything, but she didn't say *anything.* And the soot on the carpet? That singed hole right in the middle - it'll be impossible to cover up. Ned, are you *listening?* Have you heard a *word* of what I've been saying - "

"Belle! Give it a rest? Your brother, you know, William? So high, so wide, five-foot ten and perhaps seven and a half stone?" Ned acted out William's body. "How are we going to get him back? If you're that concerned about what your Mum thinks - of the carpet - , she's expecting a family tea, *with* William - *tonight.* I heard her say so when we snuck away. So we better get your brother back, unscathed, before night really *does* fall."

Baby-ette Fireplace looked cold.

Ice cold.

It was calm.

Unlit.

Placid.

No flying soot and *certainly* no seething dragons.

Ned put his head up inside the chimney. "Ouch!" he hissed as he cracked his head hard inside the tall thin black grate. He rapped his bony knuckles on the interior. *"Definitely* has a back, and I can see *right* out into the night's sky up there. No way at all in to another world - "

"Let *me* look," Belle stuck her hair right up inside the chimney. *"I feel sick!"* she collapsed back onto the floor; a cloud of chokingly black smoke blurring her vision, and a heap of soot in her face. "I think I've got vertigo."

“Let me look again - ”

“No, *I’m* in here now,” and Belle stuck her head back inside again. “Looks like an ordinary fireplace to me,” she spluttered, rubbing her eyes free of grit and cinders. “How *are* we going to get back to Anouka? We just fell in before. There’s no portal *now - ”*

“You *think* so?” a deep bottomless voice sounded from somewhere.

“HUH? Who said *that? Who’s* there? We think *what?”* Belle dropped back inside the attic, searching for a person to link to the voice. “Who *are* you? *Where* are you? *Show* yourself, come on, *show* yourself,” but before Belle could work out from where such a lurk-some tone lay, a rumbling came from within the fireplace.

The hugest logs rolled from the back to the front of the grate leaving an opening that looked azure and luring.

“Come on,” the voice demanded.

“No!” Belle replied shrilly.

“Sorry?”

“YOU come on. Into the attic. We’re not coming in THERE!”

“Come on *quickly. Get* in. *I’ll* take you to William,” the deep voice continued.

“You think we’ll just **get** in there?”

“Yes, of course! But you have to be quick, that Smock woman is on her way. Your Mum *can* deal with her, but she *is* rather clumsy and can’t hold her away forever, but you both better get in *quick.* The *last* thing we need is

Smock seeing you, me, *this* old fireplace in use. Come *on* - ”

“It’s Rupert, it sounds like *Rupert,* it really *does* - ” Ned rushed towards the logs which were now rolling out further and further from the fireplace, “ - Rupert, it’s you, it is, *isn’t* it? *Tell* me it’s you?”

Silence.

“I’m not waiting here for an answer when there’s an *escape* route at our fingertips!” and, before Ned even checked the fireplace for its supposed tunnel in existence, in he leapt.

“Ned! You’ll hit your head again,” but all Belle saw was the soles of Ned’s feet as he held on to his flapping anorak and shut his eyes.

Thud.

“I guess I’ve arrived,” Belle heard Ned cry back. “Come on - ”

“If you say so, but on your head be it - ”and soon Belle tumbled into the forest too.

Rupert was leant up against a tall dry oak tree, with an *enormous* green velveteen trunk.

“Rupert! It *is* you!” Belle hugged the man tightly.

“Yes, well, enough of this *hugging* stuff child, I don’t really *do* empathy,” Rupert blushed.

“Did you say Smock was after us - ?”

“And *Mrs Joy* could deal with her?” Ned remarked.

"Mum? *Our* Mum, she can't *possibly,* she could never at all deal with the likes of Smock - we *have* to go back, we must!"

"Without *William?* Go back home without your *brother?"* Rupert replied, calmly stroking his chin. "Can you imagine your Mum's face at tea-time?"

"I'd rather not," Ned muttered.

"Where did he go?" Belle looked about.

"Who?" Ned asked.

"That little boy, *where* did he go? I *saw* him, I *saw* him just before *you* appeared, Rupert. *Where* did he go? You *must* have seen him, Rupert?"

"There's been no one here but me, Belle. No one but me," Rupert spoke slowly. "But, we have to go. She's doing well, Mrs Joy, I can tell, very capable, for *now,* but we mustn't be in this forest too long," Rupert started to look stretched and worn. "Follow me, and be quick about it."

"Are we off to get my brother?" Belle jogged by Rupert's side.

"Sssh, lie low."

"But, William, is that where we're headed?"

"Yes, yes - "

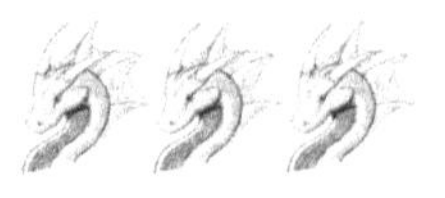

"What's wrong?" Belle ran along, exhausted.

"Nothing, stay *quiet* I told you."

"You sound worried? *You* have the book, yes, Rupert? *The Book of Immortality,* so Smock *can't* get it from Ned now - so why are you so worried?" but Belle was met with panicked flicking eyes.

"Ssssssh, I *keep* telling you - "

"She'll *never* listen," Ned caught up. "Haven't you learnt that by now? On and on and *on,* girls keep talking - "

"These trees," Rupert spied about. "You *never* know who's listening, but if we don't get back, your Mum will be wondering. And - we can't have that. She'll be setting that Stick on you."

"She'll *just* be scolding the fish, or cooking-up a spell to iron pants in record time," Belle tried to pick through the thicket. "She shan't be looking for us. Where are we going, Rupert?"

Rupert did not answer.

"Rupert, are we looking for something? Do you *know* where we're going?"

Silence.

"Rupert, you're turning white. I mean *really* white," Belle stared at Rupert's face. It was distraught, as if a plan was faltering. "Ned, *come* on," but Ned was nowhere to be seen, and instead, as Belle turned back around to face Rupert, who she then saw invading her space in the forest was Jacintha and a very *very* worn looking Miss Smock.

Miss Smock was bedraggled.

Her clothes were ripped.

And, she was being dragged by Jacintha's talons across the dry forest floor.

"Here, Rupert," Jacintha spoke lowly, her voice pulsating. *"Do* with her what you will, but **I** *have* to get back," and the green-scaled dragon, nostrils flared with anxiety, dropped an unconscious Miss Smock at Rupert's long bony feet.

"Thank you."

"You're welcome, Rupert," Jacintha huffed, and slunk off, breathing a sigh of relief. She looked exhausted.

"Jacintha?" Rupert cried to the dragon as she started to head back through the trees the way she had come. "Jacintha, thank you, *thank* you for bringing that beast," Rupert turned back to face the inanimate looking frail crimson body as it lay, motionless, between himself and the emerald dragon figure within arm's reach. "Are you okay, *are* you? It is okay, you know."

"Why of *course,* Rupert. What on *earth* has come across you? You sound absurd. If I didn't know any better I'd think there was a faint tinge of emotion in your voice," Jacintha protruded her talons, less sharp and not half as pointed as Belle remembered them to be, and scratched the inside of her nostril. It flared. *"Really,* Rupert, that's *quite* enough of this ludicrous nonsensical banter," and Belle could have sworn Jacintha's hardened rough cheeks flashed a hint of rosy embarrassment. *"Really,* Rupert, stop this baffling questioning, I simply *must* return home," and the mild-mannered dragon turned, clumsily, on her heel and stumbled off into the thicket of trees.

She was gone.

"Ouch!"

Not quite gone.

"*Dratted* gorse bush, *who* put that there? *Really,* indeed. *Huh?* Where *is* my tunnel, or mountain peak, yes, *mountain* peak, that I *have* to rectify, can't leave him there, quite ashamed I am, oh Jacintha, you left the boy there, heavens, quite simply wronged I must be when it comes to directions, and correct faces, you are Jacintha, quite simply unblessed you are when it comes to navigational skills, that's me, dear, oh dear, oh *dear - "* Jacintha's crabby tone got fainter and fainter. "That boy, I *must* retrieve that boy."

"Oh Mrs Joy," Rupert whispered to himself. "Mrs Joy, you lovely old fool."

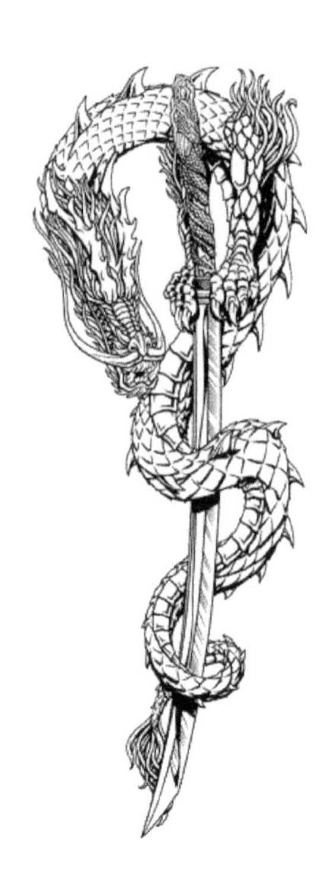

Beyond the Unfinished Chapter

William sat, cross-legged, and frowned.

"The *last* place I want to be is *here,* wherever *here* is," he moaned, and carefully touched his wounds. Both

elbows were black and blue, bruised from the severe plucking from the comfort of his warm bed. "I'm *starving.* Where's a mug of hot chocolate with marshmallows when you need one? Eh? *EH?"*

Silence.

"Guess not, then."

William sighed.

He pushed the air around him.

"How on *earth* am I to get out of *here*?" William pushed the air again. It was no use, the daggers surrounding the nest in which he had been strewn from a height were getting progressively closer and closer together, and the air between each blade was getting remarkably thicker and thicker.

"IT'S SIMPLY NO USE!" William shouted to the abyss where nobody was present.

The green dragon had gone, left William alone, and as far as he could see it was not coming back.

"HELP ME! *HELP* **ME!** *Anyone?"* William cried, but his question was answered with more silence.

No reply indulged him.

"Anyone?" William asked again, more sheepishly this time.

Then he stopped.

And he looked around.

And as William peered closer at the array of daggers before him he noticed that one, one in particular, hovered in mid-air quite freely. He put out his hand.

"Oh!"

The ruby-encrusted dagger jumped right into his palm. *"Double cheesecakes and more!"* William exclaimed. "Did that just happen?" and William clenched the dagger's ridged handle even tighter, and as he did so the strangest most overwhelming feeling came upon him. William felt immediately strong, ever so curiously intelligent, but most of all, the place from where the ruby dagger, now in his grasp, had sat an image was forming. No, *many* images. In fact, an *entire* collection of scenes began to materialise from the high misty nest surround and William found he was looking at a story – a pictorial story of which he had already been part and of which was about to occur. A Book was visually playing itself to William, chapter by chapter, from the loss of Ned's Mum to - "Crikey, bloody 'ell, *Mum? MUM?"*

William stared closer as the images set themselves out as clear as day.

"Mum? Is that really *you?"* William gasped so deep he could barely breathe as he spied his *own* Mum striking Miss Smock to the ground in his *own* kitchen. And what *was* that she quickly concealed beneath her skirts? "Mum, is that a *tail?"* William slanted his eyes. *"It is, it's* a sweeping emerald tail, the same tail I saw fleeing *this* scene, from where the dragon, huh, where *you*, dumped me? *Mum?* Mmm, a Jaffa cake? What's that doing under my finger nail?"

William carried on looking at the Book.

The last image was himself. Sitting alone. On the peak of the mountain top - the ruby dagger protruding from the lifeless body of his most hated woman. And he heard his

own voice speak lowly; "Aha. The future. Miss *Smock,* your end is nigh," he stuttered to himself.

"William?" Mrs Joy's quiet tone slowly roused her son. "William, goodness *gracious,* did you sleep walk again? I thought you'd grown out of that. Been in the garden this time have we?"

"Huh?" William's eyelids flickered.

Mr Fireplace glowed crimson.

Belle stared at her brother, sitting half awake and half droopy, in the kitchen rocking chair.

"Huh?" William muttered, slowly, again. "The *garden?* No."

"William?" Belle whispered into William's ear to avoid her Mum's earshot. "How did you get back, from Anouka?" she asked. "We left you surrounded by daggers, Miss Smock tearing along behind us and, well, a bumbling dragon saved us but that's for later. How *did* **you** get back?"

"I don't think he went *anywhere,*" Mrs Joy pricked up her ears and then cleared her throat. "Come on, Belle, now. Give your brother some air, *please,*" Mrs Joy flapped her tea towel about to clear pickled egg fumes from her nose. "Blasted chickens, never trust them to lay a perfect pickled egg. I *shan't* be buying my poultry from No.6 again," and she tripped over her skirts and landed on top of

the invalid. "You feeling dizzy, William?" Mrs Joy peered so close William went cross-eyed.

"Well, I wasn't until *you* fell on me," William rubbed his stomach. "I'm starving."

"You do look a little *pale,* dear?"

"Any wonder?"

Mrs Joy brushed her fingers across William's perspiring forehead, and he felt her dry cracked skin more than he had *ever* done before. And that *smell,* an old smoky fog circling under his nose from his Mum's own clothing.

"Mum? Are you really just my *Mum*? *I* saw you as something *else?"* William whispered, holding his mouth to her ear.

"Mr Joy? Mr *Jooooooooooy?* Your son, gracious me, he's *hallucinating* again, for pity's sake. Let's get him back to bed. Mr ***Joooooy?"*** the run-ragged woman snapped. "MR JOY, WHERE *ARE* YOU?"

"Fixing the washing machine," a muffled voice replied. "That *darn* belt's gone again."

"Washing machines are for sissies! Get here, at *OOONCE!"*

"Coming, dear, coming, dear," Mr Joy shuffled along the corridor for what seemed like the seventeenth time that morning, and ended up in the kitchen to lean on the wall. *"What,* dear? *What* did you want?"

"You're absolutely *drenched!* What *have* you been doing?"

"I *told* you, woman. Fixing the washing machine, and for love nor money, you wouldn't let me finish - "

"But, Mr *Joy,* you're dripping rancid water *all* over my floor!"

"As I said, you *wouldn't* let it lie. You summoned me as if I was that Stick of yours."

The Stick juddered on the spot.

"Good idea, GOOD IDEA, Mr Joy! I *knew* you would come up trumps," and Mrs Joy snapped her fingers and the Stick immediately jumped to attention. It grew hundreds and *hundreds* of woolly threads until it no longer looked like a Stick at all. "Oh wonders, WONDERS!" Mrs Joy clapped her hands four and a quarter times, twisted thrice on the spot, smashed three partially pickled eggs onto the floor and the Stick started to mop. *Mop, mop, mop* it went, backwards and forwards whilst Mr Joy just stared in disbelief.

"Can I get one of those in my bedroom?" William muttered. "Could do with it."

"Your son, Mr Joy, your son, he's having one of those *funny* turns again," Mrs Joy tried to heave William from the rocking chair, but her strength was weakening. "Oddities, pure oddities, he's rambling, he is."

"I'd like to call it quirky, Mum, not odd," William rubbed his head. It was throbbing.

"Call it what you like, you're *still* spouting nonsense."

"Am not!"

"Here, here. Let me," Mr Joy shuffled further across the kitchen, Mr Fireplace roaring as if to pull him inside. "Come, son. Come along, my boy. Let's get you back to your room. Perhaps you need a rest, but for *what* I *don't*

know, you never seem to be doing much exercise to be needing rests, but I'm not getting the end of that Stick up my - "

"Quite enough obscenities, Mr Joy, that's *quite* enough, we don't *all* need to hear where that Stick's been - or hasn't been," Mrs Joy's eyes twitched.

"UGH! Where *has* it been?" Belle screwed up her face. "Because I've been drinking from cups it's *definitely* touched. I think I'm going to be sick."

"I'm fine, I am. There's no need to fuss," William suddenly sat bolt upright, and spoke quite competently for the first time since he woke up.

"But you *won't* be fine in a minute if Mum lets that Stick dish up the chargrilled remains of that bulbous-eyed reptile who's bubbling away. What IS that? I'm not eating."

"It's called nutrition, Rosabella. Not that you'd know anything about that with all the marshmallows and custard knock-off varieties on the shelves these days."

"Belle, where's *Ned?"* but William's interrogation was met with a stern silence.

Belle shrugged.

"Really, Belle. I haven't brought you up with manners of shrugging ones shoulders? I'm sure Ned is fine, just *fine,"* Mrs Joy's twitching eyes seemed to be getting worse.

William kept silent.

He just itched a series of incisions in his arms, that dragon's talons. He *had* seen Ned, and he racked his brains to try and remember where.

"Ned?" William had a vision. "Ned, who is that *lady*?" William started to pace about the kitchen towards Mr Fireplace. The Stick followed him, tap-tapping just one eleventh of an inch from his bottom.

"Are you *quite* sure you want to be that close?" Belle screwed up her nose at the Stick. "I wouldn't if I were you, Stick." But the Stick still clipped itself along the floor, slipping on a drowning cockroach and falling into William's pyjama bottoms.

"William, *come, come* now, come now, will you - Willia – aaa*aaaaam - "* Mrs Joy clicked her fingers and immediately William twisted a sharp forty five degrees away from Mr Fireplace and stepped, one shuffle of a foot followed by the other, towards the voice. "And quick march, and stop, STOP, I SAID STOOOOOPPPP!" Mrs Joy stared at the Stick. "That's *your* fault, that is. Allowing my guinea pigs to dive themselves headfirst into chairs. Imagine if I'd tested the real thing and William's head ended up in there?" and Mrs Joy glared at Mr Fireplace's roaring flames.

"Imagine," Mr Fireplace blazed green.

"Having the tip of your Stick inside William's pyjama trousers you can't hear a *single* command," and Mrs Joy hurried William's head back out the rocking chair and begun spouting nonsensicals again, knowing he was about to shed knowledge that was not particularly appropriate.

"Ned, who was that girl, that old female, in your arms? I saw something else, that Book showed me something else," William muttered in a trance, but before

he could say much more, Mrs Joy had pulled his over-sized pyjamas by the shoulders and heaved him across the craggy tiles.

"Who on *earth* fitted these wretched things? Mrs Joy skidded. "Always such a tiresome passageway this has to be," she cursed to herself. "Not enough sleep? Not enough *sleep.* A rest is what you need, William, to stop all this vivid and rubbishy chit-chat," and Mrs Joy, not realising her own strength, had managed to clear two flights of curvy staircases and throw William into bed.

"What *girl*?" Belle spat up the stairs. "William, ***what*** girl?" but Mrs Joy chivvied her daughter back downstairs before William could divulge much more.

"Aaaand – WAIT FOR IT STICKKK! Sleep," Mrs Joy stared at the boy.

William's eyes shut like concrete.

"Phew, that *was* close," and Mrs Joy wiped her brow. A tap tugged her skirt. "And *you? YOU? You* can go away and don't come out until I call you. Do you understand? *Hum?"*

The Stick rolled under a rug.

"Insanity, what ***is*** *Gladiolus-Viola* teaching you nowadays? Goodness me, you'll be saying there are dragons in the closet soon," Mrs Joy shocked herself at her over-ripe mouth. "Forget that."

"Mum?" Belle stood there.

"Mrs Joy, really. You and your mouth," Mr Joy scorned.

The Dark Hole

Ned rubbed his eyes.

It wasn't dark yet, but he could barely see.

"Hello? *Hello?"*

Nothing.

The rakey-looking boy felt his surrounding curiously.
"Belle? *Belle?* Are you *there?"*

Silence.

"I say, can *anyone* hear me?"

Nothing.

Ned stood up.

"Oh, yuk, what *is* that?" and his long white fingers felt about. "Sticky, it's so terribly *sticky,* and hard, strangely hard. Where *am* I? Belle?"

Still nothing.

A small chink of light emerged in the distance and Ned squinted to try and make it out. Not sure if the bright white vision was daylight forcing its way through or something more sinister he just stood on the spot, not daring to move forwards or backwards, or even to stretch out each side. Ned stood motionless, the air around him quiet and the atmosphere out of ordinarily tense.

"Son?" the tiniest flutter of a voice pitted the air.

"For heaven's sake, *who's* there?" Ned quaked and pushed his hands further into his pockets. "I said who's *there*? *Show* yourself."

Then, the oddest thing happened. Ned's fingers felt a movement, an awakening in his deep pockets, and the token photo of his Mum, that he always kept hidden, started to flinch. And then to struggle. And then before he realised what was happening, the worn old brown picture of his young Mum flew out of his pockets, right through his fingers and exploded, right there, in front of Ned's eyes; the bright white vision cascading into a million tiny pieces.

Ned shaded his eyes, but even with his eyelids tightly closed and his palms forced over his face, chards of light still pierced through. "Who *are* you? What *is* it? What do you *want* with me?" Ned cried, and

collapsed to the dry dusty floor, his knees denting the earth, and sobbed.

"Don't fret."

"Don't tell me not to fret! I'm stuck, alone, in a forest, and the most treasured item I possess has just been wrenched from my life and destroyed right in front of my eyes. And, you tell me not to *fret.* A stranger telling me not to fret. How *dare* you - "

"I'm no stranger, Ned. Really, I'm not."

"Reveal yourself then. If you're so sure you know me, why won't you show yourself?"

"Of course, but I want you to be calm. I shan't want to shock you."

"Shock me? I think I've had enough shocks to last me a life-time. Nothing can shock me anymore. Yesterday's breakfast for starters. Nothing could be more shocking than *that."*

"Glad to see you still have a funny side, dear. A sense of humour, just like your Father - "

"You know my *Father?"*

"Of *course* I do."

"Stop telling me *of course* at everything. Why is it so obvious that I should be knowing things?"

"Oh, Ned, *dear* Ned - "

"Mum?"

"Yes?"

"Mum? Is it *you*, *is* it?"

"Why, of *course."*

"Don't believe it. You're just pretending. A sick pretence. Reveal yourself, trickster!"

"Have faith. You need to have faith or Anouka shall fall foul, and - "

"And *what?"*

"We'll all be dust."

"Right," Ned whispered in a boyish tone he had not heard in years. "Dust? What can *possibly* turn us to dust? Tell me that, stranger."

"You'd be surprised what lurks around these parts, Ned."

"Try me."

"I'm not here to *test* you, Ned. I'm here to *help* you."

"Well, we haven't really got very far, have we?"

"You keep thinking I'm here to harm you. We're going round in circles. But, you must have the *faith."*

"So you keep saying."

"Well, *have* you?"

"Have I *what?"*

"Got the *faith?"*

"I don't know. I don't know *much* anymore."

"Trust me then. If you don't know what else to do, you might as well trust *me."*

Ned's mouth suddenly felt soft, warm. And a tender, less than stoic feeling, rushed throughout his own body. He felt like he did that day when another world had taken his Mum, then his Father. He had felt nothing but hatred and fear, but now that fear masqueraded as a strength and a

sudden realisation that perhaps now was the time for *him* to help *them*. “Mum?”

“Thank the *heaven’s* you’ve come to your senses, Ned,” a translucent crimson figure appeared, blending in with the dark brown cracked interwoven sticks surrounding him. The sticks were long and old, ancient in fact, but Ned did not feel fear, fear of the unknown, he just felt like a matured mind inside a young body, *his* adolescent body. He looked down to see that he was eight again, and his Mum’s wings were touching his skin like he had *never* remembered before.

“Mum.”

“Ned, it *is* me, it *is* your Mum, and what can I tell you? First, that your hair is abysmal, but never mind. You *are* brave, *ever* so brave, and so *handsome,”* Magenta spread her wings, and the thinness of them shuddered as Ned stifled a curious laugh. “I was taken as a sacrifice, to save this world, and you, *you* Ned were the thread that stayed on to defeat *her*. That *beast,”* Magenta hushed her own words.

“Miss *Smock?”*

“That name *haunts* us,” Magenta shook, and Ned could see right through her body to the sticky cocoon behind.

“Us?”

“Yes, dear.”

“Us? You mean yourself and Father?”

“Indeed. This cocoon, this *growing* chrysalis, has been spinning for *hundreds* of years, and now, when *you*

break that thread, you will release the protective casing and that beast will vanish into her own black hole. I entered into this cocoon to protect myself from the harsh and unfriendly environment that could cause the fall of Anouka for eternity. Now you are here to release me, and rewrite the last Chapter, Chapter 14 of Father's book, I can retreat, and Anouka can prosper. Son, I am *so* proud," Magenta sighed. "Our cocoon threads have stuck together as we have emerged and then grown hard until the fresh air that you breathed upon me awakened them. This cocoon is a miracle of nature itself. Oh Ned, *save* Anouka and prosper."

"No pressure, then."

"Ned, dear. Humour shan't save you now."

"Guess not," Ned's eyes started welling with salt-ridden tears as his own Mum, his own Mum whom he barely knew, enveloped her wings around him, and released herself into the most beautiful-est of butterflies imaginable. Her image just as was in the photo.

And then, Magenta was gone.

William looked at the scene from the mountain peak.

Ned was dumbfounded.

"NOT AGAIN!" Ned shrieked. "YOU'VE LEFT ME AGAIN!" and Ned collapsed.

Pale.

Desolate.

Heart-broken.

"Ned?" a voice echoed. "Are you alive? Ned, *are* you?"

The Awakening

"He mumbled."

"Did he?" William looked at Belle. "I don't *think* so."

"Don't be so mean. Don't write him off."

"I'm *not.* I'm just saying."

"He *did,* I'm *sure* he did," Belle stared at Ned. He lay there, lifeless.

"You've said that *every* day since we found him like this. Don't get your hopes up," William screwed up yet another chocolate bar wrapper and threw it on the floor.

Crumbs rolled under the rug, but although he saw them, he didn't care. In fact, William rubbed his feet over them to grind them in further.

"You're *such* a pig, William."

"Honk," William grimaced and scuffed his heels further into the decimated crumbs.

"Save some for Ned, *greedy*-guts," Belle threw William the dirtiest of looks. "Glutton."

"Well, I'm *bored.*"

"Doesn't mean you need to eat and *eat.*"

"Nothing *else* to do."

"Ned *mumbled!*" Belle jumped up again after three days of waiting; three days of deathly silent unconsciousness. *"Ned?"*

"Stop *saying* that, he's not conscious."

"How do *you* know?"

"I can *see!* He's *deathly* pale."

"So are *you!* No nutrition, just high calorific, melodramatic, synthetic vitamin-fuelled bars of disgust that'll fur up your insides - "

"It's tasty high calorific, melodramatic, synthetic vitamin-fuelled bars of disgust that'll fur up my insides though - "

"And, you *don't* want to admit Ned's alive because you *don't* want to share the chocolates. *And,* I'll *have* you know, the hearing in a person is the strongest, most sensitive part. Even if a person cannot see, or feel or even *move,* then they can still *hear* you. So we should *talk* to Ned, keep him feeling - wanted."

"Talk to a *dead* person? No *thanks."*

"WILLIAM! Ned's not *dead!"*

"If you say so."

"Urrrrrrrrr - " Ned's bed covers juddered. The curtains blew in all of a sudden, although the window was shut tight. It hadn't been opened since 1903.

"William!"

"What *now?"*

"He *spoke!* You *must* have heard him that time? Ned spoke, look, and he *moved, and* the curtains got sucked in. It's Baby-ette Fireplace, trying to suck Ned back to Anouka," Belle shook Ned's hand and tugged at his fingers limp with hope. "*William?*"

William just sat at the end of Ned's bed. He stared at the floor, and didn't utter a word.

"What's that rustling?" Belle glared from her ears without taking her eyes off Ned. *"Don't* tell me you've got *more* chocolates stuffed in your pockets?"

"And what if I have?"

"Huhhhhhh," Ned moved, just a little.

William rustled, a little more loudly this time.

"Huhhhhhhhhhhh," Ned's nose twitched a little and his nostrils started to sniff. "Chocolate? Is that *chocolate* I can smell?"

"See, I'm *not* a glutton. I actually woke him from beyond the grave. I helped - "

"He was never *dead!"*

"Huhhhhh, urrrrrr...marzipan chocolate?"

"See William! You *must* have heard *that?* Ned, he's coming round. Isn't that great?" but Belle could plainly see that William was not at all happy. Not at all. "William, what *is* it? You've been morose for *days* come to think of it. Although how I noticed any difference - "

"I shouldn't have rustled so loudly."

"I thought you said it *helped* him? An ulterior motive?"

"Umm," William ugged a short snorted response and looked around the attic.

It was quiet, an *eerie* quiet, a far cry from the overwhelming pace and noise spread over the last few days.

"William, why are you looking so *pathetic?"*

"Am NOT! Take that back. Just - inquisitive."

"Shan't."

"Suit yourself."

"Aren't you just a little bit happy that Ned seems to be conscious again? I don't understand. Why are you so glum? Imagine if Ned opened his eyes to *your* sour face? I think he'd feign death, *then.* I know ***I*** would."

"How well do you know Ned? I mean *really* know him?" William twisted around, Ned's bedclothes tangling in his arms.

"What do you mean?"

"I mean, you've only known him for one term at *Gladiolus-Viola.* What if he's not entirely who you think?"

"What, he's out *kill us?"*

"I never said anything about Ned *killing* us. Just that we don't really know his motives, *do* we?"

But Belle was spared giving any reply by Mrs Joy bustling in.

The door barely stayed on its hinge.

"Less chit-chat, less of that - " Mrs Joy pushed past William and Belle to reach Ned who had started to stir and try to sit up, *" - Ned,* dear - "

"Huh? How did *you* know he'd come round?" Belle stared at her Mum who put her glass to the floor. "Were you spying on us? *Were* you? With that glass? Were you *eavesdropping?"*

"You *poor* old thing having to wake up to Belle's questioning, and *William?* What *has* happened to you? Your face looks like someone slammed a door in it? Well, *did* they?"

"Mum! That's horrible, but well, true. William's been sour forever."

"Mmm, you *don't* need to tell *me,"* Mrs Joy peered so close in to Ned's eyes that he shut them tight and pretended he'd fallen back into unconsciousness again.

"Err, excuse *me?* I am *here,* you know," William nibbled under his fingernails. Mmm, a Twixler nougat bar!"

"More fool us, William, dear. More fool *us.* I can quite see that you've emptied the *entire* biscuit tin, *and* the chocolate larder? You've managed to eat your way *far* further back than your arms could *possibly* reach - "

"I was hungry."

"Greedy, more like," Belle muttered, and she turned to Ned.

"Chocolate? - did I hear that word again?" Ned opened just the one eye this time so as he didn't have to see double Mrs Joys.

"Yes, dear. Yes, dear, you *did - "*

"Mmm - "

"BUT, you've got *William* to answer for the fact that. There *is* none - "

"Huh?"

"He ate it all, the greedy *pig,"* Belle spat.

"Can't you crack that Stick of yours on the floor? Generate some more?" William ground the crumbs now so far into the rug they disappeared altogether.

"Feeling *guilty* now, *are* we, William?" Belle stared at Ned. His eyes were shutting and opening like he had no control.

"William, I've *tried,* and if *only* the recipe book hadn't been drenched in boiled milk," Mrs Joy tutted and looked with irritation at the Stick.

Stick had followed Mrs Joy up to the attic and was now trying to wind his way around her legs like a cat. "I *tried* to tap this Stick three times in succession and swing a banana around my head six times, but no, I think part of the recipe is *beyond* repair. There is an *entire* other section I *cannot* read, smudged *right* threw, it is. I ended up with a rotten flamingo thigh and a new belt for the washing machine, that's what three taps and swinging bananas gets you. I mean, we are *in* desperate need of the belt, but an insipid flamingo is *no* substitute for oozing, melting chocolate when you haven't eaten for *days - "*

"Mrs Joy, I feel sick, *please* can we stop talking about what we can't actually have. I'll happily eat the flamingo," Ned moved his neck slightly higher.

"Did you catch a chill, dear? Out there, in the snow? Are you *terribly* ill, Ned? *Please* don't be. It has been the *worst* snow fall for 140 years the newspapers are reporting. You stumbled back, quite blue-looking you were, and it was *all* we could do, Mr Joy and I, *alllllll* we could do to just tuck you up inside these thick feathered covers and hope for the best - "

"Mum! That sounds *awful. Hope* for the *best?* I don't think it was quite *that* dramatic," Belle gawped.

"Remember what we said about the fish, Rosabella? Close that mouth of yours before you end up like a Salvelinus Agassizii."

"A *what?"*

"That's a silver trout to you, Belle - "

"Right."

"And at worst, you could become a Moxostoma Lacerum - "

"Is that any better?"

"Only if you fancy being a great big Harelip Sucker."

"No, thanks."

"SO - Ned, dear. NED, DEAR! It *was* that dramatic, if not *more!"* Mrs Joy wiped her hands on her apron.

"I was - *dead?"*

"Yep!"

"NO! No you *weren't,* Ned," Belle glared at her Mum.

Ned sounded disturbed.

His voice was croaky as he spoke ridiculous words, jumbled they were, and made no sense at all. But, as he got used to using his throat, William could see Ned's fear and he glared at the invalid.

Ned glared back in some sort of weird trance.

"And?" William glared more.

"And *what,* William?" Belle stepped further towards the bed. Her toes crunched on the crunchiest of chocolate wrappers, and she kicked it out the way. *"Glutton pants - "*

"M, M, Ma - " Ned's voice wobbled and his bed shook; each foot reverberating on the floor - the crumbs that William had so banished forever resurfacing again.

And William sensed there was something very, *very* wrong.

"William, I *found* her. She's beautiful. I *finally* found her."

"Huh," William turned back to simple grunts.

Ned tried again, a whisper into just William's ear. "William, I found the *most* beautiful lady in Anouka, and she's - " but William cut Ned short.

"I've *always* been sceptical of *you – creep -* " William hissed back, " - warned my sister about boys like *you.* Why on *earth* would I want to hear about your *new* love when my own sister's just over there?"

"Didn't know you cared so much - "

"I care more about *her* than I do *you*," William snapped. "I *barely* know you. Belle's an ignoramus at times, most of the time actually, but she's not a - "

"A what?"

"Does she *know,* Belle? Does she *know* she's dicing with a - " William cracked his knuckles, " - a player, that's right, a player, a *charmer* even, a *chancer?* Does Belle know you've been stringing her along until you found someone else, in Anouka? *Huh?"* William kept eye contact as he whispered his atrocities. *"Player - and you've not got the muscles for rugby - "*

"William, no, you've got it wrong, stupid. *Completely wrong!"* Ned cried out, forcing fourteen blankets away. "It's my Mum, I found my *MUM."*

"Magenta?!" and Mrs Joy fainted.

William and Belle glared at Ned.

And Ned just glared back as white as one of Mrs Joy's starched to death bed sheets.

"Mrs Joy?" Ned peered over the woman lying long and flat on the floor. "Mrs *Joy?"* but before Ned could peer closer still, his eyelids larger than life itself, Mrs Joy had disappeared, tripping over her emerald frills, crying, "Those fizz wallop biscuits *shan't* be taking themselves out of the oven, never have done before and I can't imagine they will do today. *Magenta Marvels,* yep, that's what I cried, *my*

Magenta Marvels, which only ever rise up when the time is right, oh, for the love of death itself, please let that self-raising flour come up trumps," and Mrs Joy glared at that Stick which for the first time in his life wasn't trying to wheedle out of his responsibilities. "Let's hope those *Magenta Marvels* survived the course and live to save our souls - for tea, I mean, for tea - "

Ned sat up.

"Are you really related to that lunatic?"

"'fraid so," William replied.

Ned's eyes reddened, his palms hot and sweaty. "Has anyone got any honey?"

"Honey?" William's eyes widened. "Now *there's* a novel idea, and I know where *all* of that's kept. You're a genius, Ned."

"My body, I feel like I've been through a mincing machine," and as Ned looked down at his feet, all he saw was elfin toes. In fact, frail and crystalline was all that he could see as his skin began to disappear before his eyes. "My limbs, my feet and, hang on, my *body* and - " Ned pulled his bed sheet back and forced his head between his legs, and what he saw shocked him through and through. "Belle, look *away* - " but Belle had already shoved her head under the covers.

"Ned!"

"I said don't *look."*

"Ned, where's your *body?"*

"I, I, I don't *know!* I feel a bit funny," Ned shot completely under the covers.

"You *look* a bit funny. Ned, there's - "

"There's *what?"*

"There's - things," Belle whispered.

"What *things?"*

"Long sticky *brown* things; growing out your eyebrows. Ned, you've got *feelers.* Ned, you're, you're an *insect! Oh my God!* You've been infected with cross contamination?" and the chimney's flames threw silver sparks out into the room - William's chocolate crumbs melting into a bubbling pool under the rug.

"I'll have *that,"* William surreptitiously licked his toes which oozed down into the melting pot. "You've turned into a *mothy-thing,* Ned! Yuk - "

" - what *now?"* Ned tried to move about but his flimsy bits of body didn't let him.

"A sticky, peeling, brown *dying* butterfly," Belle prodded Ned's wings and then looked further down.

"Get *lost,"* and Ned fainted, vocal-less once more.

"Oy, Ned, *Ned?"* William shook Ned through the covers. "Blimey, there's nothing of him. He's limp."

"Fragile, I think that's the word you're looking for William. Fragile, and well, a little less than manly, but I'm sure he'll overcome that."

"Are you *sure* about that? *I* wouldn't. Have you *seen* yourself in the mirror, Ned? Man, I *wouldn't* look."

"What shall we tell Mum? We can't say *oh and by the way, my boyfriend, the one who I just brought back here with no warning? Well him. He's turned into a dying butterfly, so, what's for tea?*

"What *is* for tea?"

"What shall we to **do** with *him*?" Belle could barely look at Ned. She forced a smile. His face was petrified. And his veins? They were becoming so prominent she could see bright red blood running at speed round and around inside him.

"Where's Ned?" Mrs Joy suddenly appeared in the doorway.

"Oh, he's turned into a dying butterfly, practically dead," William coughed.

"I'm *sorry?"*

"So, what's for tea?"

"Don't think I've quite met anyone like you before, William. They certainly broke the mould when you entered this world," Mrs Joy walked closer and scratched her elbows. "And tea? That'll be the chargrilled remains of that bulbous-eyed reptile which seems to be getting more aromatic the longer it bubbles away. What's *that?"*

"What?" William moved closer to the end of the bed.

"That wriggling?"

"What wriggling?"

"That wriggling. In the bed, *Ned's* bed?"

"Urm - "

"Never mind, I've got better things to be investigating than moving beds," and a sharp whistle from the fish kettle blasted up her skirt.

And she swept back off downstairs.

"Magenta, thank you, thank you indeed. Perhaps we're saving Anouka after all, just that elusive Rupert of

whom I'm not too sure. Wise beyond his years, I feel, I just hope he's up to the job? Whoever pulled him out the woodwork needs their head examining. Elusive, that's all I can say."

That Little Boy

"Hello?"

"Who said *that?"* Belle put her ear to the top of the attic stairs and strained. "Someone's arrived."

"So?" William picked his teeth. Some of the chocolate had caked itself to his gums and he could barely speak. "I'm sure it wasn't past its sell-by date, was it ? - "

"Sorry?" Belle frowned back. She was leaning so far over the bannister rail her fingers were pale from gripping on so tightly. "What's past its sell-by date?"

"This chocolate, I'm *sure* I checked the packet. Some bits taste a bit off, that's all."

"You're *unbelievable!* How are we going to cover for Ned, you ignoramus? Stop talking about chocolate! And what's that disgusting brown stuff on the rug? Don't say - " Belle peered closer and bent down, " - it *is!* It smells, *chocolatey?"*

"Hello, anyone *home?"*

"That's right, it *is*. It's the lemon drizzle chocolate from the depths of Mum's cupboard. That's how her recipe book got spoiled. Don't tell," William licked his lips. "I'd have a scoop if I were you, to drown the taste of chargrilled bulbous fish that'll be working its way through your intestines in a minute."

"Why's it down there?"

"What? Your *intestines?"*

"No, that *chocolate lake?* Why's it mashed into the rug? And, how did rifling about in Mum's cupboard spoil her recipe book?"

"I was saving some chocolate for later, so I tried to stamp it in - and I guess that later is now - and the milk on the recipe book? Well, *that* escapade was *bound* to happen, couldn't help it really. I was leaning *so* far into the cupboard that my foot slipped and it kicked the mop, and the mop tipped up and hit the saucepan which in turn was boiling the milk and the *entire* thing just seemed to turn right over.

Trust the recipe book to have been in the way. Splat it went. But at least I got the chocolate - "

"Is that *all* you think about?"

"Ye..."

"Don't answer that."

"Well, if *you're* not going to take advantage, *I* will," and William bent down and licked the rug. His tongue looked like a depraved tiger.

"You're *disgusting!"*

"It'll only be trodden in further - "

"You're *still* a skank."

"I don't mind that."

"Now that you've joked about Ned's predicament, what are we *really* going to say to Mum? We can't say Ned just up and went for a walk, passing her in the kitchen without her even seeing him - after he's been laid up for days."

"Mum notices *nothing*, she's only interested in passing that spell exam and keeping that Stick out of mischief. She wouldn't know if we were dead or alive until our corpses started rotting in our beds," William was still licking the rug, down on all fours now.

"Rupert, oh how *nice* to *see* you? Oh dear, oh dear, my hair!" Mrs Joy's dulcet tones floated up the stairs and lingered in Belle's ears. "My hair, it looks a state - "

"It was *Rupert,"* Belle hissed to William and then went back to eavesdropping. "Funny time for *him* to be coming."

"Must have smelt the bulbous fish. He can have mine. I might be sick," William picked globules of chocolate from his ear lobes.

"She doesn't sound *too* fussed that Rupert's come, does she?" Belle crept down the stairs to the bottom of the attic room and opened their door right back.

Her heart raced.

"Family dinner," William hissed back. "That's probably why Rupert's here. Mum wanted a family dinner, and now Rupert's turned up. Suits me. Less bulbous fish to stomach per head," William slithered down the stairs.

"He's not family - " Belle glared shrilly.

"Mum'll invite anyone."

"I guess so."

"Saves us having to explain Ned's disappearance. Mum'll just be swooning into Rupert's eyes, slopping fishy soup into his lap. I wonder if that Stick cast a spell on her? And, I'm sure Mum thinks he flirts with her. Don't you? You must admit, Rupert *is* a bit of a lady's man?"

"Disappearance, did you say disappearance? Ned hasn't disappeared, he's upstairs," Belle retorted.

"Well *I* know that, and *you* know that, but to all intents and purposes he's *far* from normal, so let's assume Ned's just disappeared. Easier that way."

Belle and William crept down to the kitchen and peered in through a crack in the door.

"He *sure* has," Rupert's head suddenly shot up.

"GEES!" Belle leapt back. "Don't *do* that!"

Rupert's hair was a little greyer than usual. He smiled. "You talking about your friend, Ned?"

"Might be."

"Well, if you *are,* I saw him taking a hike in the village just now."

"Oh, *did* you?"

"Definitely him. Tall, lanky, almost flying he was, he walks so fast," Rupert winked.

"Having a party, are we? In the corridor?" Mrs Joy suddenly popped up behind Rupert, that Stick herding her along like she was about to be put in a pen. *"Ned? Walking?* In the *village? Don't* be so absurd, Mr Gvist," Mrs Joy raised her voice over the hacking of the fish from the tray which she had randomly brought with her. "I did *try* to crisp up its skin but it appears to have got stuck - stupid fish."

"Oh, never mind. Can we just have toast?" William slumped into the rocking chair. "I'm not really *that* hungry, in fact, I feel rather ill," William's face was green, and his tummy was making disgusting gurgling noises.

"It's all that chocolate," Belle scowled. "Pig."

"A walk? Ned? Are you *absolutely* sure it was him, Rupert?" Mrs Joy chipped and chipped away, completely ignoring William.

"Toast, Mum?"

"Sure as the flames rise *tall* in a fire place like that, it was Ned," Rupert eyes widened. "Fine one that is you have there, Mrs Joy, the fireplace. Fine one that is. What a

multitude of pictures seem to emerge once you *really* take a good look."

"Late, late, *always* late that husband of mine. Why can't he be back from fossilling, paleontologing, whatever he's up to this week on time just once, just *once,* it's not *too* much to ask, is it? And the Broccoli Bakes are about to spoil and those Magenta Marvels shan't be marvels *all* night - " Mrs Joy pottered back to her pots and pans.

"Broccoli *Bakes?* Magenta *Marvels?* You *do* spoil your family, Mrs Joy," Rupert smirked, pulling up a chair. Its wooden feet scraped across the tiles, their rubber stoppers having been lost years back, and sat down.

"Oh, Mr Gvist, make yourself at home," Mrs Joy started to fumble about.

"Thank you."

"She was *being* sarcastic," William hissed.

"So was *I,*" Rupert smirked back.

"So, urm, Rupert - "

"Yes, Mrs Joy?"

"Have you eaten? What I *guess* I'm asking is would you like to stay for tea, supper now I suppose, the time is rather taking over?"

Mr Clock ticked on the wall, and as the night drew in colder and darker and more sinister, so did each tick of Mr Clock's hands. They seemed to be speeding up.

"Now your sarcasm has come and bitten you on the behind, *hasn't* it, Rupert?" William hissed, again, as he peered into the incarcerated dish. Six chargrilled eyes, and

a tail that William swore was still flapping, stared back. "Mum's asked if you want to stay and eat *that!*"

Mrs Joy rolled her eyes and looked at Mr Clock.

Mr Clock ticked, toneless, but his hands moved round regardless, faster and faster as if at any moment they would snap off completely and fly around the kitchen.

"Oh Mrs Joy, delighted, I'd be *delighted* to stay. Brought my own."

"Sorry?" Mrs Joy fussed with her hair. It had started to itch.

"Supper, I brought my own. Couldn't *possibly* rely on you to supply supper for *everyone* - and your *hair,* it's turning grey - " Rupert leant further back. "Comfy chairs you have in this place - "

"But Rupert, there's *plenty* to go around, *more* than enough for even quadruple the amount of mouths to feed - " Mrs Joy's Stick hopped about. "And *you* can stop acting so enthusiastically, you can't even subtly persuade guests to stay for tea." The Stick hopped about even more. "What *is* it?" Mrs Joy stared at the Stick's tip, her pupils *so* large even the dead fish scuttled to the back of the dish, shivering in the corner. *"Well?"*

"NO, NO, *NO,* I IN*SIST!* I think I'm allergic to - " Rupert's eyes peered into the same dish into which William was *still* staring; he had not yet retreated, the dead fish's eyes were definitely still moving, *definitely, " - that.* Yes, I'm allergic to *that.* Makes my tongue swell up so much it fills my entire throat *and* my nostrils and if I don't act in time I'll be asphyxiated. So, if you *don't* mind, I'll just heat

up my Shepherd's Pie with extra mash and *extra* thick gravy in the microwave?"

William's mouth watered.

The Stick wet itself on the floor.

"What *is* it, Stick? Stop yelping," Mrs Joy's skirt started to soak up the yellowing water that the Stick was making. "You are *vile,* I shall *never* know why you can't just work like the other Sticks in the shop. But, I suppose that's why I bought you at a discount; your legs sawn off in that *tragic* accident, I couldn't bear to leave you alone, but I should have listened to my head and *not* to my heart."

The Stick wriggled and tipped its head to the floor.

"Never mind, never mind. *Please* don't cry. Not again, we have *guests - "*

"Guests which help themselves to the microwave," William hissed for the third time.

"Oh, you're *stuck,"* Mrs Joy peered down. "Mr Gvist, *please!* Your chair leg, it's squashing Stick, *please* can you budge up, *poor* thing. I'll not be putting you in nappies, again, Stick. Now *stop* that crying I say, STOP!"

Stick froze mid wail.

"But, how *kind* of you to think of me," and Rupert just pinged the switch and his plate of sweet aromatic hot food started to turn on the microwave plate. He smiled and twitched his nostrils.

"Cretin," William hissed for the umpteenth time that Rupert had stopped counting and just assumed that this was the only way the boy knew how to behave.

Belle cackled.

"Lovely of you to ask me to stay, quite thoughtful and *most* spontaneous," Rupert sniffed the air.

But Mrs Joy didn't think it spontaneous at *all.* "Don't wait for us, *do* tuck into your Shepherd's Pie," she frowned.

"Don't mind if I do," and it was all Rupert could do to not have already started munching the over-crusty loaf which appeared from Mr Fireplace and onto the mat, and hoover up his plate of overly-gravied-mash. "Delightful," Rupert spat out drops of gravy. "Aren't you lot joining me?"

"The fish is dead," William hissed, again. "I *think.*"

"You like hissing, sonny, don't you?" Rupert spat out even larger globules of gravy which seemed to be getting thicker and thicker as he ate. "And, the fish, it's *supposed* to be dead."

"Well, what I *meant* to say is, it, the fish, should actually be in a *coffin.* It's *so* chargrilled it needs a funeral all of its own, and if its eyes keep on moving, I'll actually vomit, so no, *I shan't* be joining you *any* time soon - especially as you haven't even left us any bread, and you practically choked that Stick to death to avoid having to eat bulbous-faced-fish over there, *Rupert - "*

"Oh dear *Lord,* so I haven't, left you any bread. Never mind. I'm *sure* you've got a stash of something somewhere, sonny. *Hmm?"*

"And, *stop* calling me, sonny."

"Did you *really* see Ned?" Belle leant across William to reach Rupert's ear. "We left him in rather a strange set of circumstances, you see."

"Course he didn't - " William answered for Rupert, " - he's covering for us, and thank you, I *s'pose. Still* don't forgive you for not leaving us any bread, though."

"Gossip, gossip, what *are* you all talking about? Why, there's *all* of the Broccoli Bakes left, getting cold. Dig in - " Mrs Joy pushed the tray across the table, but as if a hardened rope was tied to the tray and to Rupert, he moved further back as the tray grew closer, " - they're a speciality of mine, not cooked them in *years,* must make them more often but quite simply where *does* the time go?" Mrs Joy tapped her long fingernails on the kitchen table, faster and faster in time to Mr Clock who was now speeding so incredibly fast that his entire face had started to rattle on its hook.

"Mrs Joy, relax, for once. I'm sure Mr Joy will be home soon. Better save him one of those green broccoli things, oh and at *least* two of those Magenta Marvels, he hasn't tasted one in years. Will it put him to sleep again? For three weeks?"

"How do *you* know about that?" William hissed. *"And,* I *shan't* stop hissing."

"Ned?" Mrs Joy sat Stick up against the oven. Stick relaxed against the heat from bulbous-face whilst a last little bit of yellowing water dribbled down his stubby new growth of a leg.

"What *about* him?" Belle stuffed a Broccoli Bake in her mouth. "O abou' 'im?" she could barely speak.

"Darling, you *like* them?"

"Um?"

"Well, *do* you?"

"You only stuffed one in to stop Mum investigating Ned, didn't you?" William whispered.

"Well, Belle, dear? *What* do you think?" Mrs Joy caressed the Stick as it ran circles around her legs again like that distempered old cat. "Another?" she moved closer like a possessed old witch.

"I couldn't, *possibly - "*

"Oh, of *course* you could," Rupert intervened. "One isn't enough to be able to make a judgement."

"Oh, it is, I tell you, it *is,"* Belle's mouth had started to burn and the feeling in her gums had completely *disappeared.*

"Gracious, *poor* old Ned, how awful of me, these vegetable bullets seem to be taking over. I must head upstairs and see him. And Belle - "

"Hmph?"

"Ned's Mum, what's the number? - "

"Of *course* I'll have another broccoli thing, perhaps three more, Mum?"

"HELP YOURSELF - " Mrs Joy's skirts swept across the floor, " - her telephone number, Rosabella? We are *sure* to call her tonight and let her know her son practically *died."*

"Can I eat the entire plate of these, Mum, PLEEEEASE? Watch me, watch me Mum - "

"Despite her *not* knowing *anything* of her son's predicament, that indeed her son's predicament is now just fine, and he's not unconscious anymore, I really should tell

Ned's Mum that he's fine, just fine - no I really *cannot* tell her that - may be best not to say anything at all - yes, that's best, just, um, *lie,"* and Mrs Joy stumbled back to the sink to dab a damp wet cloth on her forehead.

Rupert walked up behind her.

"Your tail, Jacintha, it's sticking out," Rupert poked it in.

"Mr Gvist, *indeed,* your hands, *stop* it, there's no Magenta Marvels up there - "

An icy wind whistled outside.

Hard snowflakes cracked onto the window panes. In contrast, hot flames in Mr Fireplace's grate rose tall, *bright* orange, and Belle became mesmerised.

She yawned.

Then she rubbed her eyes; she felt *excruciatingly* tired. The last few days had been long, *very* long.

Belle sighed, and then she frowned. *What was that, no, who was that?* Belle squinted and rubbed her eyes a second time. *Who are you?"* Belle spoke quietly to herself but the roaring flames heard.

Belle looked around.

Mrs Joy was still scrubbing bowls for dessert. Rupert was looking worried. The oldest pot sat precariously on the hob, bubbling up something else inedible, he thought. A

browny-green sludge rose up and up and *up*, that Stick jiggling on the spot.

"Don't you start wetting yourself, again," Mrs Joy eyed Stick's antics. "I've still got the receipt. I can take you back and exchange you for one of your second cousins twice removed, I *can* you know."

"Grrrrrrr - " Stick grizzled, trying its hardest to tap the pot, jumping from its spot on the floor and just managing to scrape the pot's side each time.

"Oh, are you *helping?* Are you *WORKING?"* Mrs Joy stared in disbelief. *"Are* you?"

"GRRRRRR - "

"You *ARE*! Heaven's above, you've taken your time to adjust, but I *do* believe you are finally starting to work some of those powers of yours, Sticky, my DEAR!"

"GRRRRRRRRRRRRRRRRR," and, each time, before the pot nearly bubbled over its rim in excitement, Stick *leapt* up, *hit* the pan, and the increasingly disgusting sludge simmered back down again.

William just sat, eating his *third* Broccoli Bake, like he had not another care in the world.

"Who *are* you?" Belle spoke a little louder this time and slowly ventured over to Mr Fireplace. His flames grew tall, and the little wisps that appeared at the top of each flicker seemed to be tipped her way, and little hands from which grew fingers drew themselves towards her, - then *flash.*

She was gone.

Huh? Belle muttered, not to William, nor to her Mum, nor even to Rupert Gvist, who was indeed otherwise engaged trying to shove more and more and *more* prunes back into the oldest pot that appeared to be hungrier than ever. Mrs Joy had boiled the custard in it at the same time and it was all turning rather nasty.

Belle did not even speak to herself. But instead, she was speaking to a small brown-trousered boy who just stood, staring at her. And Belle, she just stared back. "*You?*" she finally spoke again.

"Yes, I, I, I *was* me when I *last* looked," the little boy sounded surprised that he'd actually been acknowledged. "You can *see* me?"

"Of *course* I can see you, plain as day," Belle replied, taking a step closer. The little boy took two steps further back. "Don't be scared."

"Me, me, *I'm* not scared," the little boy retorted, flicking his hair and cracking his fingers.

"Don't do that, that's *horrid.* My brother does that, it's not becoming you know. He gets it from my Dad, when he's actually at home that is. Imagine, if my Dad was around *all* of the time, William would be a nightmare. He'd probably turn into him. Yuk."

"*That's* not nice."

"I'm only telling you not to crack your fingers, it's disgusting. Sets my teeth on edge."

"Don't tell *me* what to do, you *don't* even know me," the little boy snapped back.

"Who *are* you then, and *why* are you in this wood? I saw you the other day, I did, running away from me, you stopped, looked at me, and then made your excuses that you'd been told not to stop and talk to *anyone,* under *any* circumstances."

"I don't remember that, I've never *seen* you before, honestly, I've just arrived myself."

"Oh," Belle frowned. "What are you doing here?"

"That's the *least* of my worries, what I'm *doing* here, I want to know where here *is* first! Where actually have I *come*? I stepped indoors, out the path of a *raging* wind that was blowing up at home, and I ended up here, in this forest. I came through the back door, and my house, well, it wasn't really my house at all, it was *here.* The wind was *so* ferocious I'd covered my eyes, that's right, covered my eyes before grit and dust flew in from the trees, and when I opened them, I saw, well, *here*, and then *you*. Who are *you*, I should be asking?" and the boy looked even more puzzled than Belle. "Who *are* you, I said?"

"Belle, my name's *Belle,"* Belle stared into the boy's eyes.

"That's a nice name, I *s'pose,"* the little boy moved a little closer. "And who *are* you Belle, and why are *you* here?"

"Don't know," Belle replied honestly. "I mean, I don't know why I've been summoned quite *this* time, but Anouka always has a reason, a very good reason to pull you back."

"Anouka, what's *that?"* the little boy looked curious.

"Don't you know *anything?* That's *easy,"* Belle smiled. "Anouka, that's *this* place - *and beyond,"* Belle whispered.

"But why are you *here*?" the little boy asked. "And, why am *I* here, come to think of it?"

"Well, we need to prevent this place, Anouka, from *ultimate* sin, *ultimate* devastation, and finishing Chapter 14 of *The Book of Immortality* can achieve that. But, ssh, there are others, *an* other who is after the book, *The Book of Immortality*, so perhaps pretend I never mentioned it at all, or, let's perhaps pretend we've never even met," Belle wished she had William with her to prevent her mouth blurting out secrets that should be well left alone.

"That's okay then, because you *are* rather scary, Belle, *really* you are. Has anyone ever told you that before?" the little boy started to reverse. *"Sin? Devastation?* I think I'll be making tracks."

"No don't, don't go, we've only just met."

"That's enough for me, we don't need to do any *more* meeting."

"Where are you *going?"* Belle shouted after the boy who had decided that talking with Belle was *not* very comforting. "Wait for *me!* Perhaps we can take on the evils of Smock together? I mean, you *did* run away from her when I saw you last, in the forest, *this* forest. And I didn't catch your *name? WAIT!"* but the little boy was well into the bushes by now, and even if he *had* heard Belle's question, she wasn't *entirely* sure she could have convinced him to take part.

The Forest's Ears

"Who was *she*?" the little boy spoke aloud to himself. "I thought the girls in my class at school were hawkish, but

she was by *far* the clingiest, most *half*-witted one I've *ever* come across. Sin? Devastation? *Books of Immortality?* I hope I wake up from this crazy dream soon. *Well?"* he spoke louder, to the trees, as they seemed to be the only objects listening. "WELL?" he rustled and turned back hoping he had lost the apparition; she was *rather* white and particularly bony for sure. "Immortality? Books of *Immor-whatity?"* the boy repeated. "Can't say I understand a *word* she said - - OH!" and the boy fell, face first, into a ditch quite ridiculously deep. "Ouch! My forehead! That *quite* hurt."

"Psst!" a low voice disturbed the forest's otherwise silent ebb.

"Huh?"

"Psst! Up *here,"* the voice came from above, half-way up a velveteen oak tree.

"Where's *up here?"*

"UP HERE! Look UP!"

"Shan't."

"Nicholas, you *can* see me? I'm positive of that. I've *never* been more positive of anything in my *entire* life."

"I don't want to talk to *anyone.* I've had *enough,"* the boy stood up, alert. More alert than he had *ever* been. "Go away."

"Shan't."

"That's *my* line."

"Now, look here, Nicholas - "

"Ridiculousness! How do you keep knowing my name?" the boy, Nicholas, cried back.

"I can't *keep* knowing it, I either *do* or I *don't,* and it just so happens that I *do.* But don't you worry yourself with tiny dynamics like *that,* just get up here, come *on,* before anyone *sees* you, or *hears* you. *Come on,"* and Rupert stretched out his long-clothed arm and offered it to Nicholas to pull him aside himself on the branch.

They sat together.

In silence.

"So - " Rupert smiled at this younger counterpart.

"So *what?"*

"So you *were* telling the truth that day, I *always* thought you were, I *always* believed it to be so, but everyone led *you* to feel bereft, idiotic, a *fibber* I believe was one term used by those *hoitey toity* ladies," Rupert stroked Nicholas's hair.

"Urrr, get *off* me, you utter *weirdo."*

"Now now, *that's* no way to be talking to your elders, and wisers, and those growing grey hair."

"Is that *actually* a word, *wisers?"*

"It doesn't really matter where I come from. You know what I mean, and that's all that counts, don't you think?" and he patted Nicholas's arm. "So, well, chubby, you shouldn't devour *all* of the rice pudding in one go, you know."

"Don't you have *any* idea about personal space? Stop *touching* me," Nicholas was starting to feel a little more that uneasy.

"Oh to be *young* again - and *believed.* I was convinced this day *had* happened, *so* convinced, I was

Nicholas, but others plainly convinced me otherwise until I was too pickled to know *what* to believe. They all thought I'd been taken ill with a debilitating disease, memory loss, a needy obsession for attention, attention seeking, *that* was it, and they also thought I'd been kissed by the devil - "

"Who did?"

"Oh, just a sack of old ladies with no imagination, that's all. But *we* know better, *don't* we?"

"S'pose."

"Why, *thank* you, Nicholas."

"Sir, who *are* you? And how *do* you know my name?"

"Hush. Keep still. I *hear* someone," Rupert pushed Nicholas's head between his own knees, and held him close. "Don't utter a *word.* When I say run, *run* as *fast* as you can, don't stop for *anything,* under *no* circumstances should you stop, or talk, for *anything* or with *anyone.* Now go - oh, and take *this,* so dizzy I am, take *this,* and run as *far* back to your house as you can - and put it there, safe, deep, but within arm's reach. Now *go* - and remember, *don't* stop and *don't* talk to anyone. *Promise* me?"

"I promise," Nicholas mooched and then jumped down from the branch and dropped quietly to the forest floor. "Weirdo - "

"I *heard* that. Speak for yourself! NOW - " the voice above cried, *"R---U---N---!"*

Nicholas could hear a commotion, a raucous commotion, happening deep, *deep* inside the forest but he kept to his word and he just ran as fast as he could the

opposite way, the beige satchel crossed over his body flying out behind, but, Nicholas, he did not stop and he did not falter from the fastest pace he had ever run.

“Wait, *wait!* Hello, young lad, where are you headed?” Nicholas heard a girl’s voice. “Wait!” she continued to call out to him, but Nicholas kept running, his legs felt like they had never *been* quite so worn, and his feet had turned numb.

“Sorry, I *can’t* stop, I was told *not* to stop and talk to *anyone.* I *really* mustn’t. You look *awfully* nice, but I really *must not* stop,” Nicholas sighed breathlessly and clutched his satchel even tighter.

“Who *are* you?” Belle’s cried. “Where have you gone, again? *That boy, he’s vanished into a bright light of embers.”*

Silence.

Nicholas tiptoed down the passageway.

His cottage was old, dark, and chillingly archaic in places, but he held the satchel tight. Nicholas ventured to the furthest corner of the corridor where no one *ever* passed. Spiders lived there. Cobwebs and nasties that *never* scared *him* lived there.

Today seemed quiet.

Nicholas curled up.

Prising his fingernails into the sandy grouting, the corner tiles moved freely, far easier than Nicholas *ever* expected, and as he dug deeper and *deeper* still the oldest quarry tile just fell away leaving a gaping deep black hole beneath. He pushed the lone tile to one side. It was heavy, and it graunched across the others as he pushed and pushed. *Sssh,* he spoke to the floor, not realising the ridiculousness of his words, and he simply dropped the satchel inside. It fell from his tight grip with ease. Nicholas placed one ear to the black hole to hear it land.

He listened.

Hard.

Very hard.

Nothing.

Soundless.

The satchel had been heavy, *really* heavy, and Nicholas had spied a leather bound book inside peeping out, but when he dropped it into the hole, Nicholas heard no resounding thud. *Strange. This day's getting stranger and stranger. Weird girls, weird men, weird everything,* but he jumped back when a dusty moth-like insect flew into his eyes from the hole below, fluttered incredulously in his face, and then fell back deep inside the sheer, black abyss.

"Where *is* that slovenly child, boy?" Nicholas heard mutterings coming from the kitchen. A gathering for the Women's Institute had arrived, and he was filthy. *"I'm going to be in so much trouble. I'm so grubby,"* Nicholas whispered to himself.

But it was too late.

"BOY?" Nicholas' nanny, the strictest *ever* they could *possibly* come, threw open the kitchen door and stood there, large as life, and *that* was quite *incredibly* large. "Boy! You…..are….. FILTHY!" the nanny, Clarissa, drew closer, bent double as she walked, stinking of old booze covered up with lavender eau de toilette, and squinted in his direction. "Dis*grace*ful! An absolute *disgrace* boy! You are *covered* from head to toe with dust, mud and what is *this?* Moss? Grass stains and *moss?* That will *never* wash out! Mark my words you shall *not* be allowed tea tonight. Your filth will surely embarrass your poor Mother who has guests, very *important* guests I'll say, from the Women's Institute, and you cannot *possibly* sit in the kitchen with your clothes in such a state. Where *have* you been?"

Nicholas stood tall.

"Well? Speak *up!"*

Nicholas had not uttered a *word* throughout Clarissa's *entire* speech, and now he still just stood, silent. What should he say? He *ought* to tell the truth but *no* one would believe him, though it *was* wrong to lie.

"I'm waiting, boy!"

"Anouka. I was in *Anouka,* and a kindly man gave me a satchel, a satchel with a *book* inside, a book that was *destined* to come back home, with me, here. I had to run, run *fast* through the forest and not stop for *anything,* for *anyone.* So I did. I'm *deeply* sorry my clothes are dirty and my fingernails are a mess, but I *had* no choice. *The Book of Immortality,* you see, Chapter 14, it *has* to be written, and if

I didn't bring it home? Well, we would *all* fall foul to - - - - - *sin, devastation,* and *Anouka?* It would be *destroyed."*

Silence.

Nicholas couldn't decide if even *he* believed his story, but at least it ceased Clarissa's dulcet tones.

"Oh!" a voice hissed from somewhere.

"Huh?" Nicholas frowned.

"What a *delightful* little boy," Nicholas heard one lady from the kitchen speak out. "How *nice* he can spin such tales to keep himself amused," the voice laughed, falsely Nicholas quickly realised. "Keep your eye, mind - " the lady whispered in Nicholas' Mum's ear, "- once prone to telling tales, he won't know *where* to stop - "

"Quite *right,* Mrs Evans. *I* once heard about a little girl who told reams of tales about a silver time travel chalice, and she grew up quite a snitch, associated with *boys*, she did," spoke a rather rotund ginger-haired lady in reply.

"Really? *Boys?* And at *such* a young age, well I never," Mrs Wilton piped up. "*Boys?*"

"Did you *hear* him though, it *was* quite a *fine* speech, you *do* have to admit?" Nicholas' Mum pushed her way through the crowds. "Nick, are you feeling quite okay? You *do* look rather pale?"

"Beneath that dreadful dirt, how *can* you tell?" Mrs Evans rolled her eyes.

"I'm fine Mum, really. Belle and Rupert I think, *they* saw me right," Nicholas started to scratch his head. His

forehead was sprouting the most enormous green bruise from the fall.

"*Belle?* See, he's talking of *girls* already," Mrs Wilton scowled and poked her nose into the air.

Bloody Women's Institute, Nicholas spoke, underhandedly, to himself.

"Nicholas!" Clarissa tugged the boy's over-sized shirt, dry dirt and cobwebs falling from his shoulders. "Nicholas! Your foul *scrupulous* mouth," and Clarissa dragged him, ashamedly, up the stairs. "You little *fibber,* trying to pretend you had been with *girls* and *odd books* and in *forests.* You little *fibber,* that's all I can say. We're not falling for your antics of pretence, you'll be passing off your rude mouth as an illness soon, to be sure - *that's* a thought we might have to pursue. Yes, an *illness.* You were taken ill with a depraved *brain* disorder, *that'll* be it. We can't have the W.I.'s reputation being ruined by the foul mouth of a dirty little boy," and Clarissa pushed Nicholas up to his attic room, but not before he could kick the loose quarry tile back in place.

Well, roughly anyway.

The Ruby Sword

William sat back.

His stomach was *totally* full. His head told him so. He sighed. His intestines felt a bit uncomfortable and he

rubbed his chubby little hands on his tummy. He felt quite sore. *What was* ***in*** *that Broccoli Bake, I feel really sick.*

The kitchen felt odd, and William opened one eye. "Nice, that was nice, Mum," he lied.

Silence.

Not even that Stick was tapping.

William opened both eyes and looked up. "Where's *Belle?"*

No one replied.

The kitchen was dark.

The room was empty.

"Oh, there's **no** one here, just me. Did I drop off?"

William looked at Mr Clock.

It was still only early evening, but he had been left, alone, at the table.

"Belle?" William called, but there was no reply, just his echoed question bouncing back like a boomerang. *"Belle? Belle? Belle?* - Huh? *Anyone?"*

Mr Fireplace crackled.

"Belle? Are you **in** *there?* In Mr Fireplace? Stop messing. I'm *sure* I can see you, Belle?" William became mesmerised as he gazed deeper and *deeper* into the flames the grate offered, until his thoughts were disturbed by voices.

He sat up taller.

"Ow, my tummy really does hurt," and William glugged a pint of water that was sitting on the side as if being purposefully left for him to devour.

"Ahh, that's better."

"Rupert, *please - "* William heard.

"Huh?"

"You *are* an extremely, how shall I put it? Extremely enthusiastic, and persuasive, if not dashing might I add, young man, and I *suppose* I should be flattered but, *really,* my husband will be back imminently, *really* he will, and he might not like you rattling about up there?" Mrs Joy's, half-chortled, words sounded down the corridor.

"What is that man up to?" William scratched his head, and, remembering Belle's quite adamant assertions that Rupert was a lady's man, William scraped his chair as far back across the kitchen tiles as the kitchen cupboards allowed and took giant steps into the living room.

William cleared his throat. "Rupert, I think you *really* ought to leave my Mum alone, she clearly has *no* interest in or claim to your advances; chasing her down vulnerably whilst my Dad is - *oh,"* William's voice petered out. "Oh, sorry, I thought - "

"Yes, I *know* what you *thought,"* Rupert glanced back with his charming eyes. "Really, and with Mr Joy away fossilling or paleontologing. Now, if I can *just* clear out this bit, *just* here, if I can *just* reach that step in the fireplace chimney the blockage will be sorted, I think it will," and Rupert reached higher and higher and *higher* still, faltering on the most unsteady bit of old brickwork, until he could *just* about reach inside Flaming Fiona's tallest bit.

"You'll probably find my custard doughnut from last summer up there, Rupert," William stepped closer. "I

dropped it in the garden, and some heartless bird swiped it before I could take a grab at it. But luck would have it, it fell from his beak and down the chimney. Didn't ever fall out the bottom, though. So it's probably some mouldy old mush by now."

"Very helpful, William. I can see you're full of the best suggestions," and Rupert pushed the *oldest* chimney sweep ever in the life of chimney sweeps up into the darkness of Flaming Fiona's choking, gaping abyss. "Does anyone *ever* clean in here?" William heard Rupert splutter.

"Wouldn't have thought so," William muttered.

"That was a rhetorical question, William."

"Are you *sure* you know what you're doing, Rupert?" William squinted across the room. It was filled with black soot. "And, if my doughnut is even half edible, I'll have it back?"

"That's it, *that's* why the smoke has been whirling back into the room, this blockage, this blockage right here, got it, got it, *got it, this* is the cause," and with one last *enormous* final shove, the blockage released itself and fell, together with absolutely clouds of black dust, into the middle of the room.

And Mrs Joy fainted.

"Belle?" William stared. "What on *earth?"*

Belle choked and dragged thick handfuls of soot from her hair.

"What in *heaven's* name are you *doing* up the *chimney?"*

"Quick! Get Mrs Joy upstairs, before she sees you and remembers," Rupert started to shovel up the lady from the carpet into his arms. *"Help* then, you two?"

"She's *hardly* likely to forget seeing Belle fall from inside the chimney, *is* she?" William thought Rupert, divine intervention that he was, must be joking. "Belle - she fell - from up *there!* Remember?"

"Don't be so facetious, boy. She's as scatty as they come, Mrs Joy. Trust me, she'll forget. Let's just get her back to the kitchen. Act as before. And, I knew it would be you up there, Belle. That *Amdoch Atlas* showed the black outline of a person, with wild hair and lips talking incessantly, and I knew in an instant it would be you, Belle. Did you get confused, in Anouka? Came back through a different portal?"

"I guess so," Belle tried to brush herself down but all she succeeded in doing was mush the dirt even deeper into her clothes. "I suppose a fireplace *is* a fireplace; from the other side it looks as plain as the next - "

"Hu-hmm," Flaming Fiona blurted out.

"Sorry, I wasn't being mean, Fiona."

"Cheesecake, did I leave my *Amdoch Atlas* lying around again?" William groaned.

"That you *did,* boy," Rupert narrowed his eyes. "Good job only people with good intentions are managing to make use of its information."

"Sorry - "

"I met a boy though. Nice lad, he was, in a bit hurry with some secret satchel. Perhaps *he* took *my* portal and *I*

ended up tumbling down *here;* amazed we actually get back at all really, come to think of it."

"Boys, it's *always* boys with you, Belle," William rapped his fingers on Flaming Fiona's grate looking a little green. "I still feel sick."

"You shouldn't have scoffed all the bakes, then," Belle choked up a massive bit of something.

"How do *you* know? And, let's look at that."

"What?"

"That *thing* you just choked up?"

"What, this gloopy bit of something or other?"

"That gloopy bit of something or other, I'll have you know, is my custard doughnut!"

"It's horrid, William!"

"It wasn't horrid last summer. It was divine, before the crow nabbed it."

"I can see disgusting stringy bits hanging from your mouth. How many did you eat? Mum's Broccoli Bakes? I hoped it was broccoli and nothing else even more disgusting."

"You're disgusting, Belle."

"COME *ON!* We haven't got time for tit for tat, just get her into the kitchen," Rupert pulled Mrs Joy's arms as William tried to help heave her over Rupert's shoulder. But, it was *no* use, she was a dead weight when out cold. "What's the woman got in her pockets?"

"There's an *entire* series of books in here!" William rummaged around in his Mum's dress and pulled out at least eleven hard-backed recipe books *For the Novice Witchety*

Cook Series No. 1-12. "Number 12, it's not here. That's the one I ruined and we ended up with Flamingo thighs. Oops."

"Don't really care about *that,* another book and she'd be collapsing through the floorboards. Now PULL!" and Rupert started dragging the body along the floor, but it was still no use.

"It's STICK!" Belle cried.

"What is?" Rupert's eyes had started to look angry. "We can't be all day. Things might start to happen. Irreversible things."

"That Stick, *look!* It's jiggling about all over the place and closing its little eyes as tight as can be. That Stick, it's making Mum as heavy as a horse and cart. Look at Book 5, that page is flapping," and Belle grabbed Book 5 and forced it onto the floor before it flew out of the room altogether. It wriggled and tried to snap shut, but Belle was just about strong enough to read page 77. *"How to make a fainted woman feel as heavy as a horse and cart. One: make sure Stick has eyes. Two: make sure Stick isn't wetting itself,"* Belle looked at the Stick. It was as dry as a bone. *"Three: make sure Stick can wriggle and outstare you (the fainted woman) and hence, you will become as heavy as a carthorse if not heavier."*

"I think that Stick is more intelligent than we thought," Rupert stared at it as if to try and outwit it, but as he continued to hold its gaze, he felt his *own* legs start to feel like lead weights. "Mrs Joy has programmed that Stick to adhere to these books without even knowing what she's doing. If she could stop meddling in spells that hinder and

only suffice in making fishety-soup, and start to think more about the death and demise of the entire universe then we might be able to live to see another day."

"Another day of fishety-soup?"

"SHUT UP, William," Belle heaved at her Mum's feet to see if dragging her another way would work. "She's like concrete. Where's that Stick? I need to reverse the spell. She's as hard as nails."

"Just like the soup, then."

"I thought I told you to *shut up.*"

"Belle? Belle? I wouldn't try and use that Stick, if the rightful owner isn't in control, heaven's knows what will happen. We're in enough trouble as it is," Ned's voice muttered from somewhere.

"Where *are* you?" Belle dropped her Mum's left foot to the floor, and William heard her toes crack.

"What on earth *happened* to you? You're black, completely black. Have I missed much? Did dinner blow up in your face?"

"Where ARE you?"

"Here!"

"Where's *here?"*

"Right in *front* of you."

"It's that *Stick,* again," Belle made a grab for the Stick who seemed to be cackling and its little eyes, newly formed in its bulbous head, seemed to be getting larger and larger and blacker and blacker. It was jiggling on the spot, but not slowly, really fast and making Belle's head spin.

"I'll get Book 7, if *you* grab that Stick," William cried. "It's getting out of *control,* I think it's getting a life of its own! That Stick's controlling the Books," and William pounced on Book 7 which had pages and *pages* flapping uncontrollably around the room, buzzing right in Mrs Joy's face. But she was still out cold.

Flaming Fiona's flames drew in.

Cold.

Austere.

Severe and stormy.

Then, before Book 7 could try and outwit Book 5, and Book 6 fought to get in-between, Ned's face, and then his *entire* body, limbs shooting out from his lanky carcass, alive, materialised in mid-air. He fell to the floor with an almighty thud. "Anyway, as I was saying, why are you so *filthy,* Belle?"

"I don't care about *filth,* where are your *wings?"*

"I don't care about my *wings,* at least I've got my *other* bits back," Ned rubbed his bottom which was pounding with pain, and then put his hand down *there.* "Phew!"

"Ned, that's *awful!* Why are boys so *gross?"*

"Bloody awful," William replied, "but I like it."

"That *Stick,* he helped me, you know. He gave me back my body in return for a tap on the head for eyes, proper *big* eyes, and strength, yes, *that's* it. Stick asked for strength, and I found a great recipe for that in one of those books," Ned tried to point to the books that were still flitting about everywhere. Little wings were sprouting from their

spines, and Book 9 was trying to find its way into Ned's trousers. "I gave Stick a newly found strength," and Ned looked really pleased with himself.

"Yes, we *did* notice, idiot," William spat back. "Our Mum's a morsel of concrete, and that Stick nearly killed the lot of us. *And,* I didn't *ever* get to eat my custard doughnut."

"Mrs Joy? Mrs *Joy? Hello* there? It's me, I'm back. *Ludicrously* cold and the roads full of ice, good job you've got the fireplaces roaring, clouds of black smoke shot out the chimney just now. *Please* don't say you've got another *newbie* dinner being tested? I'm coming to thaw out - " the voice echoed, and Rupert shot up the chimney from where Belle had shot down. "Mrs *Joy?"*

"It's Dad. *What* shall we *say?"* Belle stood rigid, Book 8 trying its hardest to wriggle out of her hands. Belle's fingers clenched on tight.

"Get the Books back in Mum's pockets, quick," William shouted his whisper. "All Dad wants is his dinner. He shan't care what it is, just not a *newbie.* He *hates* newbies. Turned him into a broomstick that last time, and he spent three days circling the chimney, out there, in a blizzard."

"Oh yeah," Belle made a grab for the Books, but she could only get four.

Ned wrestled on the floor, eying Stick the whole time, and whispering beneath his breath.

"What's he saying?" William glared at Belle. "Well?" he whispered. "What's he up to?"

"I dunno. Something *I've* never heard before. Can't work it out. Funny stuff. Like witchery."

"But Stick is *sort* of calming down," William watched Ned as he tried to send the Stick into a trance. Ned's lips moved quickly, snapping open and shut like lightning.

"He's got *something* going for him anyway. At least the Books aren't trying to *eat* each other now. It's quite amusing, isn't it, watching Ned try and hypnotise a *Stick?"* William cackled.

"Stop it, you're putting him off," Belle kicked William.

"I'll ask Ned to hypnotise *you* in a minute, that *hurt!"*

"Putting *who* off *what?"* Mr Joy crashed into the settee room. "Oh, you're *all* in *here,"* and Mr Joy blew hot air into his hands and rubbed them briskly together. "Mrs Joy, what-*ever* is it?"

"She's, err … - … asleep," Ned retorted.

"Asleep?"

"Yep, you know, *newbies* took it out of her," Ned cocked his head and winked at Mr Joy as if they were sharing some kind of a private joke.

"Newbie?"

"Yep!"

"Oh dear *Lord,* not *newbies.* When will she *ever* learn? That *Stick* I suppose? Tried to cut corners did she, Mrs Joy?"

"Huh?"

"Cut corners. Try to cook something out of her league? She's only on, well, Book 3 at the very most, actually, no, Book *2.* She tried to skip to Book 3, but the author noticed and turned her fingers into blunt tortoise claws and she couldn't cook for three weeks, so, if I remember rightly, she's only read about five chapters in all, and the first three were teaching a Recipe Witch how to wash her hands, and *you're* holding - " Mr Joy peered into Ned's arms. He was holding *masses* of books, *" - all* of them it appears. She's got ten books to go and she's trying newbies *already?"*

"Yep! Getting a *bit* out of control they were, the Books, so, I just calmly gathered them up and Mrs Joy must have worn herself out, *that's* it. *That's* what happened."

"Hmmm."

Ned smiled, the Books wriggling in his arms. He carried on smiling, falsely; the tips of his ears burning holding his fake grin.

Mr Joy dipped down, squinting, and shook Mrs Joy's shoulders. "Why *is* she *half* hanging on the floor? Sort of, well, rigid? Her leg, it's a dead weight! What *is* it with this woman? Can't leave her alone for, well, any time at *all,* truth be told."

"Rupert! Oh *Rupert,* did you *see* what just happened?" Mrs Joy was starting to come around. Her legs were still planks of concrete, and her hair was shot to the ceiling like wallpaper paste, but her eyes were wide open, and her mouth? It would *not* stop jabbering.

"Huh?" Mr Joy scratched his head. "Rupert?"

"Hallucinating," Ned couldn't look Mr Joy in the eye.

"Hallucinating?"

"Yep! She's been hallucinating for *ages,* keeps shouting all *sorts* of men's names, she does," Belle cried over the sounds of her Mum reeling off plenty of stuff. "Must be the names of the *newbies."*

"Belle! She, she, she fell out the *chimney,"* Mrs Joy started to crawl about on all fours searching for Belle. "The *CHIMNEY?* Did you *see,* Rupert? *DID* YOU? Chimney? *Belle?"*

Mr Joy stared at Belle who just looked at the ceiling. "Care to explain yourself?"

"There's a crack, Dad, did you know?"

"What?"

"A crack, in the ceiling. Needs a bit of plastering, I'd imagine - "

"STOP changing the subject, child. Explain what on **earth** your mother is wittering on about. Mrs *Joy?"*

"Oh - dear, *hello* dear, Mr Joy, you're *back,"* Mrs Joy scratched her head. "My hair? It's, it's like *plaster."*

"We can use it to fill the crack in the ceiling," Belle squinted at her Dad, but it was really no use.

"Stop this deceit. *And,* there's *nothing* wrong with my handy-work, I'll have you know. It lasted one entire season last year. Imagine that, an *entire* season? The first time we've *ever* seen that, thank the Lord. *And* only seven albino squirrels managed to get in. But only as far as the bulbous fish picture - "

"You mean Mum's made that bulbous fish soup *before* and she *still* hasn't got it right despite taking all those pictures of it? Did she put it on, you know - *social media?"* Belle whispered, rolling her eyes.

"Probably, that's why Herman Kooplunk from Sweden knew about it before I did - "

"Who's *Herman Kooplunk?"*

"Exactly," Mr Joy rolled his eyes back. "And, yep, appears so, *doesn't* it, that she's made that bulbous fish soup before? And that Stick, *why* is it *staring* at me? It shan't be trying any new tricks just because it seems a bit, well, I can't *quite* put my finger on it," Mr Joy peered closer. "It looks different. You, you look *different.* You don't look like a weak little Stick anymore."

Stick wriggled and hopped up and down closer and *closer* to Ned as if it were trying to earn a new master.

"What? What ***is*** it?" Ned shifted his shoulder sideways on to this weird new acquaintance, but Stick just shot around the other side. "Stop *following* me!" Ned demanded. "What did I *ever* do to *you?* Well, apart from giving you eyes, and strength, and basically a complete overhaul - "

Belle dragged her Mum up onto the settee. Only her arms moved, and that was just because Belle was stretching them. Her legs and feet twisted and dangled from the self-inflating cushion. And her eyes started to focus, slightly.

"You're, you're dirty, no, you're *clean?* Come closer," Mrs Joy glared. "You're clean?!"

"Belle, your *neck,"* William hissed, staring at Belle's neck and chin. "Get rid of that last bit of soot, it's evidence."

"Oh," Belle wiped her sleeve across the soot, and smiled.

Mrs Joy had a double take.

"Belle, I don't believe you, and *please* don't say you've rubbed the soot on the furniture?" Mrs Joy tried to move closer, but her body felt like a ton of bricks cemented together.

"No, Mum. I mean, *what* soot, Mum? Are you *hallucinating* again?"

"Hallucinating? *Me?* What about *you?* Are you hurt?"

"Hurt? From what?"

"That fall, Rosabella."

"What fall?"

"Don't be facetious - "

"I'm *not,* just wondered why I'd be hurt?"

"The fall, from, you know, up - *there,"* Mrs Joy flinched her chin towards the Flaming Fiona's chimney, and scratched her head. Flaming Fiona's chimney *looked* normal. And there was nothing broken. In fact, it looked just as it always did. Mrs Joy rubbed her eyes. "There's *something* suspicious going on here."

"Isn't there *always?"* Mr Joy was still glaring at that Stick. "And if it's another ill-prepared newbie for tea, I swear I'll *not* come back."

"Perhaps you meant I could be hurt when I just flew to the floor - after eating your *Magenta Marvels,* Mum? But me? I'm fine. *See!"* Belle flipped her arms up into the air.

"Belle," William spat under his breath. "You've just showed off the *worst* of the soot, under your armpits!"

"Your *Magenta Marvels* aren't *that* intoxicating, Mum. I'm not dead. They, they, they … just exploded, Mum. *That's* it. Right under my armpits, would you believe?"

"No, no I *wouldn't.* Just sit me up straight, will you. These mid-afternoon naps are becoming *quite* disconcerting. And pass me Stick," but Stick hopped back and hid behind Ned.

"Doesn't appear to want to come to you, Mrs Joy," Ned groaned. "But, PLEASE, make him?"

"Stick?" Mrs Joy demanded.

Stick wiggled its eyebrows that were starting to grow thicker and thicker.

"Come here, I say. And, what *have* you got stuck above your eyes? They, they look suspiciously like … *eyebrows?"*

"They do, don't they?" Ned butted in.

"But, but how did Stick get *those?"* Mrs Joy stared at her witchety friend.

"Stick doesn't know," Stick replied.

"Stick? STICK? You, you can *talk?"*

"Of *course* I can talk, woman."

"Well, that's enough of your cheek if that's the best you can do? Back-chat!"

"Well, I've been tossled *all* these years, and now there's someone who has given me a chance without any silly wooles ..."

"Wooles? What are *wooles?* This new master of yours, whoever he is, or *she,* hmm - "

Stick just stuck out its purple tongue.

" – this new master doesn't *seem* to be able to *talk."*

"Wooles, you know."

"Err, *no,* Stick. Enlighten us. Enlighten us *all."*

Belle glared at William. This unusual situation wasn't really going to plan. What if Smock had something to do with it?

"Well, Stick? Has the cat got your tongue?" Mrs Joy tapped her concrete-heavy finger on her other hand. The terrible sound echoed around the entire room and up Flaming Fiona's chimney.

"OUCH! That tickles!" Flaming Fiona grinned.

"I *think* you better had go back to Book 1, Mrs Joy. *Chapter* 1 to be sure," Mr Joy slumped down.

"And *you'll* not be having any Suet-Apple-Dumpling-Fritter-Fratters, Mr Joy, speaking so out of turn to the one who fills your stomach!" Mrs Joy retorted.

"Oh, never mind, I'll just have toast. Or a Chinese take-away, now *there's* a thought."

Mrs Joy scratched her head, again, and smoothed down her ruffled strands of black hair as if her husband might guess she had been entertaining of sorts, but actually he could not appear more disinterested if he tried.

Stick still stood tall, its purple mouth parched.

"Mr Joy?" Mrs Joy managed to move her left eye.

"Hmm?"

"You've eaten, I hope not. There's *plenty* left aside for you that I'll simply just reheat," and Mrs Joy frantically up-sticked from the dishevelled cushions which had deflated under the weight and stumbled for the kitchen. "Right, plates, let me get those plates, what an extraordinary afternoon it has turned out to be, *extraordinary* indeed. Stick? STICK? I need a hand, *pleeese?"* Mrs Joy trotted about like a wooden doll.

But Stick did not come.

"Go ***on,"*** Ned pushed Stick out into the corridor.

"Shan't, shan't, *shan't,"* Stick spat back shrilly.

"What's *wrong* with you? *I'm* not your master, ***she*** is; *Mrs Joy."*

"Not," Stick just stood rigid and did not budge.

"She *is,"* Ned tried to pick up Stick with both hands but he did not budge. "Come on, you *can't* hang around here, you'll spoil *every*thing."

"SHAN'T!"

"So, Belle," William whispered. "Who was this boy, the boy with the satchel? Was it him, you know, that same boy from before? Did he look, you know, dangerous?" William kept one eye on Belle, the other on that Stick. "You're *definitely* listening, aren't you, Stick? Who do you work for?"

"Him," Stick pointed at Ned.

"Me? No, you *don't* work for *me. No* one works for *me,"* Ned stepped back. "I'm not responsible for *anything,* let alone a needy Stick."

"Yes, absolutely, that *same* boy," Belle mouthed, cupping her hand so as that Stick did not see.

"Stop keeping me out of things, **don't** be so MEAN!" Stick hopped about, enraged.

"We don't know anything *about* you," William snapped back. "Now you can speak, and you're acting totally weird, *I'm* **not** taking any chances."

"Weird? *WEIRD?* I'm not *weird! You* take that back! *All* my life I've been at the end of the chain of friends. I know Mrs Joy only bought me because I was cheap, and she bought me at a discount and she felt sorry for me," and before anyone could say anything at all, Stick wailed SO loudly the remains of the deathly mouldy doughnut that William had been so adamant he wanted to eat dropped out the chimney.

"AWESOME!" William made a swipe for it before all the sugar was lost into the carpet. "You're wicked! Thanks, Stick!"

"You're incorrigible, William," Belle snapped shrilly. *"As* I was saying, he didn't recognise me initially, this little boy, and I was *most* confused, but then I realised I'd entered Anouka at a slightly earlier point in time. The little boy had *no* idea where he was, just that he had come in from the cold outside, through his own door, and had ended up back outside. But a *different* outside. An *Anoukan* outside. He had *no* idea where he was headed or why he was

there, and I tell you, he was rather startled when I blurted out about our mission, and about the Book - "

"Hmmm," William snorted.

"Belle, you can *never* hold your tongue, honestly," Ned whispered.

"Stop leaving me out," Stick cried. "I can't hear a ***word*** you're saying. You should have given me ears, BIG ears, so I can hear *every*thing … "

"That would be *terrible!* I don't want *you* butting in all the time," Ned smirked.

"I'll, I'll, I'll … turn you into *THAT!"* and Stick leapt up and tapped the last mouthful of William's sugary doughnut. "Ned, I'll, I'll, I'll … make you look like a *doughnut!"* And, the doughnut fell out of William's mouth and onto the floor. Immediately, the grains of sugar beads melted into the carpet.

"You IDIOT! That was *mine,* and now it's going to be just a hard old piece of savoury dough," William shrieked.

"You said I was *wicked* before, I *still* want to be *wicked,"* Stick wailed, his eyebrows rising up and starting to fill with salty tears from his eyes below.

"I meant awesome. You were wickedly *awesome* when you saved my doughnut. But, you're **not** *wicked* if you ruin my doughnut, *stupid.* And you *have …* " but before William could finish his words, Ned's eyebrows started to twitch. His eyes started to turn a jammy red, and his lips the same. His teeth turned all yellow and gooey, and his hair a mass of what looked like sugar.

"NED!" Belle's eyes widened as far as they could go. "NED! Your, your face - "

"What about it?"

"It's a doughnut!"

"A *doughnut?"*

"Yep! Your head is as round and as sickly as that jam doughnut William was scoffing. Stick, that Stick, it's *actually* turned you into William's doughnut!"

"AWESOME! Can *I* have a bite?" William leapt forward, licking his lips.

Stick smirked, "Am I back in your *wicked* books again, William?"

"S'pose," William flared his nostrils. "So, Ned, can I have a bite? After all, it *is* actually *mine,* the doughnut. Just that it's now part of your head."

"Get lost, no!" Ned stepped back, but lost his footing as his feet had become as wobbly as jelly.

"Why not? That's *stealing* if you don't let me have a bite."

"Because *if* you take a *bite* out of me, I'll be missing an ear, or a nose, or worse still, my entire mouth!"

"S'pose," William retreated. "You're not in my *wicked* books anymore, Stick. You've *failed.* Failed *miserably.* That doughnut, Ned's head, looks the biggest, most juiciest doughnut in the world, and HE gets to actually BE it."

"I'd rather NOT be it. It's actually starting to make me want to vomit. Stick, turn me back to being me."

"SHAN'T!"

"PLEEESE?"

"Give me big ears, then?"

"What?"

"An exchange. *I'll* turn your head back into a head, if *you* give me ears, and make them BIG!"

"I can't just do anything - "

"I'd TRY if I were you, or your head just might start melting, and where will *that* leave you?"

"Okay, OKAY!" and Ned tensed up his fists, stared at the Stick, and started to shake and shake and *shake* harder and *harder* and fiercer and *fiercer* on the spot, his entire face turning as red as a boiled tomato. "PAZANG!" Sparks shot out of Ned's eyes and struck Stick's entire body.

"OW!" Stick wiggled and was nearly sick. "My head! It's going to explode!"

"Well, you said you wanted BIG ears, so BIG ears you've got!" and Ned looked and *looked* at Stick's head as the biggest ears imaginable started to sprout larger and *larger* out of the side of his rather bulbous head. "You look like that FISH!"

"DON'T laugh at me. I've spent my entire *life* being - "

"Oh, cut out the violin music, *pleeese!!!*"

"How did you learn to cast spells like *that?*" Belle peered into Ned's eyes.

"Those Books, your Mum's Books. A bit pretentious, have you seen the bit about cleaning out your ears with dirty sweet potato skins? Gross. But, they seem to work if you try

hard enough. I managed to make your Mum as hard as concrete, didn't I? - "

"That was *you?"*

"Yep! Course it was me," Ned looked smug, but as he glanced across the room back at Stick, he realised that Stick's ears were getting BIGGER and BIGGER, in fact they were *so* huge they were making stick bend under the pressure.

"Make it STOP!" Stick cried. "My ears! Make them STOP growing! They're getting fatter and **fatter** and *far* too heavy. I'm going to break in two if not ten!"

"I , I, I don't know *how,* Stick, *really* I don't!"

"You LIAR! You *must* know! *You* cast it, the spell!"

"I don't! I *don't* know!"

"You just want me dead, *don't* you? You just want to *kill* me?! You just want me out of the picture just when it was starting to get exciting!"

"No I don't, that's a *ridiculous* thing to say!"

"Well, why cast such a mean, *evil* spell on me then?"

"You asked me to make your ears big, didn't you?! *You* demanded that I do something in exchange for my head being turned back into a head. I did that, *didn't* I? I just wasn't planning on the spell being SO huge! I *am* a novice after all. I didn't *mean* to make your ears grow *so* much they'd block out the sun!" Ned cried back. "WOAH, Stick, duck! You're going to hit the ceiling!"

"MAKE…IT…STOP!"

"I…DON'T…KNOW…HOW!"

"Reverse it - "

"Reverse *what?"*

"Reverse the polarity!"

"Reverse the *what?"*

"The *polarity.* I read it in Book 3."

"I haven't *read* Book 3!"

"Ignoramus!"

"I AM *NOT* AN IGNORAMUS! And, if you *keep* insulting me, I shan't help you at *all* and your ears, they'll grow soooo big, they'll cover your eyes and your nose and eventually, they'll swallow you up completely!"

The *spell,* then. *Reverse* it. If I *have* to speak in laymen's terms, the spell. Reverse the SPELL! If you can't stop this BIG spell, cast a *small* one. Make my ears tiny, Ned, QUICK! I'm going to burst on the chandelier!"

"PAZANG!" Ned screamed the same words, staring at Stick and shaking tiny bits of anything that he could grab.

"OUCH! That's my *hair!* Belle slapped and thrashed the air. "Can't you do *anything* normally?"

"Your Mum doesn't, when she casts her spells. She nearly drowned out the kitchen that time - "

"But *she* doesn't turn us black and blue and try to blow us up *soooo* big we explode!" Belle rubbed her bruised scalp.

"I'm sure she would if she could, she just hasn't got to page 73 of Book 2 yet. You won't just be destined to eat bulbous fish once she's read *that* part, I'm telling you! There was more than just *PAZANG I* had to say to Stick, I needed to complete the spell with, what was it? Ohhh. Oh YES! PAZANG Zwosting-Packa-Moomin-Marq!"

"What would have happened then?"

"Um, if I remember rightly, pink ears, pointed at the top with little brooms painted on them, and a few thistles for tomorrow's breakfast ready to infuse - "

"Stick would have *hated* you!"

"Oh well, never mind, rotten luck happens to everyone at some point."

"I *can* still hear you," Stick rotated on the spot scratching his miniscule ear lobes. They had started to itch and Stick had started to scratch them *so* hard bits had actually started to fall off.

"Is, is , is that a *thistle* I can see?" Ned squinted more closely at Stick who was just levitating on the spot somehow.

"I don't know, but it's horrible! Make it stop! Make it stop itching RIGHT NOW!"

"You're always complaining, Stick. I liked it better when you were stupid and your tongue didn't waggle so much."

"Well, that's a *horrid* thing to insinuate - "

"Oooh-y-ooooh, did Stick swallow a dictionary?"

"Stop talking about me as if I wasn't here."

"Wish you *weren't,"* Ned uttered, snooting his nose Stick's way.

"Now now *now! Swords* at *dawn,* is it? Hmm?" Mr Joy squirmed into the conversation. "Why does that toilet never seem to flush? I once knew of a couple - "

"Here he goes again - " William muttered.

" - Not much older than you both, Belle and Ned, who argued and tossled with their emotions *so* much, one never believing the others antics and tales that they nearly caused the end of time, but they became the best of friends, they *had* to - "

"Well, *that's* a stupid idea. I'm not being the best of *anything* with *her,"* Ned spat back.

"Stick together, or we may all end up fossils in a dead old world."

"Well, *that's* always something to look forward to, why don't you *really* try and depress us, I don't think that *death* is *far* enough," Ned still just stood and stared at Stick. Not only were Stick's ears getting *smaller* and smaller until they were the tiniest of dots on a bit of old wood, but so were Stick's new eyes and even his new feet were shrinking and shrinking until the bug on his tummy looked like a giant.

"Anyway, hot chocolate with marshmallows? *That's* better than swords at dawn. Follow me," and Mr Joy seemed to sort of float down the corridor in a floaty-like state.

"That archaeological trip has turned Dad a bit loopy, I'll say," Belle whispered. "Did he not *see* Stick wailing and moving and talking? TALKING?"

"He doesn't care, your Dad," Ned still just stared at Stick. "He's his *own* master of doom," and Ned followed Mr Joy down the passage to the kitchen, Stick hopping behind, his miniscule ears reaching and reaching as *far* forward as possible to even hear his own tap-tapping along the tiles.

Swords at dawn? What does he mean? William trailed behind the others. *The only sword I've encountered is that demonic ruby dagger that slain Miss Smock,* William shuddered.

"What, William?" Belle turned around. "What are you muttering on about now? Not still that jam doughnut, pleeeease?"

"No, actually."

"What then?"

"Nothing to bother you, nosey."

"More hot chocolate? Are you *sure,* Mr Joy? That boy'll turn into a walking talking lump of sugar soon with a tummy barely small enough to fit into his trousers," Mrs Joy stirred a pot of sludge, a *huge* pot of sludge that got sludgier and sludgier whilst she stared at William's waistline and flicked through numerous yellowing pages of goodness *knows* what Book. "Carob Indigestives, Carob Indigestives, Carob Indigestives," she muttered, with a frown. "There's not a chance in hell I'll be making hot chocolate," and she continued to eye up William's waistline whilst flailing her fingers, randomly, across an entire page searching for cooking clues.

"What?" William stared at his Mum.

"What?"

"Yes, *what?* Why do you keep *staring* at me? And saying *Carob Indigestives?"*

"Far healthier, dear. You're rather pale, *again.*"

"Do you *blame* me?" William stared at the sludge.

"Yes, well, as I said, I'm *still* a novice."

"But, if it's not for you, you *could* just give it up."

"Give *what* up?"

"You know?"

"WILLIAM, if you're insinuating that I should let go of my absolute heartfelt ambition in life, you can stop *right* there."

"We could just have fish and chips for tea?"

"FISH and CHIPS?"

"Urr, yep."

"FISH AND CHIPS?"

"I think we're going round in circles here."

"Where is the nutrition in *that?"*

"Where is the nutrition in ***THAT!"*** and William snaked over to the sludge pot, that was getting more tarnished as the fire on its bottom got hotter and hotter, and stared right in. "Seriously, is that meant to be a substitute for hot chocolate? I wouldn't feed it to a dog!" he snarled.

"Take that screwed up nose and ungrateful attitude *right* out of my kitchen, William, and come back when you're a little more, how can I say? Appreciative - "

"Appreciative? Appreciative of *what,* exactly?"

"My pot of nutrition! I've learnt at my online classes. I do have a computer, you know, as well as that heap of spell books. The computer allows you to pause in time and see a concoction actually being made – colourful moving pictures 'n all, it's just so clever, see?" and Mrs Joy flicked her 37 inch screen and the sludge brewing in the pot actually popped up larger in life as if it was about to star in a movie. "Wonderful, isn't it?"

"It's called technology, Mum," William groaned.

"Well, it may not *look* tasty to the eye, but you'll need a kick up that backside where *you're* going."

"Where's *that* exactly. Where *am* I going?"

"And an early night, early night, you need. Someone's got to help you conserve your energy," Mrs Joy fussed and bumbled, and tripped over her own skirts, which was not particularly indifferent, and bustled the remaining bits of *Broccoli Bakes* and *Magenta Marvels* into a dish to heat, accidentally turning the stove up to such a high temperature that golden-blue flames shot around the cast iron pan and set the food alight.

"Thank the heavens," Mr Joy muttered into his hands. "Thank the heavens it's so burnt it shan't be my offerings for tea."

"Mr JOY, how *mean* of you to say such things. I can see where that son of yours gets it from."

"Oh, she heard."

"Yes, *she* did."

"What happened to the hot chocolate?" William scowled.

"And the marshmallows?" Belle piped up.

But Mrs Joy huffed and disappeared. "Book 4, Book 4, I *must* read Book 4."

"Is she *quite* okay?" Ned spoke after what seemed an age of silence. "Mrs Joy, is she *really* quite okay?"

"Oh, goes over *my* head, Mrs Joy's larksome ineptitude at times, straight over the top, it goes. She's a whirlwind, and that's how she's always been, the love," Mr

Joy remarked, facetiously, and just shook his head. *Anouka's done that for her.*

"Swords, Dad. Why talk of swords?" William whispered.

"Applause? Yes, *absolutely* I did. A *huge* round of applause I received upon ending my talk on - anthropology," Mr Joy's eyes diverted away. "Now, did someone mention fish and chips?"

"It's not allowed. And - "

"Not *allowed?"*

"AND, anthropology?" William frowned.

"Hmm?"

"Wasn't it *archaeology?"*

"Hmm? *Archaeology?* Yes, *great* it was. Starving now though."

"No, but you said *Anthropology."*

"Sorry, what was that? What *are* you wittering on about, boy?" Mr Joy started to walk quickly out the room backwards, holding William's eye, then suddenly, as William squinted at his Dad's face, Mr Joy's eyes turned deep violet, and William felt the most *enormous* spark.

"Ouch! What was *that?"* William felt a sharp pang in his left eye. The pain shot right up to his head. "And, I didn't say *applause*, I said *swords."*

"Oh, blast and *blast* again. I guess *I'm* no whizz at Mrs Joy's Books either; trying to *Bleach the Memory of Knowledge,* that didn't work, did it? I'm sure Book 6 said *Strike a Pose, and Flick the Wrist and then your Son will have no...no, no, what was it?"*

"Swords?" Belle cried before her Dad could react.

"Yes, but stop talking about them will you? That spell should have wiped his memory," and Mr Joy then flicked his wrist at Belle.

"What swords?" Belle asked again.

"Phew, worked *that* time," and, as if for good measure, he then struck *another* huge demonic SPARK. It launched itself out of Mr Joy's wrists and then out of his eyes and struck Belle right between the eyebrows. "OUCH! Not *again!* What *was* that?"

"Yes, yes, I'll make sure, Mrs Joy. I'll make sure that there's no mistaking the break of dawn; it will, it will be adhered to, 4.56am, yes, Magenta, 4.56am for sure," Mr Joy's last word tapered off up Flaming Fiona's chimney.

"What's he on about? He *has* gone mad," Belle rubbed her head.

"Do you think Dad *pretends* he can't hear us?" William slumped down in the rocking chair. "He heard *perfectly* when Mum called him from the kitchen for hot chocolate and *Broccoli Bakes,* but his hearing became remarkably selective, if you ask me, when I asked him about *swords."*

"What *is* it with you and swords? Is there something we ought to know, William? Not getting blood on *my* hands."

"I'll let you know if you share that chocolate."

"Oh, what the waffles, are we meant to slay *you know who?"*

"Chocolate?"

"Well, *are* we?"

"CHOCOLATE?"

"Are we?"

"YES!"

"Really?" Belle's arms flew up into the air. *"Really?"*

"Chocolate?"

"I haven't got any."

"Schmuck. You promised."

"How do you know that tyrant Miss Smock, that evil-snitch of a woman, is to be slain…by *us?* US? Are you *sure* about that? I think I'm going to be sick."

"Well, it's all rather strange, but when I was taken by the green dragon - " William started to explain.

"*Jacintha* do you mean?" Ned replied, keeping one eye on Stick who kept edging further and further forward with its miniscule ears the size of a pea.

"What do you mean *Jacintha do you mean?* You *know* it, or should I say *her?"*

"Yes, oh *yes* – William, you don't know, do you? Of *course,"* Belle hissed.

"What do you mean, *of course?"*

"Of course."

"Is there a parrot in here? How? *How* do you know Jacintha?"

"We've *met* her, but she's the scattiest thing you could possibly ever lay your eyes on, William."

"You've *met* her?"

"Yes. Are you *deaf* as well as greedy, chocolate-brain?"

"Wish I was when *your* mouth opened and such drivel spouted out."

"Jacintha, she's so untypically - *dragonny,* she is, you know. In fact, not like a dragon at *all,* not in the sense that she'd flare her nostrils and burn you to cinders with fire as hot as a volcanic eruption."

"Right."

"She's a fool, she *is.* Foolish and dippy and massive and fiery, but she hasn't really got two brain cells to rub together if you start a conversation with her, not really, not really with it at *all.* You'd get on well, William."

"A conversation, a *conversation* with her?"

"Yes, *words* William. Quite a few words that string together to make what's called chatting?"

"Get lost - "

"She took you, Jacintha. She *plucked* you from your bed, William, when she was really aiming for Ned; to save him from Smock."

"So, William, the *sword?"* Ned butted in. "What makes you think you and a *sword* are involved? Who made *you* the hero?"

"Me? *I'm* not a hero."

"You're trying to sound like one."

"Do you think I *chose* this life? I just wanted a few squares of chocolate, *white* chocolate to be honest, but to tell you the truth *any* colour would have done, *anything* but

this. Why did you have to bring *him* home, Belle. It's been nothing but trouble and death since Ned arrived."

"Trouble? Since *Ned* arrived?"

"Yes, Belle. You've got to admit."

"Can you not remember *every* school holiday since we moved here?"

"No, not really."

"William, Mum's *never* been normal. When she shrunk your fish tank and your *bestest* fishy was crushed to death?"

"You didn't need to bring *that* back up. You're so mean. I was mortified all summer -"

"Only because Mum then didn't give you the money to go and buy fish food, because we didn't have a fish, and then you couldn't spend half of the money on yourself. *And,* that night when Mum nearly killed Dad?"

"Killed Mr Joy?" Ned shrieked. "I don't think I should *ever* have come here either, Belle. You didn't tell me your family were maniacs," Ned stepped back, closer to Mr Fireplace whose flames turned taller and wiser and bluer in appearance.

"Don't be so ridiculous, Mum's not a killer by trade. It was an accident."

"*What* was an accident?"

"You've seen that my Dad limps, haven't you?"

"Oh yeah, I was going to ask you what happened, but I sort of didn't."

"Well, that was Mum - one night when Dad came home late. He'd been gone for three nights, and it was so

freezing in our house as Mum couldn't find the right spell to chop the firewood we nearly died anyway -"

"Nice."

"Dad came home just as Mum was in the kitchen hanging right over her pot of green soup. Stick appeared, that's right, just as Dad opened the back door and let in a *howling* wind. Mum was trying to reach Book 12 *and* stir the soup at the same time but anyone in their right mind could easily see that there was about five arms stretches at *least* between that pot and that Book 12. But, Mum's Mum, and she *wasn't* going to let a stupid thing like impossibility get in her way. So, she used Stick to try and knock Book 12 off the shelf. She was thrashing about *so* hard that she knocked Dad right into the pot just as the flames underneath flew to the ceiling by the great gust. Dad's entire head just missed the pot, but his leg slipped and it clipped the cast iron which crashed down onto his foot. Broken in seven places it was - "

"The *pot?* The soup must have been like a river?"

"No, Dad's *foot.* The pot was fine. But he doesn't really talk about it. Just never really gets anywhere near Stick unless he thinks he can chop it in two."

"Bet he doesn't trust your Mum now?"

"Oh, he *never* did. Just hopes that one day Book 12 will be done and dusted."

"Why?"

"Well, surely if Mum gets as far as digesting Book 12, then she'll at *least* be a bit better at, well, - *life."*

"Harsh."

"Yep."

"Yeah, but Mum, she's never been faced with *him,* has she," William pointed at Ned. "I think she's trying to impress *him - "*

"I *am* still here, William," Ned spat back. "And, it doesn't sound like it's *only* me that's caused all of this. Your home was a mad house far before I came through the back door. And, you **can** *say* my name."

"Not sure I *want* to. Not sure what it might conjure up. We could all just be waiting for the grim reaper, *Ned."*

"That's a bit dismal."

"It was a bit dismal up on top of that mountain, I can tell you. Watching tales of death and blood unfold themselves right in front of my eyes. And that Rupert? What's *he* all about?"

"What about him? The last time I looked, he was watching our backs. You're getting a bit boring now, William," Belle swung off the corner of the rocking chair.

"Well, if Ned hadn't followed you here, Rupert would *never* have turned up. Ned, it's like he oozes trouble. Both of them."

"Ned? What about *Dad?* You can't blame Ned for Dad's existence. Dad's eccentric, *always* has been."

"But he has no idea about his swords, and Ned's a bit too curious about them for his own good."

"Yeah, well, so Dad *says,"* Belle looked across the kitchen at Stick. "Dad's good at pretending that bananas are *supposed* to grow on branches in the cupboard. Got Mum's back when Stick's having one of his turns."

"Huh?"

"Just saying, Dad, he's not *all* what he seems."

"That's rich, coming from *you.*"

"Stick?" Belle peered at the ageing dried out lanky piece of wood. It looked incredibly old and weary. "What *is* it, Stick?" Stick was trying to jump up, but not succeeding very well. *"What?"*

"Hmm - " Stick pattered, effortlessly, on the spot. Even his feet were practically soundless.

"Poor Stick, it can't even *talk* now."

"That's because its mouth is so small it hasn't even got one," William scorned, *"and* I don't think we should encourage it either. Remember the trouble it just got us in?"

"Sssh, William. Stick, he's trying to tell us something," Belle peered into Stick's dot eyes. "What *is* it?"

"Hmmmm - "

"I know, you just said that, *poor* Stick. But we can't *hear* you. Can you point, can you show us something?"

"Hmmmmmmmmmmm," Stick was getting redder and redder and *redder,* and the tiniest wisps of smoke had started to weep from its tiny miniscule ears.

"It's *no* use. We don't know what he's trying to tell us," Belle stamped her feet. "We're doomed."

"Don't give up so easily, Belle," and Ned peered at Stick. Stick was jumping on the spot, but, little by little, Stick was making the teeniest, tinciest bit of progress towards old Mr Fireplace. "Stick?" Ned looked closer.

Centimetre by *tiny* centimetre, Stick tapped further and further forwards until finally he was on the rug. Then,

all of a sudden, as if propelled across the room by its own backside, Stick *flew* into the grate.

"GEES! Get him *out!"* Ned cried. "He'll burn alive!"

Stick had started to turn green, and then a terrible shade of vomit-coloured brown until a crackling shade of black worked its way up from his bony feet to his thin little head. Ned launched himself at Stick and managed to grab one of his knots before he fell headfirst into the groaning flames.

"He can't even remember what trip he's just returned from, *that's* a bit odd, don't you think - " Belle tossed her hair.

"What *are* you talking about, Belle?" Ned cried from the floor, facedown. *"Who* can't?"

"Dad can't."

"What's *that* got to do with anything? *We're* trying to stop your Mum's pride and joy die a painfully, sickeningly, petrifyingly horrifying death, before your Mum hangs us from the rafters and uses us as victimised bait, and all *you* can pipe up with is your Dad's abnormalities," Ned threw Stick from hand to hand. "He's burning my skin a*live!"*

"He doesn't even know *where* he's just been or *what* he's just been doing, William, so life hasn't *all* been normal, it's *never* been normal as far as *I* can remember, so don't blame me bringing peeps home -"

"Peeps?" William just stared at Belle.

"Well, Ned."

"Oh."

“Stop harping on about *that,* and help Stick!” Ned cried as he grabbed a wet towel and wrapped it around and around and *around* Stick’s sticky body.

Stick wriggled, fervently.

“What *is* it, Stick?” Ned glared. *“What* are you trying to show us?” and, as if even the slightest of movements were a matter of life and a gruelling death for Stick, he managed to move his tiny little dried up arm and shakily point to a Book, high up, shoved on the topmost shelf that was barely ever used. “A Book? *That* Book? Book *12?”*

Then Stick collapsed.

Motionless.

Cold.

Brittle.

“Dead?” William looked at the burnt offerings wrapped in a towel. “Stick, is, is, is, he *dead?* Gees, what are we going to tell *Mum?”* William just stared at the incinerated piece of wood lying flat out on the floor.

“More to the point, what if Stick was *supposed* to help us? What if Stick was part of the plan?” Ned tried to squeeze drips and drops and splots of water from the towel into any little crack and crevice that Stick had.

“What *plan?”* Belle tried to pick a dried up old bit of sprats and goulash from the sink. “Who said there was a plan? How do we know there’s a *plan?*” but, before Ned could ask Belle to zip it, Belle stopped dead still as the most *excruciating* rumble groaned from somewhere. *“HUH?”*

“The plan. Of *course!* Book *12,* the rest of the *chapter,* the *chapter* that *I’m* supposed to write. It must be

in *there,"* Ned stared at Book 12 sitting innocently wedged in between *A Life Less Dreadful* and *Best Ever Fish Disaster Recipes.* "Your Mum, she must know more, *much* more, than her scatty brain has ever let on. Cunning old fool. Buying Stick was no error, letting poor little disabled Stick into your house was no little accident or sad misfortune because the other Sticks were more expensive. It was all-*purposeful.* All-*powerful.* Stick came to this house to save it, to save us *all,* to save the ENTIRE WORLD! Stick and that Book 12. Your Mum, she's a genius!"

"Well, I wouldn't go quite *that* far."

Dragon Fest

“Rupert! Rupert, where *did* you go?” Belle looked into Mr Fireplace as a silhouette tried to come out.

Heat filled the kitchen.

"You left *us* to explain to Dad why Mum was lying on the floor, and now she's actually questioning her own sanity," Belle snapped into the blackening grate as Stick still lay out cold whilst fingernails attached to long fingers started to pierce through Mr Fireplace's flames. "What are you doing hanging about in *there,* get in *here.* I know it's you, I could tell those knobbly knuckles anywhere."

"I'm more concerned about why Rupert's fingers, which are obviously attached to the rest of his body, are able to hang about in the fireplace. Why isn't he burning to death?" William gaped into the flames.

"Shut up, you wooden windbag, you're ruining the moment. Rupert might know something," Belle glared further and *further* and deeper and *deeper* into the flames as they wisped and wavered and lingered in the air. "Well? *Do* you, Rupert? *Do* you know something?"

"You're talking to his palms, Belle."

"Well, help him out then, William - "

"Help him *out?* Rather you than me sticking my mitts in *there!"*

"We need to get Rupert in *here,* so just *do* it, William - "

"No, I'm not a complete moron."

"Just *half* a one then."

"Snitch."

"Look, William, we all know Mum hasn't actually got any sanity, not one ounce, but perhaps she *thinks* she has and now she's trying to test it. With Stick. Thinks I fell from

the chimney, well I did, and she knows that. She's playing us."

"She's not *that* intelligent to know how to do one thing and actually mean another."

"I think you'll find she *is,"* Ned butted in.

"She's a woman, William, of *course* she is," Belle turned to Rupert. His fingers and his palms were now pulling their way in, crawling themselves across the rug and letting in his elbows and then his shoulders until his entire head just popped right out into the kitchen.

"Did you *have* to heave such massive logs into the fireplace just as I was coming out?" Rupert rubbed his scalp. "You could've killed me, and where would *that* have left you?"

"Killed you?" William snapped. "And dragging yourself out of a burning fireplace, slowly, through flames which could easily incinerate a man in seconds, that wouldn't have done the job? *Killed* you?"

"S'pose not. I'm here," and Rupert glanced his body up and down. "I'm actually here! It normally takes some serious mind games to get myself out of *there* and into *here,* I can tell you," Rupert slapped his legs and his arms and his head. "Ouch, forgot about that brain dent from your logs. *Please* try and refrain from stoking up the fireplace when people are using it."

"You're not normal," William muttered. "How on earth are we to know when someone is planning on popping in, through the flames? They would generally use the back door."

"Well, *she* doesn't," and Rupert pointed at Belle.

"Well, *she's* not normal either. You shan't catch *me* knowingly walking into death by fireplace. Unless there's guaranteed chocolate, *white* chocolate on the other side, that is. Anyway, what did you do with *her* - you know?"

"No, *enlighten* me, please do, William."

"Smock," William shuddered.

"She's dumped," Rupert clicked shut the back door, but his eyes looked needy. "You shouldn't leave it open. Anyone could just come in."

"Dumped? As in, gone, disposed of, never to be seen again dumped?"

"Ur, no, not *exactly.* Dumped where her sister is keeping her at bay. And, there's a strange-looking dumpy dragon by their side. Not sure *his* intentions, no idea *where* that head-cocked, short-tailed beast came from but he's not looking too hot just sitting and staring at two young sisters who are just waiting for the other to bite."

"Another dragon?"

"Yep."

"And, you've no idea about this other dragon?"

"Nope."

"What if it's going to throw a curveball and mess everything up?"

"How could you *possibly* tell? We have *no* idea what's going to unfold. But Smock, she's *still* searching for that Book; you still *have* got that rogue book, Ned?"

Ned nodded in reply, and patted his inner pocket. "HUH?"

"Not lost it, have you?" Rupert peered into Ned's eyes.

"No, *course* not."

"Well, *where* is it then?"

"I, I, I hid it in *here.* I've been keeping it on my person for days, I *promise,"* Ned looked panicked and started to search frantically in every part of his clothing. He ripped off his coat, and shook out his boots.

"Your socks?"

"Nope!"

"Your trousers?"

"Gross, it wouldn't have survived in *his* back pockets. Would have been gassed to death," Belle snorted.

"I'm not *him,"* Ned poked his knobbly finger in William's direction.

"Gotta rid your body of toxins *some*how," William muttered.

"It, it, it's gone!" Ned looked blank. "Rupert, the **Book,** it's ***gone!"***

"Gone?"

"Yes, gone!" Ned couldn't make eye contact.

"You mean, you haven't got it anymore?"

"Yes, Rupert. Do I have to spell it out? I've, I've, I've *lost* it - " Ned looked at the floor.

"But, I think it's time we *accidentally* gave it to Smock, don't you think?" Rupert looked sly.

"But, but, but, how *can* I? I, I, I seem to have *lost* it - I keep telling you that!"

"LOST IT?"

"For heaven's sake!"

"Rupert, my Dad - " William spoke. "He mentioned swords, swords at dawn and it was too obvious he was trying to tell me something. I wouldn't ordinarily believe a word that mad man says, but I *did* see an image - an image that *I* slayed - you know …"

"Oh for goodness sake, say the name!" Rupert shook his head. "If you can't bring yourself to even *speak* of the eviltan, then how on *earth* are you to slay her?"

"Smock, there, *did* it! And, um, can we back track a bit here? Did you say that I, I, I - "

"Spit it out!"

William hesitated, and his feet shook. *"I'm* to *slay* her?"

"Well, *you* told me that."

"Yes, but *you* acknowledged it."

"So I did."

"I was holding a dagger, a *ruby* dagger, and then the next vision I saw was me, *me*, standing over *her* with that same dagger thrust into Smock's disgusting body. Does that mean - "

Stick moved.

Stick grunted on the floor.

And, little by little, Stick started to tossle on the tiles. Stick's fragile arms that were once an incinerated pile of dust started to reform. The kitchen got hotter and hotter and *hotter* and the tiny specks of black started to stick themselves back together.

As the flames in Mr Fireplace drew taller and taller and *taller,* forcing their turquoise heat up the darkening chimney, Stick's shoulders, and then his elbows and then his fingers started to appear, drawing the flames their way, and wending and twisting their heat higher and higher towards the topmost shelf, higher and higher towards the ceiling, and higher and higher towards *Book 12.*

"GROSS! There's bits of arm and, look, knuckles and, and, *and,* what *is* that? I'm going to be sick," Belle gagged.

"It's Stick's *bottom!"* William cackled.

And, sure as the night was black, Stick was gradually becoming stick-human again. His bony fingers, long and stick-like, grappled along the tiles to find their hands. Toes, of the most sickly dimensions with yellowing nails, ran around everywhere. They bounced off the cupboards and flew through the air.

"Catch 'em!" William screamed. "Catch all Stick's toes, *quick,* before they launch themselves into the fireplace and be lost forever!" and William flung himself about the kitchen grabbing hard wooden toes, and fingers, that had escaped again. "Belle, come *on!"*

But Belle, she couldn't move. "I, I, I *can't - "* Belle shook on the spot. "My feet, my arms, my mouth, it's no good, I can't do *anything - "*

"Well, at least her irritating mouth's having a well-deserved break," Ned retorted.

"S-H-U-T U-P!" Belle managed the loudest of words to creep through her gritted teeth.

"I think she's *petrified,"* Rupert stared at Belle, but William wasn't listening. "I think Stick is prising all of Belle's strength trying to reinvent himself, I *really* think he is!"

"Don't thound tho pleathed about it," Belle's tongue was now so dead she could barely speak.

"Oh, what's a bit of love lost between friends," Rupert marched about the kitchen flinging his arms everywhere.

"GOTCHA!" William stuffed the second to last of Stick's toes into his pockets which had started to bulge and get fatter and fatter and *fatter* as if the toes imprisoned inside were growing and growing and *growing* in size. "Just *one* last toe, Stick, just *one* last one," and William threw his entire body across the room. Leaving the floor, William's feet shot fifteen metres into the air.

"Huh? Why hathn't be banged hith head?" Belle forced out her sentence.

"Because, because, *because,* the ceiling, it's, it's, *it's* not *there!"* Ned panted back.

It was true.

The kitchen looked fuzzy, and Belle became dizzy.

As Belle looked around, the kitchen was gradually becoming fainter and fainter and more opaque. A thin white mist blew up around her, and the soles of William's feet

lingered above her head as he flew higher and higher and *higher* until his head disappeared right through the ceiling and out the other side, goodness knows where, and faded from view.

"William, William - are you *still* up?"

"Oh bo, Bum!" Belle tried to speak.

"He certainly is, still up! Still up THERE, Mrs Joy!" Ned muttered. "Most sensible thing that woman's ever said," Ned tried to hide behind the crashing flames that had started to take over as Mrs Joy's voice echoed everywhere.

"I *did* say you were far too ashen and sickly to remain out of bed, so come, come *right* back down now - " Mrs Joy's footsteps sounded on the stairs and Rupert? He simply vanished into the flames as Jacintha dragged him in. "WILLI*AAAM!"*

"Here's the fool's book, crisp and waiting," Ned whispered to Rupert through the burning fireplace. "Look, even the same ancient pen to inscribe Chapter 14."

"How did you *get* that?" Belle winced.

"Stick, it was *Stick. He* gave it to me."

"That pen, Ned, that pen- it's ruby encrusted, you've only gone and found the ruby encrusted dagger!" and William fell back to the floor, and fainted.

"And *who's* been tampering with my Books?" Mrs Joy stared at the shelf. "Book 12, where *is* it? *Where's* BOOK *12?* And what on *earth* has happened to Stick?"

Jacintha & her Sister

"You're ***great***, *aren't* you, Stick? It's like you're some immortal body who just keeps bouncing back. And, you're mine," Jacintha heard from the *other side.*

Her house.

Where her parents and her toys and little dog lived.

And herself.

And *Veronica.*

The house where she was never quick enough to get the candy floss because her horrid sister always grabbed it first. Veronica; she never shared.

"It's *my* Stick?" Jacintha whispered to herself. *"MY* Stick, not yours."

Silence.

Jacintha plodded about in her garden. "I think I'll play alone, then," and the little girl with the little hands and the little toes and the very large eyes looked around.

"You'll *never* be part of Anouka, *my* Anouka," Veronica suddenly sprung up and viciously spoke out to her little sister. *"Never!* Did you *hear* that, Jacintha? I said *never. I* discovered it first, I just *allow* you in, but it's *my* place," and Veronica skulked off.

Jacintha sighed. "How can such a girl be *so* vindictive?" Jacintha sloped off in the opposite direction. "This place is enormous. We could both be here and not even know. Anything could be here."

Jacintha was alone.

Alone in the forest.

But she preferred it that way if the only other alternative was to play with Ver*onica.* Her sister was just so spiteful, and for no good reason; no reason that Jacintha could fathom out anyway.

Crack.

"Who goes there?" Jacintha slipped behind a bush. Only her nose peered out. "Is there someone there?"

The air felt suddenly very hot.

"I said, WHO goes there? I'm only 8, and a half. Go away!"

"Bonjour, *bonjour!* Hallo, *hallo?"* a small, but rather oddly robust, dragon with a wild misshapen head and a tail so short it was a wonder it could walk at all, popped up right next to Jacintha's nose.

"What the waffles! You *did* scare me! Who *are* you? And what are you *doing* here? I mean, I've been playing here, in Anouka, for years, alone, well, I say *alone,* but my sister's *always* here too. She's a snitch, always ordering me around, so I choose to occupy myself, amuse myself, alone, well, that is until *you* turned up. Who *are* you, and how *did* you get into Anouka?"

"Gracious me, gracious *me,* I thought *I* had a tongue on me, but you beat me for sure, for *sure,"* the, up-to-now-nameless, *thing* replied. *"And,* before you start jabbering on again, I'm Dod. And, I *suppose* I entered into, *Anouka* did you say, the same way as you - ? "

"Well, hello Dod, or should I say *Hallo* or *Bonj*- what was that other word you used?" Jacintha frowned. "I'm Jacintha Potts, and *I* came in from over *there,"* Jacintha whispered and peered about and pointed through the trees to an orange flickering. "Through those embers, in through the fireplace. It's my house the other side, you see. I don't *live* in this forest, I just *play* here, with *her*," and Jacintha rolled her eyes towards the thin pale dry-skinned girl

kicking dusty leaves about on the spot. “She’s my sister, Veronica. *Terribly* spoilt, she is. She hated, absolutely *hated,* the day I was born and she had to share, share everything, even our parents. We never got on. She thinks I should never have been born. She actually *told* me that one day; don’t you think that’s awful? *I* do,” Jacintha jabbered on.

“Who are you talking to?” Veronica sauntered over and kicked dust at her sister when her feet stopped. “Well, *answer* me, Jacintha Potts, right *now*, I said. Or are you plain mad, that’s it, stupid *and* mad. Idiot - ” Veronica curled her lip up at her little sister Jacintha as she spoke.

“Now, now, *that’s* not nice. What a rude, *rude,* un-delightful child you are,” Dod spoke his words right down inside Veronica’s ear hole, but Veronica did not flinch.

“Dod!”

“Yes?”

“Veronica, she can’t *hear* you, *or* see you, now that *is* delightful,” Jacintha flung her head back and cackled; realising it was probably the first time she had *ever* laughed at her sister’s expense. “I’m *soooo* pleased *I’ve* got something that *she* hasn’t. Will you be my friend stumpy old dragon? And *Ronny - ”* Jacintha knew that her sister despised that name, “ - oh Ronny, *I* can now scorn at *you.”*

“Now, *now* Jacintha, there’s no need for *that,”* Dod frowned. “If you’re going to use me to play off your sibling rivalry, that’s not why I’m here at all, why *am* I here, in fact?” Dod speculated, and Jacintha Potts realised he was indeed rather doddery and his name suited him perfectly.

"So, as I was saying, no *battling* angsts between sisters, please, or I'll just go back the way I came - *that* way, oh, or was it *that* way? How uncanny and most ridiculously silly that all these paths in the forest look alike? Which fireplace did you say you came in through?" Dod looked particularly confused and rather peculiar.

"That one, over there, next to the velveteen oak trunk, the *largest* trunk by far," Jacintha replied.

"*What's* over there, stop leaving me out of your game?" Veronica stamped her foot hard, dust flying up into the air.

"Ouch! That grit, it's flown right into my eyes, oh, oh, oh - ATISHOO!" Dod sneezed and complained simultaneously. "It's nestled *right* up inside my nostrils too, that gritty old dust," Dod dug around inside the two large holes in the middle of his face. His claws wriggled and he wrinkled his nose. "It's, it's, it's coming – again - ATISH*OOOOO!!!* Oh, I am just *so* seemingly allergic to dust; dry dust, wet dust, cave dust, forest dust, log dust, coal dust. I have *no* idea how I *ever* stumbled through a fireplace to get here, Anouka, what a strange name, without sneezing from all the dust?" and the rotund dragon sat down all of a sudden on the forest floor, exhausted. "ATISHOO! Oh *dear.*"

"Well perhaps you *didn't* come in that way, through the fireplace like us?" Jacintha replied. "It's not impossible that *other* gates to Anouka exist? Why ever not?"

"Jacintha Potts, stop talking insanities to yourself," Veronica mumbled. "If you don't let me play, or at least tell me with whom you're speaking then, then, then - "

"Then *what,* dear?" Dod retorted. "You'll turn her into a dragon?"

"I'll turn you into a dragon," Veronica stunned herself.

"Veronica, so you *can* see Dod?" Jacintha stood up and glared at her sister.

"Dod? *Dod?* What a *stupid* name and no, I *can't* see *Dod*. Who, or *what*, is Dod?" Veronica snapped, confused, but realised she didn't want her sister to think she was actually interested in playing her silly make believe games.

"Why did you say you'd turn me into a *dragon,* then? *That's* a bit of a coincidence seeing as a dragon is to whom I'm talking," Jacintha smiled at Dod who just returned the nicety with a toothless grin. "Dod is a *dragon,* and he's sitting right *here,"* and Jacintha pointed at the fat thing on the floor. "Not a scary one, mind, and rather more, how shall I put it? Circular and, mmm, dumpy than I would *ever* have imagined a dragon to be, but Dod is a dragon none the less, and he's my friend."

"You've gone potty; Mum said it's *always* the quiet ones. Jacintha Potts has gone potty! Jacintha Potts has gone *potty!"* and Veronica stomped off.

"That got rid of *her,"* Dod sighed.

"Why *are* you here?" Jacintha sat down on the dry dusty forest floor to comfort her friend who looked quite forlorn.

"Magenta, *she* sent me, yes, *that's* right. *Magenta* sent me," Dod's ears shot up and his nostrils flared with excitement that he had actually remembered something. "That butterfly, magnificent she is, she sent me. *And,* before you butt in again, *and,* she said that whatever you do, *whatever* you do, when you choose your Stick, make sure it comes with the Books 1-12, *and,* Book *12, that's* the one with the answers."

"What *answers?"*

"Dunno. Beats *me.* She said *you'd* know, when the time came, she said *you'd* know."

"Who's *she?* Oh, you mean this Magenta person?" Jacintha frowned, again.

"You'll stick like it if you keep frowning," Veronica cried from a distance away, peering out from behind a waterfall.

A thin white mist had started to form along the forest floor.

It was falling lower and lower as the minutes ticked by.

"And then your face will be even *uglier."*

"I can compete with *you,* then," Jacintha cried back even louder.

"Nice answer," Dod chuckled.

"She sounds a bit old-fashioned," Jacintha peered at Dod again.

"Who?"

"Magenta. That's her name, that's what you said, isn't it?"

"Oh, yes, Magenta. Yes, yes, that is indeed her name, and quick, stop nattering on girl, I remember now what Magenta told me, what she told me to do, so I really had better spit it out before I forget it again. She said, when I met, oh, yes, a little girl, you, it *must* be you. You are Jacintha Potts, yes?"

"Of *course* I'm Jacintha Potts, I already told you that. It's my Anoukan name, we like to play make believe here, in Anouka. Well, *I* do. I call myself Jacintha because then I can pretend I'm not who I really am. Just for the time I'm here," Jacintha whispered in laughter. "You really *do* live up to *your* name, don't you?" she shook her head.

"What *do* you mean? I really have *no* idea what you are talking about," Dod replied, and Jacintha quite believed he didn't. "Anyway, back to my story - " Dod swished his stubby little tail, " - well, my reason for coming here, yes, I was sitting with Magenta, she's an old friend of mine - " Dod recalled his sturdy friendship as if he had had a sudden knock to the head. "My old friend, Magenta, *she* sent me to find you, here in Anouka. And that's it."

"That's *it?* What do you mean *that's it?*" Jacintha was puzzled. "We're no further as to *why* you are actually here, in *Anouka*. What do you want with *me?"*

"Didn't I say? Oh how forgetful I am, really I am so. Anyway, I am here to - oh, are those *Magenta Marvels* you're eating? Lovely, may *I* have one, please? Simply divine," Dod had become extremely side-tracked and Jacintha was getting rather annoyed.

"Sure, take them *all.* But, *please* tell me, what do you need with *me?"*

And, through his crumbs, Dod spoke.

But, he was in a trance and his thoughts were totally coming from someone else's mouth.

"So, Dod, so I think you are the one, sweet dragon of mine? Do you think you can do it? Do you think you can bypass the mishaps of Anouka and find the real person who is destined to help? Don't fall foul to the prey of her sister, mind, only one of them is the key, the key to the abolition of sin, a dreadful sin that is sure to make Anouka history, so don't let her slip through your fingers –

"Are you quite alright, Dod?" Jacintha squinted at him close-up, but Dod did not bat an eyelid.

"Remember, the right girl, she will be the only one who will be able to hear you, see you, so don't pass this information to anyone else. The first girl whom you approach will be the one. Get it right, sweet Dod, get it right. And, when you come across a lanky boy called Ned, tell this girl to please please please try and savour a book that he harps on about keeping close. And, get the right stick too - it might not be one so mercenary and good-looking at first, but it'll be the one. And this Ned's the worst clutz and will misplace things for certain, so don't believe his words, don't believe him when he says everything is under control."

Dod stared, unconsciously, into Jacintha's eyes.

Then he blinked.

"Oh, did someone stir me, Jacintha Potts? I was quite happy eating my marvels. Oh, someone appears to have polished them off. Never mind. So, where *was* I? Oh yes, why I'm here? Why *am* I here?" Dod faltered and stood up as if to unreel the entire synopsis again.

"No worries, Dod. I *think* I get the picture," Jacintha leant forward and kissed Dod -

But then a strange hypnotic feeling came across her.

Dod stood taller and taller still, and then he appeared glazed again.

"And, Dod, do not let either little girl touch you, else both will always be a part of your dragony-world too, my sweet dragonite, and each shall stay quite dragonite until the time comes for the release from such a necessity."

"Oh," Jacintha muttered. "Oops."

"What, Potts?"

"I touched you."

"So?"

"Oh well, oh dear, I feel okay for *now*. I don't *think* I feel sick, and I don't *think* I'm about to turn into anything *quite* yet - "

“Well, thank you VERY much. Kissing me might make you vomit? THANK YOU VERY MUCH!” Dod welled up.

“No, no, it’s not you, well, it *is* you, but not like that. Just that maybe I shouldn’t have touched you.”

“I’m not married, yuk, *eesh,* so I wouldn’t worry about any love triangles. I can see that, you know, you’ve taken quite a fancy to the likes of a handsome dragonite, and who’d blame you, who’d blame you at all?” and Dod flicked his one strand of hair, provocatively.

It flopped back down, immediately.

“Right,” Jacintha knelt up against a tree. But her nostrils suddenly felt quite partial to the pungent smell of its bark and the emerald moss that grew up its trunk. “Mmm, strong, these plants, I must admit, quite tasty,” and then Jacintha jumped as a little boy ran straight past her, his satchel freely swinging out behind, but when Jacintha blinked, he was gone.

“Are you *quite* alright?” Dod cocked his head to one side and squinted his odd-shaped crossed-eyes.

“What a funny day, all these weird characters just turning up. I do believe I feel quite relieved to be going back through Mr Fireplace even if it does mean I have to take **her** with me,” and Jacintha scorned at her sickly-looking sister. “She’s looking a bit peaky, Veronica is. She’s as white as a ghost. Hope that means she’s been struck down with some horrible non-contagious disease and she’s bedridden for days, *weeks* even,” Jacintha started to kick up the leaves

around her feet and lope towards the glowing embers by the velveteen oak tree.

"Jacintha, I can see your mouth moving, but there's not a recognisable sound coming out those lips of yours. Just mumbo-jumbo magic nonsense. What *are* you saying?" Dod copied Jacintha's pose and loped along next to her.

"Huh? Sorry, Dod?"

"You, you were talking in some sort of a trance. Your mouth, it was moving, but a whole load of jumbled stuff poured out, most unnerving, it was, *most* unnerving."

"Oh, sorry, I didn't realise."

The embers of Mr Fireplace were insanely bright that night and the pull towards the fire became ludicrously alluring.

Jacintha called to her sister; she always got into trouble if she left Veronica in Anouka and went to play alone. Their Mum would ask question upon *question* as to where had they *actually* been all afternoon.

Veronica looked up, indignant.

"Oh, so you *want* to talk to me now, well, *I* shan't talk to *you,"* and, as impertinent as always, Veronica stalked off towards the embers.

Jacintha trailed behind; the ever-inspiring flicker of Mr Fireplace heightening her senses. Even Veronica shuddered and Jacintha caught her sister smiling as she brushed through the blaze.

Then, quite on purpose, Veronica pushed Jacintha with brute force.

"OY!"

Their bodies collided.

Sparks shot between the two sisters.

Veronica's hair sprang tall and wiry.

"Ouch! That *hurt,* Jacintha!" Veronica cried. "Why did you pinch me, cretin?"

"I didn't, it wasn't *me,"* Jacintha spat back. "I *promise* I didn't, it was a shock, a spark, like static electric when *you* shoved *me*," and Jacintha could feel a surge of heat well up within, and little did she know that her eyes shone green whilst her sister's oozed red.

"Incredible heat, to *die* for," Jacintha heard Veronica say. "Oh, to *die* for, Anouka *will* be mine."

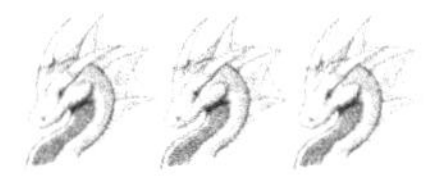

Dod peered across the forest.

He looked impish yet artful.

He knew his job was done, not quite sure what, or how, or why, but something inside, like a pulse or a beat or a shimmer of hope, rushed about his veins.

"Well, guess that's *me* done, then? I s'pose. Although *what* I s'pose beats me."

"That's foolery gone a bit *too* far," whispered Jacintha. "Just a bit *too* far, Veronica."

And Veronica, she slowly turned her neck back into the hostile forest. "I'll be seeing *you* sooner than you expected, Anouka, *my* bleak morose Anouka."

“I’m outta *here,”* and Dod popped off in a puff of black electric smoke.

The Crusade

Ned stared at the Book, Book 12, shaking in his hands.

The fictitious rogue book held the same pointed quill as his real one. He'd never really noticed, not *really,* that the quill was a *spectacularly* etched quill, the same as the one he had possessed for *years.*

Ned whispered to himself, finally managing to dull the lump forming in his throat. *This quill, it's the weapon. All this time I've been holding on to a weapon needed to save Anouka. Well I never. I can use this to write.*

"Ned, is that *you?"* Mrs Joy's shadowy outline appeared, her emerald nightie wafting out behind her thinning legs down the passageway.

"Oh, it's *her,"* Ned shrank back into the shadows.

"Who are you talking to?"

Ned stayed silent.

He didn't fancy being seen, not at that moment. How could she hear him anyway? He'd been talking to himself. He felt like he should be doing something, something else, but he couldn't think of anything helpful. So, he just stood, rigid. If he didn't move a muscle, no one would notice him. Especially *her.*

The kitchen had started to look odd.

The Books on the shelves had started to look higher and higher, *or am I getting lower and lower?* Ned thought. *I am. I'm getting lower!*

The lights had started to flicker, on and off, on and off, *on and off,* each one playing off the other as if it was only a game, until only one shimmering bulb that Ned had never ever even noticed before shone its dulling yellow sheen towards Mr Fireplace.

Mr Fireplace grumbled the lowest Ned had ever *ever* heard.

And then –

Silhouettes started to appear.

Ned squinted into the flames.

The flames weren't orange anymore, they were turning a deep, gloomy shade of burnt red.

Mr Fireplace grumbled again, so deep this time that Ned started to crouch even lower to the floor. The grumbling sound wasn't a tumbling of logs in the flames, or

the burning of tree bark, *or* the crackling of the biggest twigs.

It was deep –

Deeper than deep –

And more demonic than Ned had ever heard before.

Shadows in the burnt red flames seemed to be appearing where no visible thing could *possibly* be making them.

"Ned?"

Oh Lord, Mrs Joy?

"Yes, Ned. It is *Oh Lord, Mrs Joy.* It wasn't really *you* that had that Book 12 savoured and close now, come on, *was* it Ned?" Mrs Joy squinted at him. *"Well,* Ned?"

Oh, I'm not very well hidden, am I?

"No, you're not."

Blimey, it's like she can read my thoughts.

"Of *course* I can, I'm not a *complete* fool."

Ned tried not to think anything at all.

"Well?"

"Well, *what?"*

"The *Book. You* didn't just pull Book 12 from your insides now, quill 'n all, *did* you?"

"Sort of."

"Hmm."

"Hmm, *what?"*

"Just *hmm."*

That's a bit scathing.

"I suppose I *am* scathing. I've every *reason* to be scathing with this family to deal with."

She's a witch.

"Of *course* I am, Ned. Well, *learning* to be a witch anyway, but, if *you* ***don't*** mind, I prefer the term **SORCERESS.** *And*, I'm working my way up the series, but I'm not at Book 12, not yet. That's the key apparently."

Couldn't you just skip to Book 12?

"Don't you *ever* learn? I can still *hear* your thoughts, Ned. And *no,* you're *not* having heaps and heaps of what did you just wish for?

Nothing.

No, Ned, that wasn't it. Stop lying. You most certainly didn't request sprouts for tea? Oh, you did?"

"NO, NO, *NO! Stop* it! I *hate* it! I *hate* you being in my brain."

"Oh, you *have* got a tongue?"

Ned scowled.

"Right, the truth, then."

"What *truth?"*

"You, it *wasn't* you who found Book 12, was it? It *wasn't* **you** who hid Book 12 for safe-keeping, now, *was it?"*

"No."

"Right."

"Was it, *Stick?"*

"Dunno, and I *promise,* that's the truth."

Stick rapped on the floor with *both* his *huge* feet this time. And scowled.

"Hum-*hum,* got something *else* to add, Ned?" Mrs Joy rapped her knuckles on Mr Fireplace - and kept her hands there. On the burning metal.

Ned stared at her. "M, M, M, Mrs - "

"Spit it out, boy!"

"Mrs Joy, your, your, your *palms,* they're, they're they're on the **FIREPLACE.** I think you're going to *melt?"*

"Yes, well, never mind about *me,* child. I want to know whether *Stick* was involved? Well? *Was* he? Did *Stick* save us all like I was told he would?"

"Well, if you're asking if Stick gave us that Book 12, yes, I suppose he did."

"EXCELLENT."

"Can I go now?"

"Hmm."

"What's *that* supposed to mean?"

"I'm just trying to suss you out, Ned."

"Well, *have* you? I'm standing here, as plain as can be."

"Not everyone is what they first seem."

No, they're certainly not. Belle didn't warn me she lived with a nut-case.

"I *do* beg your pardon, Ned. I am *not* a nut-case. I'm a *nearly* fully-trained - sorceress."

"I would never have guessed."

Mrs Joy stared at William –

On the floor.

"Did you not *hear* my calls? And - *crivens above,* why *is* he lying on the floor?" but before Mrs Joy could try

and think the unthinkable, Stick crashed his enormous feet into Mr Fireplace.

Stick's eyes glared –

Stick's pupils were as dark as dark could be, and his whites as hollow as they came.

"You've certainly come full circle, *haven't* you, Stick? All this time, *all this time* I've been poking my tail back inside my knickers and now, I think, I've reached a solace. *Have* I? Yes, I have, I think - "

And you think Stick's come full circle? Have you listened to yourself lately? Ever?

"I *can* still hear you, Ned. You're such a fool. I can see why Anouka didn't entrust in you - "

That's ironic coming from a dim-witted sorceress.

"Yes, and I heard that too, Ned. Quite frankly, I *do* give up."

I should too if I were you.

"Well, it's a good job you're not me, eh? I think Dod was right, telling me that sorcery would save Anouka and a trusty old Stick with powers, and Books should be found. Just missed out the bit where *I* had to spend 36 *years*, has it *really* been that long, trying to secretly prevent fire seeping out my nostrils," Mrs Joy glanced at her greying hair in the mirror of the kettle.

What is she on about?

Stick jiggled impatiently on the spot.

"And *you* can stop acting so indignant, Mr Sticky-Pants," Mrs Joy shook her head.

But then –

Mr Fireplace roared *so* intensely that Mrs Joy's vision was blurred, and, as if a merciless demon had struck her down and turned her human bones to something far worse than she ever was, Ned swore he saw heckles, and wrinkles, and wire as thick as a beast's intestines, grow out of her nostrils. Burnt orange fire rolled up inside her mouth and then ***BURST*** out into the kitchen.

Ned bustled William up the stairs.

"Get a load of *that,* did you William? Your Mum, she's a bleedin' *dragon!"*

"I know."

"What?" Ned cried.

Rustles and huffing and the intent scraping of what Ned only thought could be talons moved across the kitchen tiles.

"He fell asleep, Mrs Joy," Ned hollered down the stairs, "don't you worry yourself about William." *Swords at dawn?* Ned repeated again and again under his breath. *Swords at dawn, we'll have to see about that,* and Ned, his fingers trembling so much he nearly pushed William back down, set his clock. "5am sharp."

"4.56am to be precise," Belle whispered. "4.56am is dawn, I heard Dad tell someone.

"Your *Dad? He's* a dragon *too,* I bet he is, Belle. You brought me back to a death trap."

"Me? *You're* the one who can walk through flames? Have you completely forgotten what I know about you?"

"Yes, but at least I've always stayed *human."*

"Doesn't feel like it sometimes."

"Sssh - "

"What?"

"I can hear a noise. Someone's coming. Turn off the light. QUICK! *QUICK!"*

Black.

Ned lay in silence.

Belle didn't dare to breathe.

"Did you bring any of those sprats up with you, Belle?" William whispered. "Belle? *Belle?"*

"Cretin," and Belle snapped tight her eyes.

Silence.

Silence.

Silence.

Not a rustle of a duvet, or a croak of a bed spring, or a creak of a floorboard broke the silence.

"Dad had undertones," Belle couldn't help herself.

"Ssshhhhhhhhhh - " Ned delved deeper and *deeper* under his duvet.

"Deep *insular* conversations as he sloped off to bed, he did. Whispering away, I *heard* him."

"Belle, shut *up."*

"Honest as that dagger lies there, Ned, I heard Dad tell someone that dawn was *surely* to be at 4.56am."

"Okay, okay, Belle, *zip* it!"

"4.56am, Ned, now don't be late - " and this time, *this* time, Ned *swore* Belle's voice in the dark sounded *just* like his Mum's.

Magenta? Mum?

But no one replied this time.

Hello? William awoke with a start.

Hello? How did I get ***here?*** *In bed, how did I get here? Huh?* William sat bolt upright.

"Who's there? Who goes there, well? Ned, are you there?" William heard a shifting of sheets and a crisp rustling of a pillow. "Come on Ned, is that you?"

"William, what *is* it?"

"Belle, is that you?"

"Course it is."

The attic room lay dark.

The silence was deafening.

Then, all of a sudden, there was that noise again.

It was getting louder and louder and *louder,* a stupendous unbearable ticking that boomed through William's head.

"Belle, that noise, that *excruciating* noise, can you not hear it? It's insufferable. I think my head is going to burst," William pressed his palms as hard as he could over his ears.

"I can't hear anything," Belle whispered. "Did you go back downstairs and eat those sprats?"

"No."

"Oh, because they were injected with Treegumph."

"Treegumph, what's that?"

"It's what comes out of a dragon's mouth, when it expels fire."

"Right."

"I read it. In Book 11. It fell from the shelf when Stick pulled down Book 12. It fell open on a page about *Treegumph.* It said *when a dragon roars its most intense roar, deep from the pit of its stomach, then Treegumph is released as spores into the air. A debilitating glue that gives you a shocking headache and the worst ringing in the ears ever. No rhyme or reason or what it hopes to gain by deafening its intruders, other than being quite annoying, has ever been discovered.* Just a thought. Seeing as you're such a glutton. Thought I'd solved your migraine. Never mind."

"I guess it used to burst the eardrums of predators."

"Yep, that's a definite possibility."

Belle's loud, annoying voice woke Ned.

"What *is* it?" Ned yawned and sat up.

"William's likely been infected with *Treegumph.*"

"What's *Treegumph?*"

"Oh, please, *don't* start that again," William pushed his forehead further into his pillow. The coldness of the cotton cooled his pulsating brain.

"Never mind, Ned."

The low burning embers in Baby-ette Fireplace shed a deep orange glow across the attic room.

The embers, they sauntered about, flickered around the room and then, finally, they fell upon Ned's satchel.

It glowed.

Ned stretched out his thin legs into the dampness of the attic but, to his surprise, the air was warm, oppressively warm.

"Ouch, my *ears!"* William rolled from beneath his bed covers onto the floor. "Ned, can *you* not hear that deafening noise, that constant beating of what sounds like the largest drum in the world?"

"I can only hear Baby-ette Clock ticking," and Ned tiptoed, lankily, an extraordinary walk it was, over to look at her face.

Baby-ette Clock glared back.

"Belle! It's 4.53am! Baby-ette Clock says 4.53am, no 4.5*4* am now. What do you think is about to happen?"

"What *are* you talking about? What's about to happen?" William momentarily unplugged his ears. "Well?" William cried out. "What are you supposing might happen, and why are you staring at that clock? Ned, Belle is something imminent about to happen? I think I'd better be warned?"

"4.55am!" Belle leapt out of bed and rushed across the room, palpitations racing so hard she thought her ribcage would burst. Kneeling at the foot of Baby-ette Clock in what William thought looked like some kind of worshipping nonsense, Ned and Belle stared.

Just stared.

And stared.

And *stared.*

"What *are* you waiting for? Tell me, *what* are you expecting to happen?" William shouted above the relentless vociferous booms –

That suddenly stopped –

"Oh. Thank *goodness,"* William collapsed into his bed.

Plain clock-ticking resumed.

But only for an instant –

As what followed next was the loudest strike imaginable and Baby-ette's flames *shot* to the ceiling.

"Creepers ***Jeepers!"*** Ned flew back across the rug from the force of Baby-ette's backdraft, his legs dangling, before he crashed back beside his satchel.

The satchel moved.

It wriggled.

It wriggled more –

And more and *more,* until a radiating incandescently gold burning heat like a furnace blew up around the room.

"My satchel, it's burning, the Book, the *fictitious* book, it's burning inside - " but before Ned could scream out again, he was sucked into the Book and there, in a green place which oozed evil, the quill appeared –

Large as life –

Serrated like Ned could not believe.

And in front of him, in the lonesome dark green forest, stood Smock –

Seething.

"So, you came, FOOL?" Smock threw back her head. "The stupid boy, he *came!"* Smock cackled to the skies, her

atrocious voice echoing through the forest; a forest that lay baron and gloomy and brick dry. "How *stupid* you are!" Smock seethed, saliva dripping from her thick fleshy lips.

She took one step forward.

Ned retreated one step back.

"This could last a while," William spoke into the pages.

"You shall *never* rule Anouka," Ned tried his hardest words.

"Oooh, *cutting* for one so thin," Veronica Smock replied. "Oh, sweet naive child!" she smiled slyly; her cruel mouth curling at the edges. "*OH, YOU STUPID NAIVE BOY! OF COURSE I WILL REIGN.*"

"Really?"

"Yeah, you *tell* her, Ned!" William leant into the chapter.

"GO AWAY!" Ned shrieked at the large dragon.

"Jesus, Ned," William clapped his hands over his eyes. "That'll get the blood pumping."

"Dark it will be, in Anouka," and Smock threw her talon-plagued claws into the deepening sky and breathed fire so incredibly high that every dry tree surrounding Ned burned with ferocity, " - and infested with dragons of what dragons are *supposed* to be; wicked and challenging, seething with fire and controlling for ETERNITY!"

"You're nice, aren't you?" Ned stood, his eyes black, his fists clenched, his heart on the outside, as he reached forward and grabbed the jewelled dagger.

"A pen, a pen, go *get* her, Ned! What's Smock doing in the fake Book anyway?" William hissed.

"Oh William, *do* shut up," Belle spat.

"Just asking."

Ned held the dagger high, high above his head. "*NEVER SHALL YOU RULE!*" he cried, his words reverberating throughout the kingdom.

"Woah! *Brutal* for one so lanky," William shot back onto the rug at the sound of Ned's voice.

"Am I?" Ned cried back.

"Urr, I *guess* so," William didn't know where to look. Ned's satchel now lay, flopped onto the floor, but as Ned cried more and *more,* the satchel glowed brighter and *brighter.*

"Intense, isn't it?" William covered his eyes.

"NEVER SHALL YOU RULE HERE!" William and Belle heard Ned's outcry from the other world.

"What are we going to do?" Belle shook William. "We can't just leave him there, in Anouka. What if he dies in the Book, and he's stuck there?"

"I guess we'd be able to have seconds of dinner?" William stared into Ned's pale face as his own intestines rumbled at the thought. "What did Book 11 say was on the menu? Does it show things like that?"

"CRETIN!"

Ned heard Belle's voice.

Her legion grew his strength and he took his
first swipe at Smock with the dagger.

He missed.

"You wretched little fiend!" Veronica Smock cackled. "I do believe you are *no* match for me. You are not deserving of taking on *me,* Veronica Smock, for I do believe I can outwit you human weaklings each time. Now *give* me that Book."

"How can I, we're *in* it!"

"Fool I can *see* it!"

Ned glanced down to the forest floor.

William riffled through the innocent satchel lying in the bedroom.

"What *is* all this commotion up here?" Mrs Joy appeared in the attic. "Well? *Explain* yourselves? William? Rosa*bella?"*

"Give me the *BOOK*!" Smock exploded, a barrage of flames shooting from her vile nostrils as she circled the boy.

Mrs Joy glared at her children. "What *Book*?"

"Nothing, Mum. Just Baby-ette learning to talk."

Mrs Joy looked about. "Belle, your voice has become the *rudest* ever. I'll be taking you out of that school."

"Mum, it wasn't me, it - "

"Ssssh, Belle, honestly, what do you think you're saying?" William whispered with indignation into Belle's ear.

"Give … me … the … *BOOK*!" Smock fired the vilest hot flames from her nostrils, the intensity of her anger shaking every bone in Ned's body.

"Oh, that woman, that simply over-zealous woman, does she *never* cease!" and Mrs Joy flew her arms into the heat-filled air and shook her head so hard Belle swore her Mum's nostrils flared far too much for a human.

"*NEVER! NEVER* shall you be the beholder of *The Book of Immortality*!" Ned snarled at Smock, shocking both himself and the fermenting dragon in his approach.

"That woman, that spoilt old lady spinster," Mrs Joy mumbled as Ned cast his dagger for the second time into the thick hazy air, its tip reaching right out into the attic.

And then –

With an inexplicable flamed flash, William and Belle were suddenly aside Ned.

Jacintha at their rear –

"Sister, sister, have you *no* morals, do you *really* not know how to conduct yourself in public? With children younger than yourself? We have visitors, can't you see?" Jacintha pointed her sprat-aroma fingers in Ned's direction as she spoke softly in the huge expanse of the woods. "Your rapaciousness amuses me so, oh Ronny, my *dearest,* you hold no prisoners," Jacintha stood afore Veronica, each dragon fixated on the other.

"Oh sister, *sister,"* Veronica replied, twisting her hard tail around and around on the floor, "have *you* no concern for *own* welfare? Can you not *see* that *you,* weasel of a dragon that you are, are simply *no* contest for *me?* We might be rivals but we cannot fight, for I fear you are sure to be doomed, *dear* sister," Veronica swished her scaly tail taking three trees clear down behind.

"WATCH OUT!" Ned shouted as half the forest seemed to fall their way, and he pushed Belle so hard she fell to the floor.

"Your revulsion *appals* me, Veronica - " Jacintha hissed.

"Does it so? What wonderful news."

"You could never cease to amaze me with your excruciating slyness and your unrelenting desire for control when we were little, but, I *do* believe the time has come when finally you realise control is *not* what life is all about, and perhaps solidarity and fairness is much better suited?" Jacintha swished her bumbling tail in return, swiping the fallen branches from the floor.

"Solitude? Selfishness? Those are all traits that I ADORE, *dear* sister Jacintha. No one gets anywhere being *nice* now, do we? Belle?"

"Huh?"

"You've always been *nice."*

"Have I?"

"Stupid and hoity toity and all the traits that I *despise,* but I guess you've *always* been faithful. And, where has **that** *ever* got you?"

"Umm - "

"Have you *ever* had apple crumble with ice-cream for tea?"

"Urr, no, but - "

"NO BUTS! There. You've been scorned and probably been the bait of burnt offerings from a blackened pot from as far back as you can remember, yes?"

"Well - "

"NO WELLS! Why don't you join me?"

"Me? Join *you?"*

"I think there's an echo around here, and I've NO TIME for parrots where *I'm* going," Veronica shrieked.

"And where may *that* be, sister *Ronny?"*

"Once I've taken that Stick, I'll be THE QUEEN!"

"Christ!" William waded over the fallen logs. "Christ, those dragons mean business, and is that Jacintha? The bumbling dragon? And, am I following this properly? Is that *other* one offering apple crumble WITH ice-cream? Can I ask what flavour, please? Is there a choice? I wouldn't mind *strawberry* myself, although I'm not sure it goes entirely with apples, so perhaps hazelnut?" and then William ducked as an entanglement of tails swept over his head, his hair taking a battering of dust-driven skin. "And, she's *good,* the bumbling one? And, the other, she's our *Auntie?* Did I miss something? Where were all our birthday presents, Auntie Veronica?"

"Oh, she's divine, the bumbling one!" Belle cried to William. "Jacintha ~ AND, SHE'S OUR MUM, WILLIAM!" Belle scrambled up on to the bark encrusted logs next to her brother. "Divine, immensely mad, but I think that WAS A COVER UP!" Belle ducked again as eight legs and arms entangled themselves in mid-air above her head. "Yep! That's our Jacintha JOY!"

"Our MUM?"

"Yep, William. Keep up!"

"Oh yeah. I remember now. From the forest. When she plucked me? From my bed? It seems to all be coming back."

"Jacintha, you were just so, mmm, *how* can I put it? Just so terribly *nice*," Veronica snarled as she swiped her pimpled damson-coloured tail in Jacintha's face. "Oh, so *awfully* accommodating and pleasant. **YUK!"** Veronica's eyes seeped the deepest blood red. "Well, pleasantries get you *nowhere*, absolutely NOWHERE. AND, I can *prove* it," Veronica twisted her body to serve Ned.

"Woah!"

"So, *stupid* one," she approached the boy, slowly, keeping her eyes fixated on him, greying smoke pouring from her heated nostrils and her eyes turning from cherry red to black as coal. "So, you *fool,* boy. **You** led this *entire* crew of people to ***me.*** All I need is simply just here, and I, *I* am all-powerful to take it ALL!"

And Veronica Smock rose higher and higher and taller and taller, more so than the tallest trees themselves, and blew the loudest, hottest most indescribable blue flame from her cave-like mouth.

The forest curled away in fear.

"You *shan't* take Anouka. You'll have to slay *me* first!" Ned leapt from his crouched position, kicking the rogue book out in front.

"THAT STUPID INEPT BOY CAN'T EVEN KEEP BOOK 12 SAFE!" Veronica cackled as Ned thrust the

dagger for the third time towards Smock, this time catching her chest head on.

"Take that, you foul heartless beast!" Ned plunged the ruby-encrusted dagger deeper and deeper and *deeper* still into Veronica Smock's chest.

She reeled in pain, her eyes bulging from their yellow-rimmed sockets.

"Her body goes on *forever!"* William stared as he watched Ned screw the dagger further and further and *further* in. *But* ***I'm*** *supposed to slay her, for sure that's what I saw* and, before William could control his feet, William found them running across the forest floor, kicking through dead black leaves and hacking holes into the earth.

But, Veronica Smock threw her body back up even taller than before, Ned's dagger popping from her breast. "You think your irksome thin body is a match for *me,* do you boy? A **match** for **Veronica Smock,** *Ned*, whose Mum left him? BOO HOO. You're mistaken," the crimson-skinned dragon heaved her body from the floor, rancid blood dripping from her wound. "You! A *boy!* A human *weakling* can outwit ***me?*** Oh, *sooooo* tiresome," she spoke with no remorse. "Well, you're wrong, SO WRONG!"

Is he now? William flung his arm, as far stretched out as he could reach, into the centre of the commotion. "We'll see who might be the weakling now!" and William made a ditch attempt to snatch at the sword, but Veronica Smock was quicker.

Their limbs collided.

Their eyes square on.

"Your death sentence, I *do* believe?" Veronica whispered into William's ear. "Say goodbye to your friends, *dear* nephew!"

"No you don't, evil sister. You can take on *me* instead," and Jacintha flew down from her nestled hiding place and threw her head square between the pair. "Repulsion, that you are!" she roared. "Freak and repulsion - "

Then, Jacintha slumped.

To the floor.

Out cold.

With William standing over her limp corpse; the ruby dagger in his blood-stained hand.

"MU-U-U-U-M!" Belle cried.

"Jacintha?" Ned whispered. "You broke the dagger, William. Jacintha penetrated the serrated dagger to save you. William, oh *how* are we to write the final chapter of the Book now with no ancient quill?"

"MUM?" Belle stood rigid over Jacintha. *Mum?*

"Oh, William, you ... *silly ... little ... boy,"* Veronica rose so tall that her words dominated the entire forest and beyond to where no one knew what existed. "Anouka is *doomed* beyond repair."

Ice-capped mountains started to rise from the earth, peppered with lava-topped volcanoes which rumbled from their roots.

"Mum?" William whimpered.

Jacintha lay motionless –

"Mum?"

"Oh, dear *sweet* nephew whom I never got the chance to BRAINWASH," Veronica carefully licked her wounds. "Oh well, no time like the present. Now, GIVE ME that BOOK! Kick it over … now! I'm to live FOREVER!"

"SHAN'T!"

"I'm sorry?"

"Oh, so you're deaf as well as mean. I said SHAN'T!"

"Well, you're more stupid that I *thought.* Mind, that isn't surprising seeing as you were born to HER, my charming, pathetic little sister married to that *fool* of a husband of hers."

"You sound jealous," William spat.

"JEALOUS? DID YOU SAY I WAS *JEALOUS?"*

"Yes, I guess I did."

"What is the MEANING of that?"

"The Collins dictionary suggests that the word *jealous* is a feeling or an emotion showing an envious resentment of someone of their achievements, possessions or perceived advantages - "

"DON'T be such a smart alec! Why would I be jealous of my bumbling half-wit of a sister who can't even bake a biscuit?"

"Because she has love, and friends and attention, and a family - "

"A FAMILY? WHO NEEDS A FAMILY? WHO NEEDS ANYONE WHEN THEY HAVE ALL OF THIS? AND FOR AN ETERNITY!" and Veronica Smock threw her arms up high into the trees, dragging birds from their

nests and throttling buds in the process of dying. "WHO WOULD WANT TO SHARE ALL OF THIS WHEN IT COULD ALL BELONG TO ME?"

"Well, you invited Belle to join you."

"DIDN'T."

"You liar. I *heard* you."

"Well, I didn't actually mean it."

"Yes, yes you did."

"DON'T MOCK ME. DO YOU KNOW WHO YOU'RE TALKING TO?"

"Yes, a lonely old spinster of a dragon."

"BE *GONE* WITH YOU, CHILD! YOU'LL REGRET THE DAY YOU SET FOOT IN ANOUKA!"

Belle tugged at the emerald dragon lying silent at her feet - Jacintha's neck torn from the blade to which she had succumbed.

The outcome was unfathomable.

Darkness fell to the utmost degree.

Jacintha Joy slumped further to the floor.

The Final Admission

The wind outside did not come that day.

The ever-falling balls of snow did not fall that day either.

In fact, the largest of deep orange suns rose from behind the velveteen grass hills and *poured* its rays upon 4 Bank Cottages.

The cottage felt lost.

Steeped in memories, but an outcome that just stood, timeless.

A solitary butterfly outside spread her wings *so* wide that their tips tapped the attic room window.

Ned opened his eyes.

"William?"

William did not answer.

But he was awake.

He did not think he had slept at all.

Then, William remembered. *Mum?*

Baby-ette Fireplace was cold.

No logs burned.

No cinders blew out around the room.

Baby-ette Clock ticked quietly –

Well, just ordinarily.

"Belle?" Ned called to her instead. "Belle, are you awake? Did we, did we - you know?"

"Yes. Yes, we did," Belle replied to Ned, softly. "We did."

"And *I* made a *right* mess," William finally spoke. "Why did I *do* that? Why didn't I just leave you all alone. Now we can't write Chapter 14, we have no Rupert, no real Book, no false Book, and we have no quill. *And* your satchel, it's empty. And, my Mum."

Ned stared across the cold, hard floor at the lank beige bag that lay lifeless.

Baby-ette Fireplace sat inanimate.

Ned put one foot outside his covers.

"It's FREEZING!"

"Well, what do you expect? *She's* ruling now," and William just stared at the ceiling.

It just stared back.

Ned tried again.

One foot followed by the other, until both heels were on the rug.

The rug felt old.

Worn.

Lifeless.

"I wonder what happened to Stick?" Ned walked across the room.

"Dunno," William slunk further down as if hiding would dull the pain.

"What's that noise?"

"Dunno," William huffed back.

"Ssh, listen, that tapping. It's getting louder. Where's it coming from?"

"You're hearing things."

"No, no I'm *not.* Listen *harder,* William."

"Anouka, it's *dead* to us now. DEAD, don't you hear? There's nothing we can do now. I'm not getting up. Mum's dead too - "

"Don't be so ridiculous."

"Ned, didn't you see? I KILLED HER! With my own bare hands. I killed my own Mum."

"Well, at least you won't need to eat sprats ever again, I suppose there's that."

"I'd eat a million sprats if I could only bring her back."

Ned rapped on Baby-ette Fireplace.

No portal let him through as he tapped each tile in turn.

"See," William hissed. It's dead. Cold. Lifeless. And Mum? She's trapped inside."

"William, it's *not* your fault."

"Leave me alone," and William crashed out the bedroom.

"OY! *Care*ful!"

"What are you doing hanging about in the doorway then, Belle?"

And William pushed his sister, hard.

And she tumbled, head first over the railings - "W-I-L-L-I-A-M - " Belle's voice trailed behind.

*"B---E---*L---L---*E?"* and William trod four steps at a time round the attic staircase.

And there she was.

Alone.

Lifeless.

Like a scene from what he could only imagine Anouka now looked.

Anouka, with Veronica Smock's head rising taller and taller and *taller* into the deathly black bracken of a dying sick world.

"Ned? NED, *help* me!" William's cry curdled back up the winding staircase. "NED, it's ***BELLE!"***

But, as William looked up, his head spun, his eyes glazed over with the brightest blinding white, and all he could see was a blur. "Ned? *Ned,* is that *you?"*

"Aha - "

"Can you warn me next time you're about to morph back into a moth and fly down?"

"I wouldn't have had the time to shove my pillow under your sister's head if I'd warned you," and Ned shook Belle with his massive black wings. "And I can't control this bleedin' cocoon popping up without any warning."

"They're a bit dull."

"What are?"

"Your wings? Why are they so dull?"

"Thanks very much, have *you* seen *your* hair lately?"

"Belle?" William stared at his sister. She'd rolled over.

And her arm had touched upon a loose quarry tile.

It tumbled to one side.

The tapping upstairs continued, louder and *louder* it was, and closer and *closer.*

"That's too loud!" Ned grimaced. "My moth ears are one hundred times more sensitive than a human's."

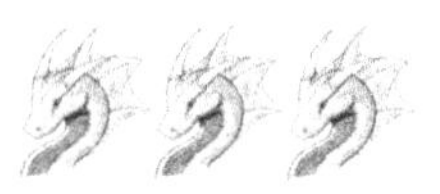

"What IS the matter?" Mrs Joy shouted from somewhere. Then appeared.

"HUH? MUM? William stared at his Mum.

She just stood there and glared back.

"You look like you've committed murder, William?"

"Yep."

"It's too nice a day to drag your feet indoors. Can I *just* squeeze past, I *must* reach those towels," and Mrs Joy stretched up.

"HUH?" William stared. *"Mum?"*

"Yes, so you keep saying. What's with you and all this adolescent lazy *Huh's?* Huh?"

"I, I didn't think it was you, that's all. You gave me a shock. A heart attack, more like."

"Well, let's not dwell on that."

"You know, don't you? You *know?"*

"I know a great many things, William, so if you could only be a little bit more specific, I might be able to help."

"You know, Mum. You know what's happened, and now I'm not sure - are, are, are you *real?"*

Mrs Joy smacked her body from head to knee; she couldn't reach her shins what with her massive skirt billowing at least three metres behind. "What *is* it William? You look like you've seen a *ghost."*

"Um, yes, I think I have."

"Well, spit it out. Who is it *this* time?"

William glared at her. "You, you, you weren't upstairs - "

"Don't be ridiculous, I've been making the beds - "

"No, no, no you *weren't.*"

"Well, I certainly think *you* were, have you *seen* the mess up there?" and Mrs Joy stretched higher. "Those blasted *towels*."

The tapping was now so close.

William started to jitter.

He couldn't hear anything, but the vibration was making him dizzy.

And he stood there.

William's eyes just stared at his Mum.

She was different.

She seemed stronger.

She was, *what was she?*

William stared more.

"William, what *is* it? And, *get* your sister off the floor. That is *no* place to be sleeping," and as she stretched the furthest ever, across Belle and right to the deepest dusty parts of the attic cupboard, Mrs Joy's neck just glared back.

A scar.

A deep red scar exactly where Jacintha would have taken her wound. Mrs Joy had got the same. "*Got* them, what a fight *that* was. The towels."

"Wasn't it just."

"Sorry?"

"Nothing."

"Always nestle them *far* too high, these towels. Oh Ned, good morning to you. We must call your Mum today for sure, tell her you're fine, *you know*."

"What *is* that vibration, can NOBODY feel it?" William hissed.

"*What* dear?"

"HUH?"

"Not *that* again, William Joy - "

Then the tapping appeared in full view and flew down out the attic door.

"Stick wasn't up there either!" William stared as Stick crashed down the stairs.

"I do feel a spring in my tail today. *Where's* Stick? Oh, there you are."

"HUH?"

"Oh, William, *do* wake up. Stick's been clearing up after *your* escapades. Stick's read the whole of Book 12, *haven't* you? Knew *exactly* what to do, *didn't* you? Did you read Chapter 14, you know, before it happened for real, for the tenth time. Have we got it right this time? I've been an age trying to work it all out."

"Work *what* out, Mum?"

Stick nodded.

There was a huge gnawed piece of his foot missing. His face, what was left of it, looked worn, and William swore he could see a trickle of crimson blood, human blood, dripping down Stick's hollowed cheeks.

"What on earth *do* you get up to in that attic room of yours, William? It's like a slaughter house up there!" Mrs

Joy peered into William's eyes. "The rug's deathly. And, as for that satchel, Ned? I don't think you'll be taking *that* back to *Gladiolus-Viola*. It's in bits!"

"No chance."

"What the waffles, it's here!" Belle cried, shrilly.

"Oh, so you *are* awake, Belle?" Mrs Joy bent down even further, her skirts rustling. "If I were you, I'd stop all this lying about on floors. It'll be the death of us if we trip over.

"I'm *sure* I can feel a hollow just *here,"* Belle tapped her toes on a misshapen tile that she'd never noticed before.

It was different from the rest –

She pushed it aside. "This *must* be where the Book lies, it *must."*

"What *Book?"* Mrs Joy butted in. "What *Book,* I say? The only Book that I know to be of importance is - Book 12. All you ever need to know is in there, *isn't* it Stick?"

Stick nodded again, and rolled his eyes this time.

The house turned cold.

4 Bank Cottages felt ancient, like no one had visited that part of the house for years.

"Rupert told us the Book was within arm's reach and where we'd been residing always," Belle squinted about.

Well, at least you remembered something.

"Who said that?"

Just trust your ears.

"My *ears?"*

"Yep."

And a faint sound of feet started to slowly walk up the stairs.

And stopped –

One stair in particular creaked.

"Who's there?" Belle's eyes shot around.

Silence.

"Stupid old house."

I wouldn't cast meanies quite yet.

"Well, I'm *not* listening."

Suit yourself.

"Tiles, *old* tiles. Rupert said a homely place, a place where the passageways to Anouka ultimately lie. *HERE!"*

And as Belle pushed her toes a little harder and a little stronger at one edge of the tile it shot up at a weathered corner - and slid away altogether.

"William, Ned, it *must* be here," Belle shoved her long leg deep inside.

"What *are* you doing? Get *out* of that hole. I'm not mending any more socks," Mrs Joy tried to squint inside but she was too far away.

Ned pushed past and spied inside. "It's *really* dark down there. I mean *really* dark. Not really in *arms reach.* I can't see a *thing,"* but then Ned's body started to shiver. He stumbled as he stretched out his long thinning arms. "The hollow goes on *forever,* and I can't really, can I, can I *see* something?" Ned squinted as much as his bulbous eyes would allow, and as each pupil became slightly more accustomed to the depth of the cavity into which he peered, an old dusty object *did* start to appear. "There *is* something

here, something *so* far down, something leather encrusted into the bricks, not sure what exactly it is, but there is *definitely* something covered in cobwebs deep down. It's so far and dim, it's hard to make out anything at all. CHARLIE! GET OFF! Belle, take this blasted chameleon away, will you?"

"It's a silhouette," Mr Joy appeared.

"What *silhouette?"* Mrs Joy bustled about. "Mr Joy, what *are* you talking about? Coming up here so slyly."

But, for once, Mr Joy ignored Mrs Joy.

"Here, take this," Mr Joy held out his hands, and, placed in his palms, was the oldest Book Ned had ever seen. "I wasn't risking leaving it in *there* for years and years. That's just a silhouette," and Mr Joy shuffled his long thin brown, almost threadbare, slippers right past. *"Take* it, then," he shook the Book at Ned. His bony feet crackled as he walked.

"How can *that* be a silhouette, down there, if the Book's right up here?" Ned frowned.

"Book 12, of course, all sorts of tricks in there, isn't there Mrs Joy?"

"You *hate* those Books, all that witchety craft - "

" - only when it turns into your cooking. Who do you think advised you to get into witchety craft? But, those were the days, time for adventures and snooping in uncertain undiscovered cracks and crevices of the cottage. Well, I *found* what I was looking for. I *should* have done. ***I*** put it there," and Mr Nicholas Joy winked, shuffled right past and closed his study door –

The latch did not completely click into place.

The dark oak door allowed a chink of daylight to filter through.

Mr Joy sat and scrawled inside.

"What *is* he talking about, scratching away with rusty pen to paper with no apparent thoughtfulness and concentration at all," and Mrs Joy snapped her fingers.

Stick wriggled towards her.

And stopped.

"Stick?"

Stick still stayed where he was. As close to the oak door as possible.

"STICK!"

"Nope. Shan't," Stick crossed his stickety legs.

Belle peered through into the old study at her Dad, through the tiniest of cracks that could barely house a moth.

"Strange," Belle muttered to herself.

Her Dad looked back.

Belle blinked. And then scuttled into the corner.

Mr Joy knew Rosabella was there, watching, assessing him. It was like he was actually waiting.

Belle pushed the door, languidly.

It creaked.

"Come in – "

"Dad?"

"Don't just stand jabbering and jittering in the doorway, girl, come in, come *right* in," Mr Joy sat, old-looking, but seeping in wisdom. "I once looked and felt quite like you."

"Me? Can't imagine *you* in ratty-plaits."

"Try me."

"I might."

"I mean young, invincible, in fact I still *do feel* like that, just my skin is like an elephant - and these bones - " Mr Joy rubbed his bristly beard hard making a papery sound that rustled around the room.

"You're still my Dad, though."

"Kind Belle. My mind has seen a multitude of happenings, rather like you, and my body, well, that's been through the works."

"Dad?"

"Yes, so you keep saying. What *is* it child?"

"You're acting - well, weird," Belle pulled herself closer.

"I always wondered, Belle, *always* wondered if I would ever know who that girl was I stumbled across that day in the forest, the pale apparition which wouldn't cease chasing me down. And now I know. She was my own daughter, who would have thought?" Mr Joy whispered so close that his beard prickled Belle's cheek.

"Me?"

"Yes. Unless you're not you? *Are* you?"

"Well, of *course* I'm me. Don't be so ridiculous."

"I don't think it's *me* being ridiculous. Have you seen your Mum's brain?"

"No."

"Good answer, I don't suppose you have – BUT, if you *did,* what do you think it would look like?"

"A jumbled mess of trifles and jelly?"

Mr Joy threw his head back. And narrowed his eyes into a wild laughter.

"And that, that *boy,* it was - *you?"*

Mr Joy clapped a long, slow, staccato-type of clap.

"I knew it! He cracked his fingers *just* like William does! Disgusting!"

The Book of Immortality shuddered.

And its pages tightened.

"*Belle*, of course. That pretty name just seemed to come from nowhere when you were born."

"Anouka – can't believe you know *Anouka - "* Belle slid her elbows even closer across the desk to this man, her feet shifting further across the ancient rug under her chair, and she stretched out her hands, and then he turned, her Dad's face suddenly being that little boy from the woods. "Clutching your satchel, it was *you*? *You* had the book in your satchel! Dad, you then came home, from that fossilling conference, but Dad, you'd been in Anouka?"

"Ssh, dear, *ssh* dear, don't tell them *all.* Youth comes but in a flash and then we are old again."

"Who's them *all?"*

"Well, we never *quite* know who *anyone* is *really* now, *do* we? Some things are better kept simple once complete," Mr Nicholas Joy scratched his head.

"Complete? I still think we're all about to *die!"*

"Simple?" Ned crashed into the study; musty dust from the crevices of inside the floorboards falling from his

hair and shoulders. "I'm not sure *any* of this has been *simple*."

"You look a bit, well, see-through - " Belle eyed Ned up and down.

"That cross-contamination will probably never wear off."

"Ah, well, let's keep it that way, shall we, Ned? Old Magenta's boy. No more unshared complications - " it was like Mr Joy was talking ridicules to himself.

Belle looked down at her Dad's desk.

It was quite empty, not a book nor a paper strewn like most days. It was lacking something.

"Dad?"

"What *now* Rosabella?"

"Are you waiting for *this*?" Belle slipped across the study to Ned and, with no eager desire to retain his own Dad's gift, Ned parted with the silhouette.

Mr Joy's book suddenly sucked it in.

It was complete.

The Book was complete.

"Bleedin' 'eck! That was *awesome!*" Ned inhaled too much air. He started to choke.

"Well, well, *you* succeeded where others have fallen," Mr Joy chuckled, "but looking at you along the way, it was a bit of a rough ride, but I shouldn't complain, we're still all here," and he burst out into a neigh-y-laughter like a horse. "She's fallen, that deathly old spinster of a sister-in-law…" and ripples of thankful desperation echoed into the chimney.

Mr Joy's hands, shaking but true, touched the tips of his fingers lightly upon *The Book of Immortality*.

Back home, complete now, are we? Mr Joy stared at the Book, questioning it in a whisper, his lips touching its cover as if it indeed had ears of its own. "Oh, you children don't know your own worth, writing the final Chapter 14 without even the slightest idea. Defeating that Miss Smock and annihilating Armageddon within the realms of Anouka itself. Your actions spoke volumes, *volumes* they did, and those volumes inscribed this Book.

"But, Dad, we didn't write a word, not one," Belle scratched her plaits.

"There was no need to *write* it at all. Can you imagine? William *writing* an entire chapter?" Mr Joy gripped his fingers tighter around the Book's spine. "And now, after *all* these years, where I placed the book as a boy, in the earth as I was instructed to do, and this cottage was built on the Book, it has been found."

"But you had it, all along."

"But *you* had its soul. That silhouette. *The Book of Immortality* was as much as dead without its soul."

"How come Mum's alive?" Belle squinted.

"Oh, must have been that wretched Stick. Full of stuff and nonsense, and some of it must have struck a chord and saved Mum. Perhaps she'd had a good cup of tea for once."

"A *good* cup of *tea?* That's *all* we needed to have done? Made Mum a *good* cup of *tea?"* William groaned at his Dad.

“Oh, *you’ve* emerged,” Mr Joy returned the compliment. “As she always says, *there’s nothing like a good cup of tea.”*

“I’ve never heard her say that.”

“Oh, just ride with it boy.”

Its plain looking title, *The Book of Immortality,* appearing innocent and suggesting freedom from any other all-powerful inscription than its own, slid, indiscriminately, secretly, and quite plainly, between two, not *quite* so empowering titles, on the Joy’s kitchen bookshelf one morning. Complete, and only fully understood by its authors and players, *The Book of Immortality* sat, and would sit, until perhaps new eyes spied it and new hands pulled it from a likely dust ridden shelf.

It was not that one soul alone had now become immortal when Chapter 14 was finally played out, but one *worldly* soul, called Anouka, became free from defeat, for always.

At least the Book could be read with no thoughts to have to scope the future, but with a mind that could read the success of the past, and with the reflection that not everyone appears who they truly first seem.

Mr Joy smiled, his hands tightly clasped, as the fireplace roared a deep burnt orange, and inside the flames Magenta’s butterfly wings appeared to resemble faint

human-like arms with hands and tiny fingers locking a door with a little old key-shaped stick and a demonic scream curdling from behind it.

"Smock," Mr Joy's ears burned, happily. "That sister-in-law of mine will never rest, but stay locked inside that Book. Forever."

Magenta winked her lashes, if that was indeed possible.

"Thank you, Rupert," Mr Joy muttered, "for Anouka now has its place in our world, if one ever again finds their way in," he spoke aloud as Magenta fluttered further and deeper into the flames. *"Rupert* indeed," Mr Joy mused, then laughed out loud. *"Rupert indeed!* Who would have thought an aging man like myself could have created such a character? I even fooled my own wife. I was still wearing the same old shoes! –

As for those children, who on *earth* has *children* who listen to their *parents?* I simply *had* to be someone else to be taken seriously, and they certainly did that for Anouka shall live on, for others to find one day…if they dare."

A pair of mean, green eyes glared through the flames in the study – another portal to an unknown universe.

"All she wanted was to be a witchety-wife and have a good cup of tea, not much to ask was it, Miss Smock? Not much to ask of your sister now, *was* it?"

A silent groan sounded deeper – and more quietly, until it disappeared, altogether, into the flames.

And the flames burned, glowed, *orange,* not green or red or black, but plain – bright – orange –

And Dod? –

Dod, he looked in the mirror, and Mr Nicholas Rupert Joy just smiled, slyly, back.

"Night Dod," Nicholas Rupert Joy spoke to his reflection.

"Well, a good night to you, Nicholas Rupert, if it is night? *Is* it night? I can see the sun starting to appear. Oh, actually, perhaps it's Mrs Joy rummaging around with her candle in the cupboard, yes, that'll be it - "

"Oh, for heaven's sake, stop doddering about, Dod," and Nicholas Rupert switched off the light.

The Anouka Family Tree

Bill Smythe m. Patty Smythe (née Klop)
Child Rosa Smythe m. Jack Joy
Children Brodie Joy & Kat Joy
Brodie Joy m. a local lass
Child Anthony Joy m. Janet Joy (née Lawrence)
Child Nicholas Joy m. Pippa Joy (née Potts)
Children William Joy & Belle Joy
Belle Joy m. Ned Argyle
Children Hetty Argyle & Drew Argyle

Naribu Zenkraw Dod Jacintha Veronica

Philippa W. Joyner has worked professionally as a P.A. for two decades, but in 2013 she was inspired by her children's whimsical offerings and active imaginations.

The author originally grew up in Hertfordshire, and completed her studies at Bangor University, Wales gaining a B.A. Hons with Distinction in French and Theatre.

She currently resides in her chocolate box village in Kent at the foot of the North Downs with her husband, two children, a bouncing puppy and a multitude of wildlife.

Plus *Chameleon-Dragon-Thing, Charlie* from North Wales.

Lots of love and dragony-thoughts,
Dod
xxx

"Life outside in the wilds of Anouka!"
Pippa and her family. The puppy appears to have disappeared through a portal to Anouka.

Other titles in the Anouka Series:

The Old Oak Tree

In a desperate plea to save Anouka from complete demise, William and Rosabella Joy are hurled into a web of strange new friends. A Black Witch is set to turn the human world into a slavery of coldness if she finds her way in. Her accomplice, an elusive goblin, is trying to capture four children, and if these children surround the Old Oak Tree only darkness will prevail for eternity. But who is it? Angus Moon, a charming Scottish boy, is bewildering and no one seems to understand his role. Alyssa too seems a rather knowledgeable dark horse. And Myriad, the elf? Well, he's just ridiculously tiny. A new headmaster, Mr Vixonight, is acting suspiciously. Miss Terrine? She just smells of old coffee. And Miss Lovett? Too bothersome she is. At the crux of Anouka, will the light or the dark side prevail? Will Mr Vixonight be able to hide his true colours? Will Angus Moon ever stop flirting. And Alyssa? Will her heroine nature help or hinder? William and Rosabella could get slain alongside their friends, or will Mrs Joy be able to rely on her son to get back home unscathed, with at least a semi-pleasing school report? For once.

The Silver Chalice

William and Belle Joy are privy to a ghostly apparition in church. The apparition is stuck in time, unable to reach home. William and Belle are determined to help this pallid little girl escape the clutches of Anouka, the parallel universe in which she appears to have found herself, but it is a mystery as to why she cannot pass back into her own world. The secrets of the Silver Chalice start to reveal why, and William begins to discover that if he does not play by the rules, Janet may never return home and his own entire existence may also lie in jeopardy.

The Hollow Boathouse

Rosa's world seems ordinary until one day she falls for the charms of a cantankerous boy who pulls her deeper into danger. But Rosa, she's used to her witchety-Mum and deaf old Dad who bakes eggs to the ceiling. Then there's Angharad, the miniscule school witch who Rosa despises. Maybe life at Gheptun's School of the Black Arts & Gastronomy is more than simply winning at cookery? Perhaps following a pre-destined set of rules is the only way to survive? Or is Rosa in too deep this time?

The Mountain & The Mirror

The Anouka Chronicles: The Mountain & The Mirror

Brodie Joy unwittingly brings home the school mascot, excited he can taunt his odd Mother with its ill-infested presence. But, Brodie is unaware this Monkey is the link to a deeply dangerous portal. And the Monkey stinks. Waking up to snarling foxes, a lisping butterfly, and a mission to battle the Ice Phoenix, Brodie realises he may be stuck in Anouka forever. With no Apple Strudel! Will Brodie and his snooty sister, Kat, get home in time for Christmas? Or will their lives be trapped in an endless spiral of darkness? What a pleasant decision.

No Ordinary Bookshop

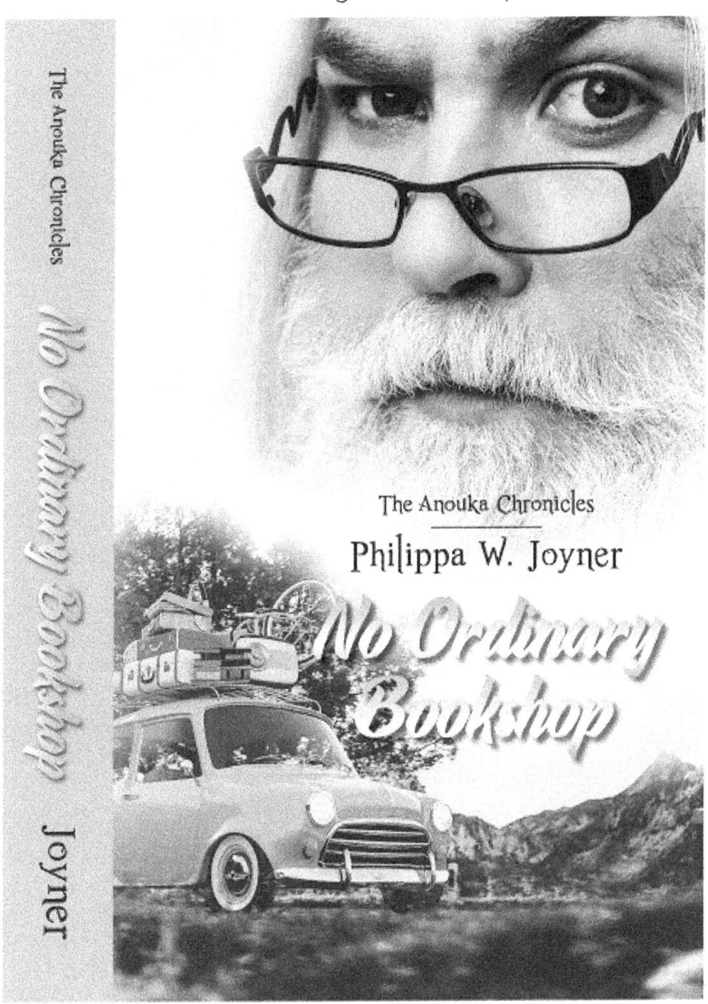

The Anouka Chronicles: No Ordinary Bookshop

Belle Joy curiously lands a place at Gladiolus-Viola, but a new boy is acting spookish. Belle confides in old Professor Argyle, but this pulls her deeper into the Professor's dark life, that is until one day she encounters Eduardo's Bookshop. However, Anouka catches up and perhaps hidden secrets cause Belle's life to be turned upside down?

The Book of Immortality

Philippa W. Joyner

Author of Children's Magical Realism, and Adult Humour

Also writes as

Honey Hollings or Pippa

Available at Waterstones, Amazon, Barnes & Noble and all good book shops!

philippajoyner@gmail.com

https://contactanauthor.co.uk/author/595/philippa-joyner

Awards:

Waterstones: "The books feature an abundance of parallel worlds, mystery, peril, suspense and well-written protagonists which readers can empathise with easily.

They bear comparison to Philip Pullman, C.S Lewis, Alan Garner and Kiran Millwood-Hargrave, and will be loved by fans of these authors."

Accolade from HarperImpulse: "We really appreciate the time and effort that has gone into your submission. There is much to enjoy in your Honey Hollings collection – you have a lovely, warm and engaging voice."

Accolade from Waterstones: "Anyone looking for a new Children's fantasy series should look no further than Philippa Joyner's 'Anouka Chronicles'. Full of magic, mystery and suspense you can't help but be drawn into their world. Perfect for readers in the 9-16 age range, great for Harry Potter fans."

Selected for Author Academy Awards 2019

The Amaska Chronicles
Philippa W. Joyner
The Amaska Chronicles
Philippa W. Joyner
The Amaska Chronicles
Philippa W. Joyner
The Hollow Boathouse

Lightning Source UK Ltd.
Milton Keynes UK
UKHW040814270522
403617UK00004B/324